al-naqba

AL-NAQBA

THE CATASTROPHE

a Novel about the Palestinian-Israeli Conflict

BARBARA A. GOLDSCHEIDER

Frog, Ltd.
Berkeley, California

The characters in this novel are fictional. Unless otherwise noted, any resemblance to actual people, living or deceased, is purely coincidental.

Published by Frog, Ltd.
Frog, Ltd. books are distibuted by
North Atlantic Books
P.O. Box 12327
Berkeley, California 94712

Cover photo by Muhammed Muheisen, courtesy of AP/Wide World Photos.
Author photo by Doreen Lis.
Cover design by Maxine Ressler.
Book design by A/M Studios.

Printed in the United States of America.
Distributed to the book trade by Publishers Group West.

"On Marriage" from *The Prophet* by Kahlil Gibran, copyright 1923 by Kahlil Gibran and renewed by Administrators C.T.A. of Kahlil Gibran Estate and Mary G. Gibran. Used by permission of Alfred A. Knopf, a division of Random House, Inc.

North Atlantic Books' publications are available through most bookstores. For further information, call 800-337-2665 or visit our website at www.northatlanticbooks.com.

Substantial discounts on bulk quantities are available to corporations, professional associations, and other organizations. For details and discount information, contact our special sales department.

Library of Congress Cataloging-in-Publication Data

Goldscheider, Barbara A., 1941–
    Al-Naqba (the catastrophe) / by Barbara A. Goldscheider.
      p. cm.
    Summary: "A historical novel dramatizing the political, economic, spiritual, and societal costs of the Arab-Israeli conflict to both sides. Interweaving the lives of Israeli Jews and Palestinian Arabs, the novel renders the human losses that result when nationalism spirals out of control"—Provided by the publisher.
    ISBN 1-58394-127-4 (pbk.)
    1. Arab-Israeli conflict—Fiction. 2. Jewish-Arab relations—Fiction. 3. Palestinian Arabs—Fiction. 4. Jews—Israel—Fiction. 5. Israel—Fiction.
I. Title: Catastrophe. II. Title.
    PR9510.9.G65A79 2005
    813'.6—dc22
                                    2005019414

1 2 3 4 5 6 7 8 9 UNITED 09 08 07 06 05

For my grandson, Micha-el, who lived only a few short days on this earth,

and in honor of my sister, Doreen, for being a beacon of light in the dark years following his death.

in memoriam

In memory of Avner ("Neyri") Etzion, Israel Defense Forces commando killed in service to Israel at age twenty-one, in the year 5733 (1972), beloved first-born son of Yemima and Yaakov Etzion, brother of Giora and Omri Etzion.

*Who can possibly know what is best for a man to do in life—
the few days of his fleeting life?*

*For who can tell him what the future holds for him under the
sun?*

ECCLESIASTES 6:12

preface

"AL-NAQBA" IS AN ARABIC WORD referring to the outcome of the 1948 war between Arabs and Jews on the eve of Israel's birth as a sovereign nation. From an Arab perspective—in particular, that of the Palestinian people—this was a humiliating defeat, resulting in the catastrophic uprooting of approximately 760,000 people, among countless other losses.

As an Israeli-American, I know that the catastrophe does not belong exclusively to the Palestinian people. We, in Israel, have also endured a catastrophe in the irreplaceable loss of lives in five major wars, in Arab riots and uprisings in the 1987 and 2000 "Intifidas," in brutal acts of terrorism, which have shattered not only the lives of victims and their families, but also the very fabric of Israeli life. The subculture of terrorism in the Middle East is now mushrooming into a global epidemic of warfare unleashed to undermine Western civilization. It is not my intention to use the title *Al-Naqba (The Catastrophe)* flagrantly, with the concomitant result of inflaming the sensitivities of either my own people or the Palestinian people. Rather, I am using it as the title of this historical novel, to serve as a reminder that there are no winners in this horrific conflict shortly to enter its sixth decade of bloodshed, violence, and turmoil.

The style/methodology of *Al-Naqba* combines fictional and non-fictional approaches, gleaned from newspapers, articles, books by historians and/or political analysts in Israel and abroad, referenced in the back of the novel as endnotes. All the characters in the novel are fictional; yet most of the events and dates are historically accurate, incorporated specifically to ensure the novel would resonate deeply and poignantly within as well as outside of Israel. I wanted readers to experience, for a brief moment, what it might feel like to be an Israeli-Jew, Israeli-Palestinian, or Palestinian-Arab. The use of the actual names of victims in *Al-Naqba* [*zichrona l'vbraha*—of blessed memory] who lost their lives in acts of terror is to underscore the brutal reality of how deeply every single Israeli Jew is affected by these suicide attacks—and how people comb the newspapers or listen non-stop to the hourly news broadcast on radio to ascertain who has been killed, wounded, or maimed, or has survived among the House of Israel.

For victims and their families, there are dire consequences the morning after the nightmare. A friend was forced to escape an Egged bus charred by a bomb blown up directly in front of her own in downtown Jerusalem. Forevermore she was haunted by flashbacks to that scene of stepping on top of the body of a dead person lying in the pool of his own blood. Years after the event she was still plagued by anguish, anxiety, and dread amid the relative safety of an American city. Never will I forget my *Magen David Adom* (Red Shield of David) instructor, Ofir, who taught me a lesson in Israeli survival during the *Ma'alot* Massacre in 1974, when schoolchildren in Israel were held hostage by three Palestinian terrorists on the twenty-sixth anniversary of Israel's independence. We subsequently met on the stairwell to the library on the *Givat Ram* campus of the Hebrew University. As I conveyed to him how distraught I was over Ma'alot, this gentle man looked at me askance, indicating in no uncertain terms that one must not allow such feelings to get in the way of living or else one could not go on. Years later, the full implication of his remarks and approach to Israeli reality became crystal clear to me: if we do not permit ourselves to feel our own pain, eventually we are unable to feel the pain of others—the Palestinian-Arabs and Israeli-Palestinians who have endured pain, suffering, deep losses, and trauma in equal measure to our own.

During the week of 9/11 when I was working in Boston, I lost a friendship of fifteen years' duration when I uttered the following words: "Now maybe Americans can fully comprehend what Israel has been enduring for years." The friendship snapped like a brittle twig—in half—in less time than it takes to blink an eye. My statement was erroneously perceived as an attempt to diminish the incomprehensible terrorist attack in America. Nothing could have been further from my mind or heart. As an author attempting to write about the Palestinian-Israeli conflict, I have approached the issues with a profound burden of caring to remain at all times detached, dispassionate, and balanced in my presentation. Nevertheless, I continue to feel humbled by the imperviousness and intractability of the problems endemic in the Middle East. It is not my intent to impel readers to take one side or the other in this ongoing dispute. Rather, the intention is to pry open eyes that remain blinded by entrenched views or passionate ideologies, which may inadvertently be fostering the dehumanization of Arabs or Jews. Such subjective, ideologically driven positions will only result in continuing bloodshed, violence, and hatred ad infinitum, hardening the polemic on both sides of the divide, fostering neither peace nor viability in the Middle East theatre of continuing warfare.

If there is no side in this conflict willing to risk for peace—and no one willing to broker compromises for the withdrawal from territory occupied since the 1967 war and the establishment of a Palestinian state whose policies and grand plan is not the ultimate destruction of the Israeli people—then a time will arise, in the very near future, when the land and its inhabitants will no longer be able to exist. Even in a land considered sacred by both sides, peaceful co-existence cannot take root under the yoke of leaders gone amok, where insanity, blindness, stupidity, hatred, greed, and destruction rule daily life.

Arabs and Jews both claim "my land." If the only solution is either a fight to the death, or the expulsion of one people by the other, or the continued subjugation of one people over another, then eventually, over time, the Promised Land will become a calamitous land, God forbid, not for a day, not for a year, not for a lifetime, but for an eternity.

Pray for peace to descend—not only in the city of Jerusalem, a city yearning for thousands of years for a peace that continues to elude it—but in all the land, so that Arabs and Jews may lay down their arms and till the soil in harmony, as direct descendants of the same forefather, Abraham.

Barbara A. Goldscheider
June 17, 2005
Bangor, Maine

acknowledgments

SPECIAL THANKS TO THE FOLLOWING PEOPLE for reviewing drafts of *Al-Naqba (The Catastrophe)* and for their encouragement and insights:

Joann Allard, Worcester, Massachusetts – for her enthusiasm, belief in the project, insightfulness, and continuous support. Special gratitude for prompting me to begin the writing by merely suggesting that I write the first chapter to "see if it flows," knowing full well that once started, there would be no stopping until the goal of completion was reached.

Yvonne Cárdenas, my project editor and copyeditor at North Atlantic Books/Frog Ltd. – for her untiring efforts to ensure a high level of literary quality in *Al-Naqba* as well as for her unstinting support, clarity, deep warmth, and friendship.

Bella Greenfield, Jerusalem, Israel – for her cogent comments, ensuring historical accuracy, a balanced portrait, and a ring of authenticity. Most of all, I am grateful for the renewal of our friendship in Jerusalem during the research on this novel in 2003.

Richard Grossinger, Berkeley, California – for his invaluable responses: first to the initial query letter and his positive response as a publisher, and all the subsequent meetings and discussions with him. His insights, astute and discerning mind, his readiness to "sharpen my edges" and to push me to a higher literary level has been a singular experience. Most of all, I value his down-to-earth, laid-back style, his integrity and his perceptiveness as a person and a publisher. Without his belief in *Al-Naqba* from the outset and his strong belief the novel would have an impact, this book would not have been produced.

Doreen Lis, Bangor, Maine – for her critical response on the first reading, her enduring support throughout the writing—giving me the space and time to conceive and carry out the writing of the manuscript—and for her lifelong friendship as my sister.

Sar-El, Israel Defense Forces – my gratitude to the Volunteer for Israel/Sar-El program, which I participated in on three separate occasions, volunteering on army bases throughout Israel.

The Bangor Public Library, Bangor, Maine – I am deeply indebted to the Bangor Public Library and its staff for research material on the Middle East, especially special requests for material obtained via the University of Maine system. It has been an invaluable resource during the research and writing phases of this novel.

To family and friends, both in the U.S. and in Israel, for their enthusiasm and support throughout the process of writing this historical novel on the Palestinian-Israeli conflict.

PART I

June 2000

one

ON A LONE STRETCH OF A DESERTED ROAD, the driver of a white Honda Civic with Israeli military plates shifted gears, turning into the Mahane Julius army base. Seated behind the wheel was an officer in the Israel Defense Forces, Colonel Neyri Ben-Ner, from the Tel Nof Air Force Base.

As the military police approached his vehicle, Neyri Ben-Ner rolled down the window, extending his army photo I.D. The MP glanced at the I.D., scrutinizing the face of the Israeli officer: light-brown hair, bleached by the sun, a pair of blood-shot brown eyes, and skin tanned to a golden sheen.

"Colonel Ben-Ner, who are you seeing on this base?"

"Commander Omri Ben-Ner, my brother."

"Go right through, Colonel."

The gate was lifted. Ben-Ner parked his vehicle. Walking across the base, he passed maintenance crews busy with tank repairs on vintage *Merkavot* tanks. This was one of the largest tank bases in the country, and where his younger brother had just taken command of the Seventh Armored Brigade.

The blazing June sun was baking his unprotected head, making him acutely aware that the humidity was even worse here than at his own base. By the time Neyri Ben-Ner reached the soldiers' mess hall, his tan dress uniform was clinging uncomfortably to his back.

He entered the massive room the size of a warehouse, where hundreds of soldiers sat eating the noonday meal. Like the hum of droning bees, the steady murmur of voices filled the packed room. Removing his dark sunglasses, his eyes readily adjusted to the reduced lighting. It was a relief to feel the coolness of the interior.

Despite a sea of khaki, Neyri sighted Omri up front, at the officers' table, wearing his field uniform, with the black beret of the tank brigade tucked under his epaulettes. They shook hands firmly, clasping each other on the shoulders. There was a strong resemblance between them, except that Omri, five years his junior, had a stockier frame that made him seem older. Under constant exposure to the harsh rays of the Middle East, his fair skin and blond hair appeared to be accelerating the ageing process.

"Good to see you, Omri."

"Same here."

They sat down to a full-course lunch of roast chicken, potatoes, assorted green vegetables, and fruit. It had been more than two months, by Neyri's calculation, since he last saw his brother. His errand on this June morning was of a personal nature. He waited until they finished eating before opening the conversation.

"Omri, I plan to take time off from the army to study in the States soon."

"How long, couple months or so?"

"More like a couple years."

"Just how do you plan to pull it off?"

"Give up my paratroop command."

"You mean temporarily?"

"No, I mean permanently."

"Permanently? Are you sure?"

"I don't have all the particulars worked out yet."

"It's a big decision. I don't envy you."

"I don't plan to tell our parents until all the details are worked out."

"Sure, no problem."

Neyri appeared more relaxed after this exchange, relieved his brother didn't feel the need to probe deeper into the reasons for such a radical decision. They were both officers with responsibility to their commands, with barely a personal life. Their relationship had shifted over the years; he felt closer to him than at any other time in their lives.

"How are Tali and the kids?" Neyri inquired.

"Tali is a good army wife. She expects you over to dinner next week. You do plan to attend grandfather's art exhibit next Thursday, right?"

"Absolutely. Tell Tali I'd love to come."

"Her sister will also be there."

"Not interested."

"Okay, Neyri, I'll tell Tali to back off."

"Thanks. I owe you one."

"Not interested in dating?"

"I'm not interested in dating Tali's sister. She's aware of this. Why does your wife persist in playing cupid?"

"Women. They like to get their way, always."

"Well, you must be one lenient husband. How long have you been married now? I've lost count."

"Me too," Omri smiled ruefully. "My oldest daughter is almost nine. Must be ten years of wedded bliss. By the way, Tali bumped into your ex-wife the other day in downtown Jerusalem."

"So?" Neyri responded indifferently, biting into a red apple.

"That's all you have to say?"

"What do you want me to admit? That you were right after all, and I never should have married her?"

"Would be nice."

"The next time I decide to get married, I'll be sure to ask you first."

"Doubtful."

"Doubtful I'll get married again, or whether I'll ask your opinion?"

"Both," Omri answered dryly.

"Why's that?"

"You seem to have difficulty with the concept of commitment, I've noticed, since your stint in Lebanon."

"And you haven't?"

"Sure, but mine is not as shredded as yours."

"How have you managed to keep intact?"

"I don't dwell on things."

"I'll have to remember this the next time I have a nightmare over Lebanon."

"We paid for our mistakes, in blood."

"So we have. The problem is, we haven't learned from our mistakes. Until we do, we'll continue to compound them."

"Why don't you consider a career in politics?"

"You must be joking."

"I'm quite serious. You have a conscience, far more than any of our politicians have."

"Precisely why I wouldn't go near the political scene."

"What a pity. *Yallah,* let's get out of here, so I can show you around the base.

⚜

ON THE DRIVE BACK TO HIS OWN BASE, Neyri reflected over the critical juncture he was approaching in his life. It was a habit of his to take stock, every now and then, of where he was and where he should be headed. He was long overdue.

From age eighteen to thirty, he had been in an elite combat unit—the Golani Flying Tigers—when he was first baptized under fire in the 1982 Lebanon war. The majority of his missions were still held classified. After switching from the Golani infantry to the Paratroop Corps, he began to miss the cutting edges of the brown beret Golani: the intensity of their training, the fierceness of their pride, the stealth of their missions, and the overall challenge it had provided him on many levels.

It was not possible to precisely identify when a sense of disillusionment began to set in. At first he thought it was because of his age—he would turn thirty-nine at the end of the month. It was actually much deeper than a mid-life crisis, he concluded, as he headed in the direction of Tel Aviv.

Ever since the ill-advised and ill-fated Israeli offensive into Lebanon, he had felt that the country was headed in the wrong direction. There appeared to be too much reliance on the strong arm of the Israel Defense Forces (IDF) to end the conflict between the Palestinians and the Israeli Jews. Irrespective of a planned August summit between President Clinton, Yasir Arafat, and Ehud Barak, neither the IDF nor Barak's government believed that signatures would appear on a peace treaty, despite the willingness of Israel to return ninety to ninety-five percent of the occupied territory held since its victory in the 1967 Six-Day War. Mainstream Israeli Jews and Palestinian Arabs living within the Israeli Green Line—and those living in the occupied territories on the West Bank of the Jordan and the Gaza Strip—expected the peace talks to break down at any moment, unleashing violence with renewed ferocity. Given this likelihood, the IDF had been stepping up its preparedness for the past several months.

By the time Neyri Ben-Ner arrived back at the Tel Nof Air Force Base, it was close to 3:00 PM. This evening, he would be conducting night exercises with his paratroops, complete with full battle gear in place. It would prove to be an arduous task, lasting until daybreak, at which time the troops would be continuing with daylight training as usual. Having had next to no sleep over the past three nights, he noted, somewhere in the remote corner of his mind, that he was burning both ends of the candle. Between honing his troops to perfection, he would have to find the time to fill out lengthy applications to universities abroad.

Neyri headed in the direction of the officers' quarters to change into his IDF khaki working uniform, or B-quality standards known in the Hebrew vernacular as *zug-bet*.

Two

THE FOLLOWING WEEK Neyri Ben-Ner drove south to Jerusalem, heading directly for the Kiryat Shemuel section of town. After parking his car next to Harlap Street #43, he rang the bell to the first floor apartment. There was no answer. It was close to 6:00 PM. Neyri headed on foot in the direction of Talbiyeh, hoping to find his grandfather. The cool breeze of the Jerusalem hills enveloped him with a sense of comfort and pleasure he hadn't felt in a long time. The air of Jerusalem is healing to the soul, he reflected, feeling vibrantly alive.

Searching the neighborhood made him recall his childhood days. Often he went directly from school to his grandparents' apartment for refreshments, with or without his two brothers. The moments spent alone with his grandfather were always special, including the long walks they would take to different neighborhoods. By the time Neyri reached high school, he knew the Old City of Jerusalem, as well as the New City, like the back of his hand. Not only the city of his birth had shaped his character and vision of life, but also the two people who had been closest to him in the early part of his life—his older brother, Gideon, and his grandfather, David Ben-Ner.

AN ELDERLY MAN, IN HIS EIGHTY-FIRST YEAR OF LIFE, was sitting on a bench within walking distance of the presidential mansion at the intersection of Jabotinsky and Marcus streets. The moments before the setting of the sun were David Ben-Ner's favorite time of day. The slanting of the sun's rays cast deep shadows over the city, splashing rays of pale yellow ochre over the streets, buildings, hills, and trees. David Ben-Ner believed Jerusalem to be a city of timeless, ageless beauty. Though built of limestone and mortar, it seemed to pulsate with the beat of a human heart.

Tomorrow evening David's watercolors would be exhibited at the Bezallal Art School. It was a singular honor, creating within him mixed emotions and penetrating feelings. Despite the decade that had passed since his wife's death from cancer, David still missed her presence deeply, and this event awakened his longing.

His reflections transported him back in time to the year of his arrival in Israel. It was 1947, he had just turned twenty-nine years old, and his last-known address had been the detention camps of Cyprus, where he'd been a displaced person. Trained eleven months later as a soldier in Palmach, the elite striking arm of the Haganah defense forces, he was deployed in 1948 to Ramle and Lydda at the outbreak of war between the Arab Legionnaire and the fledgling State of Israel.

After disembarking from the ship on the shores of Haifa, there had been no time to mourn the loss of his Polish family, of which he was now the sole survivor. Both sets of grandparents, his parents, his three sisters, and one brother had all met their death in the Auschwitz crematorium. For years he asked himself the same questions: Why did I survive? For what purpose? To what end?

During the War of Independence, David was wounded in the arm and taken to the Shaarei Tzedek Hospital, at that time still in its original location on Jaffa Road in Jerusalem. It was there that he met the nurse who would become his wife—Rachel Stern. They married shortly after the war and had two sons—Avraham and Jacob—born in rapid succession. David never again asked himself why he had been saved from Nazi extermination: He had survived in order to help build a

Jewish nation out of the ashes of the Holocaust, a nation that would serve as an asylum for persecuted Jews from every corner of the world.

Winning the 1948 War of Independencear against all odds, Israel absorbed hundreds of thousands of Jews from Europe, Yemen, Iraq, Iran, Morocco, Egypt, Tunisia, Russia, the United States, South Africa, Canada, France, Argentina, and Ethiopia. In the fifty-two years of its existence, it had since fought five more wars—the 1956 Sinai Campaign, the 1967 Six-Day War, the 1969–71 War of Attrition, the 1973 Yom Kippur War, and the 1982 Lebanon War. From a persecuted people who had just endured a genocidal campaign to exterminate the Jewish race, Israeli Jews developed a formidable and legendary army, air force, and navy—the Israel Defense Forces, known by its Hebrew acronym Zahal *(Zavah Haganah L'Israel)*. The price for this revolutionary Zionistic dream of the Jewish-Viennese journalist Theodore Herzl was staggering, both on a personal and a national level, thought David, as he watched the shadows, feeling the late-afternoon wind flowing through his thick mane of white hair.

David zipped up his dark-blue fleece jacket, thinking of the incalculable losses he had endured since his arrival in the country: the death of his first-born son, Avraham, killed in the 1973 Yom Kippur War as he crossed the Suez Canal with his troops in a counter-offensive; the death of his eldest grandson, Gideon, a promising young man selected into an elite commando unit—*Sayeret Mat'kal,* General-Staff/Reconnaissance—under the direct control of the chief of staff of the Israel Defense Forces. These had been a crippling ordeal to the entire family.

For years thereafter, his grandson Neyri had attempted to fill the shoes of his deceased older brother, whom he emulated and loved as his best friend. He had established his career as an officer in the IDF, and had also been selected to join the Golani Flying Tigers, a reconnaissance unit of great élan.

During the 1982 Lebanon war in which Neyri and his brother Omri participated in combat missions, the entire nation suffered the fates of soldiers of Israel falling in battle in a controversial war that stirred the nation into an eventual withdrawal from a deplorable offensive into enemy territory. The reputation of the Golani Flying Tigers was sufficient to ensure that Neyri was continually in harm's way. Perhaps one day, thought David, when the information was no longer classified, he would learn the details of the highly dangerous missions he was involved in, in Sidon, Tyre and in Damur, Lebanon, the vicinity of the arch-terrorist Ahmed Jibril's Popular Front for the Liberation of Palestine-General Command training camps at Al-Na'ameh, with an iron-clad infrastructure of underground tunnels and command structure.[1] He was considerably relieved when Neyri switched to paratroop reconnaissance in the 1990s, devoting all his energy as a commanding officer (C.O.) of the paratroops in advanced training, considered the elite of the Corps.

Neyri's younger brother, recently appointed C.O. of the legendary Seventh Armored Brigade at the age of thirty-five, was the father of three daughters who were the joy of their grandfather's old age.

David Ben-Ner was shaken from his reverie by the familiar stride of an officer walking toward him. It was his grandson, looking youthful and impressive as always in his dress uniform.

"Saba, it is good to see you looking so fit," Neyri bent to hug his grandfather. "Are you all ready for your showing tomorrow night?" Neyri inquired, sitting down on the bench beside him.

"As ready as I'll ever be, I suppose. I figure, what's the worse that could happen? If none of my watercolors sell, so I'll give them all to my grandchildren and great grandchildren."

"Actually, I've been eyeing several for the longest time."

"Really, which ones?"

"I think the portrait of the Bedouin Arabs and the painting of the elderly Arab man holding the hand of an Israeli soldier are two outstanding pieces."

"You should have told me before the paintings were hung. I would have given them to you, Neyri."

"Precisely why I didn't tell you, Saba. You deserve to sell all your paintings. You're exceptionally good, you know."

David Ben-Ner swelled with pride as he glanced at his grandson's face. Ever since Neyri was a young boy, he was open, direct and honest. Whenever David was in his presence, he always felt invigorated as if a window had opened and fresh air was wafting into the room.

For the longest time, he was aware that something was not right in

Neyri's world. He doubted it was a woman. He had had a short-lived marriage. When it was over, he never looked back with regret. But he never got involved seriously with another woman either. The things bothering his grandson were deeper than a love affair.

"Are you hungry, Neyri?"

"Don't you remember, Saba, there's a dinner party at Omri's tonight at 7:00 PM? That's why I'm here to drive you over to my brother's house."

"I must have forgotten. The family is making a fuss over nothing."

"It's in your honor, Saba. An art exhibit of your magnificent watercolors is a very special event to your family."

"Do we still have time to sit and talk, and enjoy the breeze a little while longer?"

"Sure."

"Remember when you were a little boy, Neyri, and I would take you on walks through the open fields surrounding the Kibbutz Ramat Rachel in Talpiot?" he asked nostalgically.

"Those were my favorite times alone with you, Saba. I felt so free and wholesome, as if nothing could mar our world. You felt it too, didn't you?"

"I always wanted to make you aware of the beauty of nature, and the special gift of living in Jerusalem. All too soon, you were forced to grow up in a city beset by warfare and violence. I always wanted to protect you from that."

"I know, but reality has a way of obliterating idyllic pictures of existence. Peace is still a dream."

"Maybe in two months' time Clinton will find a way to get Arafat and Ehud Barak to sign a peace treaty?"

"We'll have to wait and see, won't we?"

"Tell me, Neyri, what happened to the girl-soldier you've been seeing for the past couple months?"

"I broke it off awhile ago. It wasn't going anywhere. Besides, she's just too young for me."

"Sounds like you're ready for a serious relationship. It'll happen in its own time, rest assured."

"I agree, but only if I start an entirely new life as a civilian."

"Do you think you'll be able to adjust to civilian life after all these years as a soldier and officer?"

"I don't really know. This is what's been plaguing me for the longest time. One has to risk for one's future. I'm no exception. I'll pay the price, one way or another, if I don't reach out for a new direction."

"Just make sure the price is not too steep, my grandson, so that regrets, if any, will be short-lived.

"You're right, as always. Let's go, Saba, or we'll be late for your own party."

Three

THE NEXT DAY, DAVID BEN-NER decided to complete a watercolor of the Old City started weeks ago but never finished. He planned to give it to Neyri; he worked diligently on it until noon. Leaving the watercolor drying on the kitchen table, David left the apartment, heading for downtown Jerusalem to refill a prescription.

Normally, he walked the mile to the downtown area, avoiding the Egged public transportation bus system, a constant target of suicide bombers. Today he decided to risk it, with little time to spare.

David began to vary his daily routine since the terrorists had chosen downtown Jerusalem to plant bombs—in cars packed with explosives and parked outside stores; in unattended packages on street corners or in garbage cans. He recalled the time a bomb had been left inside a small under-the-counter refrigerator in the center of Kikar Zion. Despite the vigilance of Israeli Jews, none of the pedestrians who had been in the area had noticed the oddity of such an object on the street. Three hundred Jerusalemites were caught in this deadly explosion that took the lives of fourteen people and wounded many more on July 4, 1975. In recent years, bombs were planted on Muslim volunteers eager to become "martyrs" *(shahid)* for their people, anticipating a reward in heaven for their deeds on earth.

After David's favorite restaurant, the Café Atara, had been blown up several times, he never went to the same café twice. It was yet another defense mechanism that subconsciously locked into place among Jerusalemites attempting to master an environment clearly out of control. It was a mind-battle with terrorism. The Café Atara and its regular customers—writers, students, journalists, artists, intellectuals—who had been drinking coffee and eating the famed onion soup since before the 1948 war, had been terrorized repeatedly. Now the café felt forced to relocate to the heart of Rehavia, out of direct target of the downtown area. After each recurrent attack temporarily emptied out the downtown, terrorists targeted the trendy area of Emek Refaim in the southern section of the city, where the locals—particularly the youth—had switched their allegiance after fearing it was too dangerous to frequent the downtown area.

Throughout the country, each suicide bombing, with its wounded and dead, enacted a somber routine. Trucks with high-pressure hoses swept the streets clean of blood, debris, and shattered glass from storefronts or buses. Body parts were collected for burial, while the blood of victims was hosed into the gutters. Stores were repaired immediately. New signs put up: OPEN. Israelis went on living, determined to hold onto the shred of hope that it couldn't happen again in the same spot, the same locale, or the same numbered bus. Within a week, when the same-numbered bus was targeted again, in the same downtown area, one's ability to live in the midst of a sub-culture of terror would again be shattered.

David Ben-Ner descended the steps of the #4 Egged bus on King George Street. He walked toward the pedestrian mall of Ben Yehuda Street with the slow gait of an elderly man, heading directly to his pharmacy. It was a very hot day. David was anxious to complete his errand. He glanced at his wristwatch. It was 12:30 PM. The streets were crowded with pedestrians, as usual at this time of day. David entered the pharmacy, noticing a long line of customers. It was the last thing he observed before a deafening explosion reverberated on Ben Yehuda Street, shattering the surreal silence among those caught in the deadly bombing of a storefront adjacent to the pharmacy. The sound of glass shattering, of mangled balconies abutting the storefronts, and of bodies being flung by the force of the bomb like puppets in a mad dance, were followed by screams of panic and wailing ambulance sirens rushing to the macabre scene of hundreds of people caught in a savage act of violence.

It was later reported on the Israeli news that out of the 172 wounded victims requiring hospitalization, one life had been claimed: that of an eighty-one-year-old man[2] whose art exhibit would remain open to the public for a month, in honor of his life—a life taken merely hours before the show's opening.

"*YITGADAL, V'YITKADASH SHEMAY RAHBAH*... Glorified and Sanctified be God's Great Name...." The Mourners' Kaddish for the dead was recited at the gravesite for David Ben-Ner, who was laid to rest at the Givat Shaul cemetery in the presence of his family, friends, neighbors, and former associates of the *Jerusalem Post* daily newspaper where he worked as a copyeditor his entire life until retirement.

When the family returned to Katamon to sit *shivah*—the seven days of mourning—at the home of his only remaining son, Jacob Ben-Ner, at first it was incomprehensible that a beloved and revered patriarch in the family had been brutally murdered in a senseless act of terror. The family was in a state of shock and disbelief. Neyri appeared inconsolable. His grandfather's death now meant there was a huge tear in the fabric of his life, a rending that he did not believe could be easily mended. It was akin to the wrenching anguish he had once felt upon learning of the death of his older brother, Gideon. He recalled another death in the family—that of his Uncle Avraham, who had fallen in the Yom Kippur War when Neyri was twelve years old. Throughout those three weeks of the sudden Yom Kippur War, which felt like an eternity to him, Neyri had feared for both his father and his uncle. He remembered the look on his grandfather's face when the army disclosed the death of his oldest son along the Suez. It was a look he never wanted to see again as long as he lived. Neyri knew without a shadow of doubt that he now wore the same mask of grief. His grandfather had been his greatest source of comfort since the death of his brother; now he too was gone, and in his place a void of unbearable magnitude.

Unless they found a way to stop the terrorism, the hatred, and the violence, there would be more attacks in the days, months, and years ahead Neyri acknowledged bitterly. The inevitable turmoil was taking its toll on the life of every Jew and Arab who breathed the same air, walked the same streets, and lived together on the same land. It was not only the Palestinians who were without hope; so were the Jews of Israel, facing a foe who would broker no compromise, whose hatred was implacable, and whose desire for vengeance was historic.

Where were the front lines now drawn? Neyri asked himself. Not on the border between Syria, Lebanon, Egypt and Jordan; rather, it was drawn between the civilians of Israel—defenseless, innocent men, women, and children—and the terrorists whose sole raison d'être was to create a theatre of panic and sow havoc within Israeli society. The prime objective of this subculture of terrorism was to accelerate the withering and decay of Israel in order to more easily crush it out of existence.

Who, among his family, friends, Zahal, and acquaintances would be the next victim? he wondered with deep sadness. Wearily, Neyri lifted his head, glancing around the living room at all the people who had gathered to comfort them in shivah. Lastly, he glanced at his father, Jacob, whose head was bowed in sorrow. He longed to comfort him, but could not.

꙰

DURING THE WEEK OF SHIVAH, the house in Katamon was filled with members of Neyri's reconnaissance unit as well as his brother's battalion paying condolence calls on the family. When shivah was finally over, the family went to see the exhibit of David Ben-Ner's watercolors on display in Jerusalem. It was a difficult viewing, mixed with intense emotions over a man who had played such a pivotal family role in each of their lives. By the time they unlocked the apartment door on Harlap Street and observed David Ben-Ner's last watercolor taped to a wooden board on the kitchen table, they were all weeping again. With shaking hands, Neyri removed the dried painting, his eyes glazed with tears.

"I'd like to take this back with me to my base, if no one has any objections," Neyri proposed.

"Your grandfather would have wanted you to have it, Neyri. You were always his biggest fan and he knew it," observed his father as he wearily escorted the family down a flight of stone steps outside the apartment, unable to go through his father's personal possessions. It was too soon; it was too raw. Jacob wondered if he would ever be ready.

WHEN NEYRI RETURNED TO HIS BASE, he was unable to slip back into sync as he always did in previous times after a crisis. All during these summer months tension was running high in the country as both sides of the conflict anticipated that the peace process being hammered out between the United States, Israel, and the Palestinian Authority would unravel, leading to a violent confrontation. Every time Neyri attempted to return to his family in Jerusalem, he was unable to get away from his base.

The Jewish New Year at the end of September was greeted with a high alert throughout the country, the High Holy Days threatened by the provocation of Ehud Barak's controversial cabinet minister Ariel Sharon showing up in the Old City of Jerusalem with a body guard of 1,000 police, resulting in the eruption of another uprising (Intifada) by Palestinian Arabs. Palestinian youths, known as *shabab,* were immortalized when footage of them throwing stones at Israeli tanks was televised. Two twelve-year-old Palestinian boys became instant martyrs: Faris Odeh, who died of fatal gunshot wounds while slinging stones at an Israeli tank; and Muhammad al-Durrah, caught in the crossfire, whose terrifying death in the arms of his father was televised to all corners of the earth.

On October 12, 2000, two Israeli reserve soldiers accidentally made a wrong turn into the Al-Diffeh al-Gharbiyyeh (the West Bank) Palestinian Arab town of Ramallah. The city had become a virtual sanctuary in 1948 for Palestinian families fleeing from Jaffa, Ramlah, and Lod. It was known as a cosmopolitan city, housing writers, artists, and academicians from the Bir Zeit University, where the English language could be heard on the streets as well. By the time these lone Israeli soldiers, Yosef Avrahami and Vadim Novesche, realized they had made a fateful wrong turn, their car—with the unmistakable yellow Israeli license plates—was completely surrounded. They were lynched—dragged, beaten, then shot and killed—by an enraged crowd screaming "*Allahu Akbar!* God is great!" The blood-stained hands of the perpetrators were photographed, depicting the sacrificial murder of Israeli Jewish soldiers for the entire world to see.[3]

This Intifada, coined the "Al-Aqsa Intifada," was worse than the first one, which erupted in December 1987, since it involved the direct participation of Israeli Arabs, Arabs with Israeli citizenship who are supposedly loyal to the State of Israel. There was no way of knowing how far or deep it would spread throughout the land. All Israel knew with certainty was that there was no way to stop what was mushrooming out of control: the intensity of the desire of inhabitants of the West Bank and the Gaza Strip to overthrow the Israeli occupation of the territories. Within a short span of time, it would claim the lives of one thousand Israeli Jews and three thousand Palestinians.

four

"*ASSALAMU ALAIKUM!* PEACE BE WITH YOU!" Asa Ibrahimi flashed the tribal leader a warm smile, extending a hand in greeting,

"*Wa Alaikum Assalam! Tayyib?* Peace unto you! You are well?" responded Sheikh Muhammad Ahmed El-Hamed, as he approached the Palestinian youth, kissing him twice on both cheeks in welcome.

In the time-honored tradition of Bedouin hospitality, the guest was escorted to the male tent. The Sheikh motioned his guest to be seated on a thick cushion, covered in an elaborate Bedouin pattern of earth-tones capturing the colors of the desert sand dunes.

Asa Ibrahimi straddled the cushion, tucking his muscled legs beneath him. His eyes swept over the interior of the Sheikh's domain. Under the canvas of the three-poled black tent, he found it surprisingly roomy for several male members of the Sheikh's family and the occasional goats he had seen on more than one occasion wandering in after dark, seeking protection from the harsh desert temperature. Against the back of the tent, a handsome wool rug was spread, thick, wide, and richly textured, reminding him of the clear, blue, cloudless desert sky.

The tent was filled with the distinct aroma of freshly ground coffee. The Sheikh's youngest son, a boy of ten, handed Asa a thimbleful of thick, dark, Arabian coffee laced with cardamom. The process of preparing coffee—boiling, allowing it to settle, and boiling again—was

a ceremony reserved for men, taught in their youth. Sipping the coffee, feeling the liquid warming his insides, Asa was grateful the long
journey from East Jerusalem had ended.

He glanced at the Sheikh's profile, noticing the proud lifting of the
Sheikh's head as he adjusted his robe to flow over his cushion like a soft
shimmering cloud. The weathered face of the Sheikh, with the deep
lines of his darkened skin was shaded the color of the sands whipped
by wintry rains. The Sheikh, wearing the traditional white long robe
with pale gold thread, the *shillahat,* and the flowing *kaffiyeh* headscarf
roped around his head, completed the portrait of a regal leader.

"A month has passed since we last sat here together. Are you still
filled with questions about your own Bedouin roots?" the Sheikh
inquired, settling down on his floor cushion. For the past several months,
Asa Ibrahimi, a Palestinian Arab from East Jerusalem, had been a regular visitor among the Ta'amireh tribe of Ain Feshkha bordering the
Dead Sea. The youthful Palestinian wore the black-and-white striped
kaffiyeh wrapped around his dark, straight hair, framing his angular
face of dark planes and shadows. His flashing, brown, intelligent eyes
were the only sensitive feature on a face devoid of any sign of softness
or slackness. Ibrahimi's research on Bedouin Arabs was the topic of his
doctoral dissertation at the Hebrew University of Jerusalem.

"I envy you the life of a desert Sheikh. Here, in the desert, surrounded by the expanse of sand and sky, rocky mountainous cliffs and
caves, I feel something that eludes me in the city, as if I shall never get
my fill of Bedouin life and all its rich traditions," Asa Ibrahimi confessed, surprising himself with the depth of his emotions.

"What do you feel here, my son?" the Sheikh inquired softly.

"Peace. Solemnity."

"Bedouins are the only true Arabs. One day you will feel this with
your entire being."

"Why? It puzzles me."

"A Bedouin believes himself to be superior in faith and manhood.
The Jews believe they are the chosen people of God. We, too, are a chosen people, Asa, tracing our ancestry back to Noah and his descendants,
long before Islam and Christianity. We call ourselves "Urban" meaning
"Arab" rather than "Badawi" or "Bedouin." We are scattered throughout

the Arabian Peninsula as well as Iraq, Syria, Jordan, Israel, Lebanon, North Africa, Egypt, and the Sudan. Our cornerstone is the *Ahl,* the patriarchal family. Each tribe, the *Ashirah,* chooses its own name. We do not recognize any authority except within our tribe. Through inheritance, I will pass the leadership to my eldest son who will rule by strict tribal traditions. Two of our customs—hospitality and the blood-feud based on "an eye for an eye and a tooth for a tooth"—makes us cautious about the shedding of blood."[4]

"Wouldn't it be easier not to have to toil to eke out your daily bread day after day, year after year under the brutal baking sun of the desert and the cold, whipping winds of nightfall?" Ibrahimi queried.

"The only thing it would ensure would be my death," the Sheikh enunciated with forcefulness. "I cannot live anything except the life of a nomad, as Bedouins have for centuries, moving from place to place, searching for food and herding the animals as well as providing for tribal life and security. Do you actually think it would be better if I went to live in Gaza or the West Bank of the Jordan wasting my strength, destroying my spirit in order to build homes for the Jews, and humiliating myself with physical labor?" The Sheikh's voice was soft, but his words were not.

Asa Ibrahimi merely shook his head, refraining from answering. He sipped the coffee in silence, knowing how true and insightful the words of his host were. He glanced outside the flap of the tent hoping to catch a glimpse of the Sheikh's daughter. In the past month since the last visit, he had dreamed of her day and night. He remembered when they last saw each other; their eyes clung for a fraction of a second, enough for him to read the love emanating from her. She possessed dove-like deep brown eyes that stirred his soul and roused his blood to an uncontrollable longing. The women of the tribe were carrying baskets on their heads filled with clothes to be washed at the nearby stream. Every aspect of manual labor - tent pitching, water carrying, tending or herding the sheep and goats, making mantles for the men and cloaks for the women, and serving the tribal men—were the exclusive domain of Bedouin women. It was considered a stain on male honor to indulge in physical work of any kind. Instead, the men raided, hunted and protected their tribe. As Asa Ibrahimi peered beyond the tent flap, he was disappointed there was no appearance of the shy, irresistible girl named Shulha. Sheikh Muhammad Ahmed El-Hamed watched carefully over his daughter's chastity, the prerogative of all male members of an Arabian family.[5]

Turning his full attention back to the Sheikh, Asa finally replied:

"No, you are correct, Sheikh Muhammad, the Bedouins are a proud race of people. You represent a pure Arabian strain. Your tribe is superior in every way to those of us who endure life in the cities of the world. All we are as a people—superior in character, generosity, courtesy, hospitality, with a poetic classical language unequalled anywhere on earth—can only be preserved in nature with Allah at your side. In the desert, removed from temptation and isolated from Western influence and contamination, you keep the strain of Arabia pure. If only I could remain here with you, Sheikh Muhammad!" he cried out, unsure who was more shocked by his unexpected outburst.

The Sheikh appeared momentarily startled. A man in his late sixties, he always carefully concealed the depth of his emotions from others. He did not question Asa Ibrahimi's frustration; it had been pronounced even at their first meeting several months ago. He questioned the root of his desire. Did Asa lust for the desert and all it had to offer, or was there an ulterior motive, the Sheikh wondered?

"You may stay here with my family and tribe as long as you want. But, you must not take such a decision lightly. There are others to consider besides you. There is your own family and the commitment you have made to become a scholar. You are well-educated. We are an illiterate people. We have the ability to converse; in fact, we have perfected conversation to the level of an art. As you know it is our favorite pastime. How long will it take you until you tire of such a static life among my simple tribesmen?"

Asa Ibrahimi remained silent, reflecting before answering. Only in the desert did he feel superior as a man. The moment he returned to his apartment on Saladin Street in East Jerusalem a sense of inferiority enveloped him. It aroused his deep-felt rage against the Israeli Jews. He felt cornered, being treated like a second-class citizen under the occupation. Humiliation at check points, constant harassment to show his identity papers infuriated him. His subjugation by an occupier, whose ruthless wielding of military prowess outraged him, and left little energy to expend on finding solutions to the enemy in his midst. His parents and family in Ramallah felt the same as he did. Their method of fighting differed. As professors at the Bir Zeit University, his mother and father were bent on political and territorial concessions from the Jews. Both his brothers, aged twenty-five and fourteen, were involved with the Islamic Resistance Movement. He approved neither the method of his parents nor of his siblings. The only way to outmatch the Israeli Jews, in his opinion, was to outsmart them intellectually and educationally in order to change their portrait of the Arabs as caged, filthy animals.

"Would I tire of the desert, Sheikh Muhammad? Why would I? It cleanses my soul. It purges my heart. It makes me feel jubilantly alive, hopeful, and unburdened as a man," he stated eloquently, duly noted by the Sheikh.

Sheikh Muhammad Ahmed El-Hamed knew Asa Ibrahimi was a man of courage and determination. What he questioned was how he would, as a Palestinian, put such courage and determination to use—for good, or for evil. He was determined to find out. Violence was part and parcel of the life of a wandering Bedouin, in defense of one's life, based on the unwritten law of the desert known to every nomad from time immemorial. Spilling blood was never to be taken lightly.

"How long do you plan to stay with my tribe, this time, Asa Ibrahimi?"

"Overnight, if this is agreeable to you."

"In your honor, a special feast is being prepared for you. Once you have eaten to your full satisfaction, I wish to show you something that might be of great interest to you."

"I am honored, Sheikh Muhammad."

The Sheikh stepped outside, motioning to his wife to begin the feast: sheep roasted whole and stuffed with *burghul*, grain of wheat, a luxury reserved only for honored guests and festivities.

When Asa Ibrahimi was fully satiated, he stood up signifying his complete satisfaction. Sheikh Muhammad hastened away toward the women on the ridge washing their clothes, signaling with his head for his wife to follow him. He ordered her to prepare the horses and the pouches for their short journey. After giving instructions to his wife, the Sheikh glanced toward his daughter wearing the traditional black dress with a matching cape and beaded veil revealing only exquisitely shaped, piercingly brown eyes. Shulha was not looking at her father. Staring at the entrance to her father's tent at Asa Ibrahimi, she quickly raised her veil, flashing a smile meant only for him.

five

THE SHEIKH AND THE PALESTINIAN made their way on horseback to the Dead Sea, heading for the Qu'rum caves on the northwestern side, an area of intensive archeological excavations since 1947, when a total of nine hundred scroll manuscripts were uncovered, written by ancient Hebrew scribes on the Old Testament. When Sheikh Muhammad el-Hamed reined in his white Arabian blue-blood mare, he pointed toward a rock projection with two holes.

"See the smaller cave opening on top?" he pointed with his right hand. "When my cousin Jum'a Muhammad Khalil was a fifteen-year-old boy wandering alone, grazing our tribe's sheep and dreaming about finding a pot of gold, he found this cave. It was toward the end of November, in the year 1947.[6] My older cousin Khalil Musa and I were herding our sheep. Jum'a ran back to us, begging that we follow him to this site. We saw two holes. Only the top one was large enough for a small person to crawl through. Jum'a lifted a rock and said, 'Listen!'

"We heard a loud, startling sound. The rock had hit something. We would have to crawl through the cave opening to investigate. Evening was approaching. We made plans to return in two days' time when we would be free to explore.

"The morning of the second day, I awoke very early, before sunrise. I saw my sleeping cousins spread out on the tent floor. I did not awaken them. Instead, I dressed hurriedly, leaving my father's tent. I found Jum'a's cave just as the sun was rising in the east. I was twelve years old, slim and nimble. My father had nicknamed me *al-Dhib,* the Wolf, ever since I was a small boy. It didn't take me long to slide through the narrow opening to the cave floor.

"When my eyes finally adjusted to the dim light in the cave, I saw pottery, broken from ceiling rocks. Along the walls of the cave were ten jars of pottery. Tall jars, some with covers; others with handles were stacked in a row. I could barely contain my excitement until I started to examine the jars. One after another, all I found were empty jars. Then I came to the last two jars. One contained only reddish earth. I removed the cover from the last of the pottery. I felt something within the jar. Slowly, I removed a bundle, a second bundle, both wrapped in a green cloth, and the third bundle rolled in leather and larger than the other two.[7]

"Placing the three bundles in my kaffiyeh, I tied them with the cord to my waist. I climbed back up to the opening and jumped down to the ground without losing my treasures. I ran all the way back to my father's tent. My cousins were having their morning coffee with my father when I burst in, breathless and unable to talk for the first few minutes. Everyone was staring at me. I didn't realize what I must have looked like, with the reddish earth I had uncovered in the last jars smeared on my arms, face, hair, and clothing. Later I was told by my father that I had had a wild look in my eyes, and then he knew the nickname he had given me as a child was an appropriate one.

"Look, father, cousins, what I found in Jum'a's cave! I found a treasure for him!"

"I did not anticipate the reaction of my cousins. They pounced on me in great anger, beating me on my head, stomach, and legs. Apparently I had profoundly betrayed them by going off alone to investigate the cave without them. They felt they could no longer trust me. My father sided with them. He forbade me to have anything further to do with the bundles in the cave, turning them over instead to my elder cousin Jum'a.

"Do you know what Jum'a did? He brought the bundles to a Ta'amireh tribal site in southeastern Bethlehem. For several weeks, the scrolls were hanging in a bag on a tent pole! I was told later by my father that this was the largest scroll, known as the Isaiah scroll along with a smaller scroll eventually known as the Manual of Discipline. The Isaiah scroll cover was broken. The smaller scroll was split in half. He didn't even know he had a treasure. He didn't know how to care for this treasure. Eventually, by not knowing what he had, it was as if he had not found anything."

"You were the shepherd who found the Dead Sea Scrolls, Sheikh Muhammad?" the Palestinian held his gaze with a look of incredulity.

"Indeed I was, or rather Jum'a was, since he found the cave, and I found the treasure. There is a lesson here you should learn, my friend. Do you know why I brought you here, to reveal this to you now?"

The Palestinian shook his head, staring into the face of the wise man he had come to admire deeply.

"Know the following so you will not err like my cousin Jum'a: If Allah bestows a treasure upon you, treat it with great care, so you will not lose it. Only after we have lost something do we know what we had, and not until then."

"By coming here to live with you and the Ta'amireh tribe, do you believe I will lose something in the outer world?"

"I do."

"What exactly?"

"You cannot straddle two worlds, Asa. The Ta'amireh tribe lives in history. We revere only the past and the daily moments of survival in the harsh desert. We are a separate people. We need independence, freedom, and aloneness. Isolation has kept us intact as wanderers over the desert, just as Abraham and Moses wandered. Prophet Muhammad gave to our nation the holy Qu'ran. From the Jews and the Christians, Muhammad expanded the Word of God. The outer world is a world of immense conflict, bloodshed, and violence. This same world wants to erase the nomadic Bedouins, to build permanent houses for us, and to turn us into farmers and laborers. It does not care that we would disintegrate if our cultural values formed in the desert were taken away from us. All they know is progress comes with science, technology, and new discoveries. All I see of their progress is toil that is corrupt, imprisoning, defiling, and savage. Yet, they call us the savages because we sleep under the sky, with the stars as a protective cover. Are you ready to live the life of a savage, by their definition, my son?"

"Yes, I am," Asa answered without hesitation, thinking he was already considered a savage anyway by the occupiers of his land.

"You are willing to give it all up? What about your studies, your degree?"

"My thesis is written. I will defend it in a month's time and then I am free."

"Freedom comes with a price. Are you willing to pay the price?"

"Yes, I am."

"Do you have any questions, Asa?"

"Only one. You talked of the treasure, of not losing it. You meant the treasure of the desert, did you not?"

"In the desert, you already have found a treasure that the outer world does not hold. Is this not correct, my son?"

"What do you mean?" Ibrahimi asked, wondering if the Sheikh had read his thoughts.

Instead of answering, the Sheikh glanced piercingly at the Palestinian astride a blue-grey mare, looking every inch a Bedouin, wearing the traditional white robe and kaffiyeh. Seated upright, with his shoulders thrust back and his head held high as if pride were wrapped around him like his flowing robe, Ibrahimi looked the portrait of a handsome son of the Arabian desert, with the rays of the diminishing sun glinting off his face, slanting across his chest, and the reins held expertly between his slim, smooth, unworked hands. It was the time of day when stillness enveloped the desert, as the sun began to slip westward.

The Sheikh became aware of the beating of his heart in time with the gentle swirling of the wind whipping the sand around the heels of the Palestinian's mare. He knew from long experience that the mare was eager to be off, galloping as if the wind were pursuing her. The Sheikh glanced away from the rider and his horse toward the shadows gliding over the sand dunes in tempo with an artist's touch. Rocky cliffs and mountain crags jutted, breaking the landscape of its monotonous, endless miles of sand. In the vastness of the desert, time stood still as if one could bask in the timelessness of eternity and immortality.

His eyes sought out the Palestinian, wondering how many years it would take Asa Ibrahimi to be transformed into a true Bedouin in spirit. It would require more than the hold of his daughter to spear this man's heart and open it to another dimension—the dimension of eternity—where he would acquire the ability to hear the whispering silence that beckoned him to step closer to the holy and turn away from the lust for blood that is endemic in this part of the world.

"What do I mean, you ask? My daughter, Shulha—I have seen the two of you watching each other from a distance. Love is the treasure you now possess. Make her your wife, with my blessings. Don't ever let her slip through your fingers. Do not sacrifice Shulha to any other value," he warned.

"I promise," Ibrahimi choked out, with a rapidly beating heart.

"Let us return; it is time."

six

THE FOLLOWING EVENING AFTER HIS RETURN from Ein Fashkha, Asa Ibrahimi descended the steps to his second-floor apartment on Saladin Street, heading west, toward the Jewish sector of Jerusalem. A cool refreshing breeze invigorated him, underscoring his love for the most controversial city in the world, a city holy to three religions: Muslim, Jewish, and Christian including people of Armenian descent. Twenty minutes later, he turned the corner to Jabotinsky and Ahad Ha-Am streets. It was 8:45 PM, too early to attend the party at his advisor's house.

Nostalgically, he turned down David Marcus, a beautiful tree-lined street named after the American Commander who, as part of the pre-1948 Jewish military organization, the Haganah, helped excavate the Burma Road to besieged Jerusalem during the 1948 war between the Jews and the Arabs. He recalled from history books that Marcus, known by his nickname "Mickey Marcus," had been accidentally shot by one of his own sentries.

Asa Ibrahimi passed the villa with a lovely garden that had once belonged to his own Arab family. It had not been desecrated; rather, it had been smothered by the proliferation of apartment buildings dwarfing his parcel of land, reducing it in size but not in the sheer beauty of its architectural design. Parallel to the home once belonging to his parents was the Jerusalem Theatre. His parents could not bring themselves to return here. He had been back dozens of times since learning the exact location of his former residence.

Asa sat down on a bench opposite the theatre, deep in thought. His family had fled from their home one month before the British were due to hand over their mandate. It was April 9, 1948 to be exact, the night of the Deir Yassin Massacre in a Palestinian village five miles west of Jerusalem. When his parents learned the Irgun Jewish terrorists had gone into this village, slaughtering 254 defenseless civilians, including one hundred women and children, there was no further argument between his father and his grandmother to abandon their home and flee to the West Bank city of Ramallah under Jordanian control. They hastily packed as the news reports trickled in that some of the bodies had been mutilated and thrown in a well; others had been dragged through the streets by the attacking Jewish forces. Throughout his childhood, his grandmother continued shrieking *"al-naqba,"* a "catastrophe" was occurring in their midst.[8]

In panic they fled, leaving all of their possessions behind.[9] Clutched in his father's hand were the keys to his home along with the deed attesting to his ownership of the land and of the villa he had built in 1920. Subsequently, as a youth, Asa had read a history book written by the Jews, learning that the Haganah had sent sound trucks warning the villagers to flee before the attack would begin to flush out Palestinian and Iraqi soldiers hiding in the village. Did it matter? Could anything justify such a massacre? he wondered.[10]

Since his birth in 1968, one year after the 1967 Six-Day War, Arabs had lost all the wars to the Israelis—in 1948, 1956, and the battle in 1967 where the Jordanians lost the walled Old City, all of the West Bank, and the Egyptians, the Gaza Strip, with a population of 1.6 million. More than thirty-three years had elapsed since the Six-Day War. All the occupied land won during the 1967 rout was still in the hands of the Israeli government, administered by the Israel Defense Forces' Civil Administration, with the likelihood that all of the occupied territory, not just East Jerusalem where he lived, would eventually be annexed as part of the Greater Land of Israel grand policy.

His two younger brothers—Hassam, twenty-five, and Mahmoud, fourteen—were constantly urging him to join in the resistance movement. Instead, he resisted, hating violence. Hassam was a high-ranking member of Hamas. He joined the night his best friend had been killed during the 1988 Intifada, known as the "Shaking Off." Hamas, an acronym for Harakat al-Mugawama al-Islamiyya, the Islamic Resistance Movement, was established in January 1988 under the leadership of Sheikh Ahmed Ismail Yassin. Sheikh Yassin, from the Zaitoun quarter of the Gaza Strip, was almost totally paralyzed due to an illness. Despite his handicap, he became one of the most powerful men in Gaza during the outbreak of the first Intifada in December 1987. For close to a decade, it was Israel's understanding that fundamentalist Muslims were much less dangerous than the nationalist PLO. Israel learned belatedly that the fundamentalists within the Islamic Resistance Movement were actually a graver threat than the PLO, surpassing the PLO in fanatical zeal and in harboring extreme anti-Jewish hatred.[11] Hamas not only endorsed the uprising or the shaking off of the Israeli occupation forces, but also believed there was no solution to the Palestinian problem except jihad, a holy war binding on all Muslims.

Hamas maintained the same uncompromising attitude toward the land, identical to the Israeli hard-liners' and settlers': the holiness of the land requires it must not be relinquished. The Jewish settlers, most notably the Gush Emunim extremists, referred to the West Bank and Gaza as Judea and Samaria, land belonging to the Jews from biblical times.

Since the occupation, his people had seen their land expropriated by the Israeli government during the years of active settlements in Qiryat Arba, Efrat, Ma'aleh Adumim, Givat Ze'ev, Ma'aleh Ephriam, Ariel, Elqana, Emmanuel, Alfei Menashe, and Qarnei Shomron, all on the West Bank of the Jordan River. In the Gaza Strip, other settlers populated Arab land in Atmona, Morag, Gan Or, Neve Deqalim, Ganei Tal, Qatif, Netzer Hazani, Kafar Darom, Netzarim, Eretz, and Alei Sinai. The Arabs on the West Bank and Gaza were over two million people, amid thousands of Israeli Jews living in Jewish communities on occupied land.

Asa Ibrahimi left the bench to glance at the view of the city and the lights of its inhabitants. He lit a cigarette, cursing the habit he needed worse than a drug, watching the tip of the flame, knowing in his heart that it would take so little to ignite their world into an inferno. He shuttered involuntarily, wanting so desperately for his people to be freed from the bitterness of their lives.[12] Deep in his heart, he knew there was no way out for his people except a fight to the death.

The failed 1993 Oslo Accord was a disastrous option from the point of view of the Palestinians, igniting the latest Intifada. Gaza and parts of the West Bank were festering lands of poverty, overpopulation, unemployment, and a deep sense of malaise and hopelessness. When a people feels as hopeless as his, then the very meaning of existence and the sanctity of life is corrupted, leading the way to suicide bombers and martyrdom. If his people could not find happiness on earth, the only option left was dying as a "martyr" for the promised glory in heaven. Their belief in dying as martyrs, using their bodies as weapons, was sanctioned by leaders and families who could find no other way out of the cesspool of their lives.

It was not his way, nor would it ever be, he thought, as he threw the butt of his cigarette over the ravine. He lifted the collar of his black leather coat as he headed back in the direction of Ahad Ha-Am Street. The living-room balcony doors to Professor David Ha-Levy's apartment were open, enabling him to hear that the party was already in full swing.

David Ha-Levy, his thesis advisor, was the only Israeli Jew he had known for years who did not fit the stereotype or the propaganda taught since he emerged from his mother's womb. From the first exposure to Ha-Levy in a graduate seminar dealing with the current Arab-Israeli conflict, he had been startled to acknowledge a begrudging admiration for this tenured faculty member. Out of twenty graduate students, only two others were male Arabs, one a Druze from Haifa and the other, a Christian Arab from Ramle. Everyone in class seemed eager to hear the perspectives of the Palestinians. On the day Asa made the claim that Israel had to recognize once and for all it could not gain happiness at the expense of another people, there was silence in the classroom, far longer than was comfortable. Breaking the silence, David Ha-Levy concluded that dialogue between Arabs and Jews would be the only rational approach to break the current impasse of no peace.

Pressing the doorbell to Professor David Ha-Levy's apartment, Asa Ibrahimi waited to be admitted.

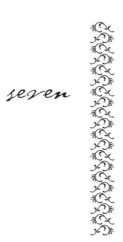

seven

IBRAHIMI DIDN'T HAVE TO WAIT LONG before he was allowed in by a smiling David Ha-Levy, extending a warm hand in greeting. Ha-Levy was a man in his early forties who had completed graduate work at Harvard, returned to the Hebrew University as an Assistant Professor, and worked his way toward a recently acquired, coveted tenure position, and chairmanship of the history department. Politically he was a leftist, insisting that the only way to end the violence with the Palestinians was by withdrawing all settlements and returning occupied land back to its rightful owners. He viewed the establishment of a Palestinian state as the only viable option for them to live in dignity and to stop the hatred, anti-Semitic diatribe, and violence against the Jewish people in Israel.

David appeared more relaxed than usual, in a white shirt open at the neck and a pair of denim jeans. He was a broad-shouldered man whose muscular body retained a toned physique. Tonight he appeared light-hearted; his brown eyes, alert and intelligent, held a look of expectation as he introduced Asa to several people in the room standing near the balcony: an American visiting professor in his department in deep conversation with two women who also appeared to be foreigners.

"Will you excuse me, Asa, while I put on another pot of coffee before I have an unruly crowd on my hands? Please help yourself to food and drinks," David pointed to a long table at the back wall of his living room.

The room was moderate in size, furnished with Scandinavian design furniture: a black leather sofa, matching chair and ottoman, bookcases from floor to ceiling, a rectangular-shaped Persian rug beneath a coffee table cluttered with drinks and half-eaten platters filled with Middle Eastern dishes to tempt the appetites of his guests.

Asa put crushed ice into a tall glass, filling it with Coca Cola. He noticed a long-legged blond with curly hair cascading down her back, looking askance at the falafel—chick-peas browned and fried to perfection.

"Tempting, aren't they?" Asa inquired nonchalantly, as he tossed several into the pocket of his pita bread.

"Very, but every time I eat those falafel balls, my stomach is out of commission for a day or two," she admitted flashing him a friendly smile. "Name's Elizabeth Dumont," she said in introduction.

He gazed into a pair of lovely green eyes the shade of an exquisite emerald, wondering if the thick eyelashes setting off her wide, innocent eyes were real.

"Would you care for a drink, Elizabeth?" he inquired. "My name is Asa Ibrahimi."

"Yes, Asa Ibrahimi, but not until you call me Beth, please."

"With pleasure, Beth" he smiled agreeably, offering her a choice of wine.

"Are you a Muslim or Christian Arab?" she asked directly.

"Muslim," he responded dryly, hoping not to get drawn into a political discussion if he could help it.

"Is that why you're drinking a non-alcoholic beverage?" she flashed him a mischievous smile, dazzling him with her white straight teeth, a pert nose covered lightly with freckles, and eyes too lovely to ever shed tears of sorrow.

Relaxing, he smiled back. It was her turn to suck in her breath, aware of his handsome, dark Semitic features and his arresting smile.

"Yes, Muslims are forbidden to drink alcohol. Like Jews, we also don't eat pork and we believe in one God. What about you? Are you a Catholic, Protestant, or Jewess?"

"A good Catholic from Ireland."

"Where's your Irish brogue, I don't hear it at all."

"Probably I left it in North Carolina where I've been living and working for the past eight years."

"What are you doing in the Middle East, may I ask?"

"I've been doing research in the Department of Antiquities," she offered.

"Are you a Dead Sea scroll researcher?"

"As a matter of fact, I am doing postgraduate research. For the first forty years since the scrolls were discovered, hardly any publications were generated. However, in the last ten years, probably due to a 'conspiracy theory,' there has been a plethora of publications to satisfy even the severest critic," she told him as they took a seat together on the leather sofa.

"A conspiracy theory, over the scrolls, surely you can't be serious?"

"Conspiracy theories die hard, I'm afraid. Apparently, since only non-Jews were initially involved with the work on the Dead Sea scrolls, eventually, after dozens of years had elapsed and not one published word to the outside world could be unearthed, it was theorized that the Christians were repressing the material for fear the nature of the findings would cast Christianity and the Church in a bad light of publicity."

Then Asa told her the story of Sheikh Muhammad who discovered the papyri in the Qu'rum cave in 1947, uncovering the first three scrolls, which now marked one of the most significant findings of antiquity. Asa saw the look of excitement in her eyes, as he described how a young Bedouin shepherd had stumbled across such a treasure.

"Any interesting findings that could possibly shed light on either Judaism or Christianity?" he inquired, with increasing awareness of the attraction she held for him.

"Actually, the findings corroborate what we already know about the Essenes, a sect who broke away from the Pharisees, living in isolation, set apart by their ascetics, the white apparel they wore, and by their prophecy of the end-times. Many postulate today that Jesus was an Essene. In fact, there are as many theories about the historical Jesus as there are stars in the sky," she admitted, acknowledging she was a former student of the well-known and highly esteemed E. P. Sanders from Duke University in North Carolina.

"I hope to gather enough material from these fragments to possibly shed some light not only on Judaism and Christianity but a more plausible hypothesis for the man named Jesus and the incarnate of God."

"Sounds like a formidable task to me. As a Muslim who believes in monotheism like the Jews, we view Jesus as a prophet like Moses and Muhammad, the last of the great prophets. The Trinity smacks of paganism to us, the idolatrous worship of a man elevated, transformed, or incarnated into a God-head. In this respect, the Muslim Qu'ran and the Jewish Torah are considered holy writs, handed to our two prophets through the mouth of God," he concluded.

"Are you, Asa, a practicing Muslim?" she inquired.

"You mean am I religious, do I pray five times a day, and do I attempt to live by the rules and regulations of the Qu'ran? Then, yes, I am a religious Muslim. And you, Beth, are you a religious Catholic?"

"No, used to be, but no longer. So, tell me, do you consider yourself an Israeli Arab or a Palestinian Arab?"

"Do you mean am I loyal to Israel, the state, or to the cause of the Palestinian people?"

"Forgive me; I'm a straight shooter. I say it like it is. Sometimes this gets me into trouble. So if I am making you uncomfortable, we'll change the subject," she suggested with a smile.

"You're not making me uncomfortable, at least not with your direct questions," realizing he may have admitted more than he intended.

She laughed, noting his double entendre with personal satisfaction. He burst out laughing as she slipped him a mischievous smile, looking extremely young and attractive in a mauve cotton dress, midi-length, revealing shapely, tanned legs in a heeled sandal. What was happening to him, he wondered? Wasn't he about to be married to Shulha shortly? In the next moment, Beth Dumont stood up, placing her drink on the table, looking around the room for David, apparently ready to exit the party.

"I'm off to get some well-needed sleep. Lately, I get so little," she confessed. "Let's get together for coffee, shall we? Are you on campus these days?"

"Yes, I am, Beth. Meet me in the cafeteria tomorrow, say 10:00 AM?"

"Sure. See you tomorrow."

As soon as Beth left the room, Asa saw his Druze friend and colleague approaching him with a wide grin on his face, saying:

"*Al-Hamdu lillah!* Praise be to God! How do you find long-legged, blond Americans to swoon at your feet, Ibrahimi!"

"Cut it out, will you, Sahidi. She's doing important research and I was just picking her brain, that's all, and besides, she's Irish, not American" he retorted, suddenly ravenously hungry. "Come on, let's get something to eat," Asa suggested, piling his plate with hummus and tehina, barekas (a pastry filled with spinach), and an Israeli salad of diced tomatoes and cucumbers.

The room had already emptied of its guests when they headed for the leather sofa. They had become fast friends as graduate students together. Sahidi Halabi was born and raised in the Druze village of Dayat el-Carmel in Haifa.

The Druze were a secretive Arab sect whose mukhtars (village leaders) orally handed down from generation to generation the rules and guidelines of their unique religion. The Druze, known as fighters of élan, fiercely proud of their exploits on the field of battle, were (with the Bedouins) the only segment of the Arabic people allowed to serve in the Israeli Defense Forces. The majority of Druze were loyal to the State of Israel, with the exception of the Druze living on the Golan Heights, with family connections in Syria. Until recently, the Druze had been held back from reaching high rank in the Jewish army. Many of the men who fought and then returned to their villages throughout the country led lives of duality and ambivalence, fitting in neither with the Jews one hundred per cent nor with their own Arab counterparts. For the most part, Israeli Arabs detested the Druze for their obsessively harsh treatment at the hands of the Border Patrol, the majority of whom were Druzim. Asa didn't pay attention to such things, knowing a true friend. For the past three years of coursework together, they were inseparable on campus.

"So, my friend, how was the wedding in Ramle?" inquired Asa, as he bit into the pita bread, referring to the third Arab in David Ha-Levy's class, who was missing from tonight's party due to his recent marriage.

"It didn't go so well, actually," admitted Sahidi as he lit a fresh cigarette, exhaling, and then telling Asa the whole story. "You see, after Hamsi took his bride to bed, he discovered there was no blood on the nuptial cushion. All hell broke loose after that."

"You don't mean they..."

"Precisely, I do mean the bride's brother was enraged that his sister did not maintain her chastity and was not a virgin after all. He crushed her head with a rock. She was killed instantly. So instead of a three-day feast and celebrations, a hasty funeral was arranged and the wailing and breast beating was the worst I've ever seen. You see, Hamsi was crazily in love with his bride and I don't personally believe it made a hell of a difference to him. He loved her and would have exonerated her, but before he could think of a plan of action such as planting blood on the sheet, his mother and mother-in-law stepped into the room demanding to see proof of virginity. They got proof all right but it wasn't what they anticipated. I understand the poor girl was as white as the sheepskin rug when they dragged her out of the bedroom into the light for everyone to see how the family had been wronged. All the while she was screaming innocence, claiming she had broken her hymen while riding horses, blah, blah, blah. No one believed this, not even the bride's parents, but all were crazed with grief after she was bludgeoned to death."

Asa Ibrahimi heard the news with mixed feelings, thinking of his fiancée and the fate awaiting Shulha if she were not virginal when they consummated their marriage. He was wild about her, yet according to their customs, it would be a sin if they touched before she became his wife. Despite the intense longing for Shulha every time they met, he dared not approach, for fear of losing control and ravishing her. Bedouins were even more strict in matters of chastity than others. Given the intensity of his physical longing, there would have to be other ways for him to be satisfied until his marriage. In the double standards that mark his culture, as a male he had resources and opportunities to learn the ways of intimacy with a woman without an iota of regret or guilt. He knew before his wedding night he would make love to Beth Dumont, loving her one moment and then forgetting her immediately after parting. It did not occur to him that this could be construed as an amoral act or perhaps that Beth might feel betrayed by his blatant use of her body. It was simply the way of the world in his society.

Sighing, he turned back to his Druze friend and admitted:

"Poor Hamsi, now who will his mother and father goad him into marrying after this fiasco?"

eight

LATER THE SAME EVENING Asa Ibrahimi was walking back to East Jerusalem when he was stopped by an Israeli patrol at the intersection of Ben Yehuda and Yaffa roads in downtown Jerusalem.

"Identity papers, please," demanded a green-beret border patrol sergeant.

While the sergeant reviewed the information on his identity card complete with name, date of birth, religion, address, and I.D. number, the other soldier started asking him questions.

"Where do you live?"

"It's all in my identity papers."

"Answer the question!"

"East Jerusalem, Saladin Street, apartment #3."

"Who lives there with you?"

"No one, just myself."

"Where does your family reside?"

"In Ramallah."

"How many brothers and sisters do you have?"

"Two brothers."

"What are their names and ages?"

"Hassam Ibrahimi and . . ."

"Did you say Hassam Ibrahimi is your brother?" This time it was the sergeant asking the question as he handed back the I.D. to Asa.

"Yes, he is."

"How old is he? Does he live in Ramallah or elsewhere?"

"He is twenty-five. He lives for the most part in Gaza."

"What is the address?"

"I do not know."

"He is your brother, yet, you do not know his address in Gaza? Strange, isn't it?"

"Not if you know my brother, it isn't."

"And your other brother, how old is he and where does he live?"

"He is fourteen. He lives with my parents in Ramallah."

"What are you doing in this neighborhood?"

"I was at a party."

"Whose party? What address?"

"Professor David Ha-Levy's party. Ahad Ha-am Street #12."

"What were you doing there?"

"I told you, I was attending a party."

"Why were you invited to Ha-Levy's party? He's the well-known historian from Hebrew University, isn't that so?"

"Why don't you go ask him, then, if you know him so well?"

"Shut up! I'll ask the questions. Besides, don't you know questions are asked only on Passover?"

"I'm an Arab, not a Jew; I don't ask questions on Passover."

"Okay, wise guy, get your ass into the patrol van."

"Where are you taking me?"

"Don't make me repeat that questions are asked only on Passover, Ibrahimi. Now get in!"

He was driven to the Russian Compound prison, located in the downtown area, for interrogation. He was finger-printed, stripped, and placed in an interrogation room. Over the next few hours, he was forced to take hot and cold showers alternately. Afterwards, a cold fan was turned on his naked body. He was ordered to stand with his arms held pressed against the wall, his legs in spread-eagle position.

For what seemed like hours, he stood pinned to the concrete wall, shivering from cold, fear, and exhaustion while his interrogators attempted to find the whereabouts of his brother Hassam. Time seemed to stand still for him. After being repeatedly slapped in the face, punched, and beaten, the prisoner finally cried out:

"I told you for the hundredth time, I don't know where he lives in the Gaza Strip!"

"Why don't you know your own brother's address?"

"Because he told my family and me it would be too dangerous to know his whereabouts. So he never gave us his address or phone number. Why don't you believe me?"

"So both you and your family know he's a terrorist working with Hamas?"

"I've told you that!"

"Then, why aren't you cooperating with us? The moment you tell us where we can find your brother, we'll let you eat, drink, get dressed, and go home."

"How can I tell you something I don't know?"

"What can you tell us, Ibrahimi?"

"That I hate your mother-fucking guts!"

"For an elite Palestinian studying at the university in Jerusalem, you need to improve your vocabulary—as well as your memory, Ibrahimi," admonished the older police officer, middle-aged, husky, and considerably overweight, nodding to his assistant to stop the interrogation, allow the prisoner to get dressed, and return him to a solitary cell.

Twenty minutes later, a man entered Asa's cell, arresting his attention with his soft, quiet voice, paradoxically carrying the weight of authority behind his laid-back approach to questioning. The prisoner was handed a tumbler filled with cold water. Ibrahimi drained the glass of its contents without stopping to take a breath.

"Would you like more water?" the man inquired softly.

"Yes, please."

More water was placed before Asa as well as a pack of Times' cigarettes. The man lit two cigarettes, one for himself and one for the prisoner.

Asa Ibrahimi inhaled the cigarette in the same manner that he drank the water, gulping it as if it were his last breath. With the cigarette between his fingers, he felt a sense of relief, erroneously believing his long ordeal was coming to an end.

Asa had no way of knowing the man who just entered the cell with him was none other than Israel's chief interrogator of Shin Bet, Israel's Security Services. Known by his nickname, Muki, his track-record for obtaining information was legendary in Shin Bet. It had been rumored, on more than one occasion, that Muki was able to break men not through physical coercion but rather through an astute psychological assessment of an individual held in incarceration. On two separate occasions—in 1984 and once again in 1989—Muki had personally interrogated Sheikh Yassin while he was imprisoned in Israel. With his mastery of Arabic—as well as the Qu'ran—Muki was able to successfully extract valuable information from the leader of Hamas.[13]

"I understand you are completing your Ph.D. defense on the Bedouin Ta'amireh tribe in Ein Fashkha," the interrogator suddenly stated, surprising the Palestinian. Asa was compelled to take a closer look at the interrogator. He was a short man with bushy eyebrows, white hair, a wide-bridged nose, narrow lips, and a solid build. The most impressive details about the man were his piercing hazel eyes and gentle, melodious voice that created in the listener a false sense of security. Asa believed this was a man of character, intelligence, and authority who now held power over him. Perhaps he would listen to reason, believe he was telling the truth, and would let him go home.

"How do you know the topic of my thesis?" Asa blurted out incredulously.

"Since your brother Hassam Ibrahimi has risen in the ranks of Hamas as an expert in explosives, we maintain a rather large file on him, including information on his family. I must admit you are to be commended for your resistance in joining a terrorist faction, given the notorious record of your brother. Can you tell me why you chose the path of an intellectual while your brother has chosen the path of the Islamic Resistance Movement intent on the destruction of the State of Israel?" Muki held his gaze as he waited quietly for the answer to his leading question.

"Violence is not my way. My parents have brought us up to believe violence perpetuates violence. They have done everything in their power to convince Hassam nothing good will come of his connection with

Hamas, all to no avail," he declared putting out his cigarette, eyeing the pack.

Muki handed him the pack, leaned in closer to light his cigarette with the flick of a match, and then coaxed another answer from him by asking:

"What do you intend to do with your degree in history once you are awarded the Ph.D. from the Hebrew University?"

"I plan to write..."

Hours later, when the chief interrogator closed the steel door to Asa Ibrahim's cell, he was convinced the prisoner was not privy to the location of his brother's whereabouts in Gaza or anywhere else in or out of the country.

The morning of the fourth day, Asa Ibrahimi was released with a warning:

"I'd stay out of West Jerusalem, if I were you."

"I have a doctorate to complete, how can I...?"

"When will you learn, Ibrahimi, to stop asking questions?"

The sunlight blasted the lids of his swollen eyes as he made his way back to his apartment in East Jerusalem. In the pocket of his jeans, he removed his wallet, stopping at a nearby kiosk to buy fresh juice and a roll. Fearing to linger longer than necessary in Jewish Jerusalem, he consumed the beverage and the roll en route to Saladin Street. Walking by rote, like a robot, he desired the safety of his apartment, wanting to sleep round the clock. Above all, he desperately needed to shower the dirt off his body, to wash away the memories of the last three nights and days in an Israeli prison cell.

Climbing the steps to his second-floor apartment, he dragged his legs one step at a time to reach the landing. He crawled into bed, falling immediately into a deep, troubled sleep. Intermittently he would awaken at the sound of the telephone ringing incessantly. It was beyond his effort to answer it. Hours later, he heard a pounding at his front door. Fearing it was another arrest by Israeli authorities, he held his breath, praying to be left alone. The noise stopped, along with the excessive beating of his heart, until moments later, when he heard a key being inserted in the lock, the front door opening, and the sound of footsteps in the hallway.

His parents entered the bedroom, in a clear state of worry and concern for him.

"We thought something terrible had happened to you! We've been trying to reach you by phone for days. Who did this to you, Asa? Who battered your eyes and face?" his mother cried out, momentarily overcome with fright for her son. Asa's left eye was swollen shut. Bruise marks beneath both eyes looked like he had been in a brawling fight. His lip was split. Black and blue marks were noticeable on his neck and the exposed part of his chest.

"I was arrested while walking in downtown Jerusalem a few nights ago.... I had been at my advisor's house.... It was late at night.... I was first picked up to show my I.D.... Then I was arrested and interrogated, finally released only this morning. When I got home, I collapsed from exhaustion. Forgive me for not calling you. I couldn't, I was in dire need of sleep, forgive me," he repeated.

"Why were you arrested? You did nothing wrong?" his father demanded.

"They wanted Hassam's address. Since I couldn't provide them with one in Gaza, they thought I was lying, withholding information. They believe Hassam is master-minding the latest series of bombings in the country...I could tell them very little...They wouldn't believe me ...even though they knew I was a doctoral student at the university, they treated me like a hoodlum...."

"They're the hoodlums!" cried out his father in anguish at the sight of his son, beaten, degraded, and humiliated.

"Don't let this change you, Asa, to become a militant like your brother. It would kill us. I couldn't bear to lose you. Promise me, Asa!" his mother begged.

The only answer he was capable of giving her was to reach out to hug his mother, feeling the soothing comfort of her arms around him. Something was churning within him. It was a strange feeling he had never experienced before. By the time they drove him back to Ramallah to recuperate with his family, he knew he was feeling an implacable hatred and the burning desire for revenge.

No sooner was Asa Ibrahimi released from incarceration, his younger brother, Mahmoud, was killed in Ramallah while throwing rocks at an

Israeli military patrol on routine duty. By the time his younger brother arrived at the hospital for immediate surgery, he was pronounced D.O.A.—dead on arrival. His parents were inconsolable.

In response, Hamas ordered militants to round up as many suicide bombers as possible for missions deep within Israeli cities in revenge for Hassam Ibrahimi's brother's untimely death at the hands of the Israeli army.

nine

AFTER ASA IBRAHIMI FAILED TO SHOW UP at the appointed time for the defense of his Ph.D. thesis before the faculty of the history department, David Ha-Levy checked the student roster for his telephone number and address. When there was no answer at his apartment in East Jerusalem, David called his Druze friend, Sahidi, and the two of them went to Saladin Street. A neighbor indicated Asa Ibrahimi was not home but in Ramallah with his parents.

David Ha-Levy and Sahidi drove back to the Mount Scopus campus of the Hebrew University rather than to Ramallah. It was not a safe area for Israeli Jews or Druze to be wandering around.

Outside his office, David Ha-Levy and Sahidi met Elizabeth Dumont, who recounted how she had been stood up by Ibrahimi the day after David's party, and wondered if all Palestinian men treated women with such disdain.

"Asa was unavoidably detained," offered Sahidi, flashing a winning smile.

"I just bet he was; don't bother to make excuses for him, Sahidi," Elizabeth answered hotly.

"He's not, Beth. We just returned from East Jerusalem looking for him," explained David Ha-Levy. "Asa missed his thesis defense yesterday, and frankly, I was worried. He's in Ramallah with his family. Come back to my office. I'll try calling his parents' home. Maybe we can clear this up."

A woman's voice answered the phone at the first ring. It was Muni Ibrahimi, Asa's mother. David Ha-Levy identified who he was and why he was calling. The conversation was brief.

When David Ha-Levy hung up the phone, he turned to Sahidi and Beth, disturbed by the events described to him.

"Asa was arrested the night of my party. After his release from detention, his younger brother was killed by an Israeli patrol on routine surveillance of the Ramallah area. The family is in mourning. We'll just have to wait for Asa to contact one of us," advised David Ha-Levy, looking grim and sober.

SOMETHING HAD CRUMBLED inside of Asa Ibrahimi. Days after his brother's death and burial, he did not know how to make the pain recede. One morning after weeks of isolation and mourning, Asa showered, shaved his beard, had a light breakfast and then took a bus to the campus of the Hebrew University. He knocked on his advisor's door. David Ha-Levy was sitting at his desk deep in papers. Three hours later, he left Ha-Levy's office feeling an enormous weight lifted from his shoulders. Such was the effect his advisor had on him.

Returning to his apartment afterwards, he emptied his refrigerator, throwing out the spoiled food. He aired the rooms and then went to the neighborhood market to buy fresh bread, assorted cheeses, and vegetables. When he returned home with his groceries and a newspaper under his arm, he turned all his attention to reviewing notes for the defense of his thesis, scheduled in two days.

Recalling David's encouragement, he felt his face flush with the warmth of his words, which he couldn't get out of his head:

"Asa, you're one of the brightest students I have had the privilege to work with in years. You will do brilliantly at your defense. I don't want to hear you are ready to throw your whole career away. Everyone on the committee is aware of the calamity that has befallen you with your brother's death, a tremendously harsh blow for you and your family to endure. But you're still alive, and I for one know if your father were standing here, he would be saying the same words to you. Go on, do the best you can, but go on for God's sake, and don't let the brutality of existence strip you of your worth as a human being..."

Asa Ibrahimi lit a cigarette, stepping out on his balcony to see the setting sun. Suddenly the tears he could not shed before were pouring down his face, releasing a flood of emotions. It seemed as if he were drowning in the sorrow and bitterness of his life. Flicking the lit cigarette over the balcony, he stepped within, pressing his forehead against the cold wall of his apartment. After many minutes, he turned on the light in his bathroom and rinsed his face with cold water from the faucet. He reached for a towel and then surveyed himself in the mirror. The light in his eyes had been extinguished as if a spotlight from the stage had been removed. His eyes were dulled with fatigue and despair. He seemed to have aged ten years in the past few weeks of mourning. It startled him into action.

He grabbed his leather jacket, which lay in the sparsely furnished living room. After locking the door, he drove back to Ramallah. He could no longer delay telling his parents he was marrying a Bedouin woman from the Ta'amireh tribe. When he climbed the steps to his parents' front door, he braced himself for what he knew would be an ordeal.

Both his parents were in the living room watching the Arabic news on television. His mother prepared coffee and assorted pastries for her son. When the television was finally turned off, Asa cleared his throat:

"There's something I need to talk to you about."

"Since when do you need to preface your remarks with an introduction? You know we're open to any discussion in this house," stated his father, looking tired after a whole day on campus.

"I don't know how you will take the news that I am planning to marry a woman of my own choice."

"Asa, we would prefer, of course, to have an arranged marriage," admitted his mother. "Given the fact that you are close to thirty and have not favored any of our matches with fine Palestinian families, we have long since stopped trying," Muni Ibrahimi revealed as she sipped the Turkish coffee.

"So, who is she? Who is her family? When will we meet this woman you plan to marry?" his mother continued without delay.

"The family lives in Ein Fashkha, from the Bedouin Ta'amireh tribe. My bride, Shulha, is a sixteen-year-old maiden. Her father is Sheikh Muhammad Ahmed El-Hamed, a man of dignity, respected and well known. I would be honored to arrange a meeting between you and the Sheikh's family," he blurted out.

Silence followed this admission. The only sound heard in the room was of the demitasse being placed on the edge of the coffee table. His mother folded both her hands in her lap, making direct eye contact with him, and then she exploded:

"You can't be serious, Asa! Have you lost your mind? You come from an elite Palestinian family who goes back four generations in Jerusalem. Not only are your parents educated and scholars, but you have also been schooled to become a scholar, with a Ph.D. almost in your pocket. Why in the world are you planning to throw all of this away to marry an illiterate woman from a family of semi-nomadic Bedouins who live in filth and poverty and who will only succeed in bringing you down to their level?" deplored his mother.

"You are highly mistaken. Sheikh Muhammad has no formal training but he is one of the wisest people and leaders I know. I have never been more impressed with a family or a way of life as I have been over the months I've spent with the Ta'amireh tribe doing research on my doctoral thesis. It was during this time that I fell in love with the daughter, who is beautiful, modest, and filled with spiritual grace. More importantly, I fell in love with the lifestyle of the Bedouins. I consider it a higher level of living than anything I have ever experienced in the city of my birth. I feel whole and at peace in the desert. I feel torn apart, inferior, and debased here."

"That's only because of your recent, terrible experience in the Russian compound. I will see to it you will never have to experience this again," promised his father, who had remained quiet until now.

"How do you propose to do this, *Abu?* Locking me up in the house? Throwing away the keys? I'm not like my brother Hassam! You both know how I detest violence. I want to fight the occupation through the use of my intellect and my education."

"Then you are contradicting yourself by marrying into a Bedouin family. You'll have no use for education or intelligence in the desert. What in the world are you thinking?" demanded his father.

"I plan to prepare my written thesis for publication. Then I will continue to do research in order to write other scholarly books."

"In Ein Fashkha? While you are watching the sheep graze?" his father asked in dismay.

"It will be the best environment for a writer, away from all the tension of city life. In desert isolation, I will be able to think and write. Please, honor my decision, and the woman I plan to make my wife. After you meet my bride and her family, I believe you will understand that all the prejudice against Bedouin Arabs has a lot of misguided notions. Won't you please consent to meet Shulha and her parents before you judge them so harshly?"

"We will do so for your sake, my son," answered his father. His mother, unable to utter a word in protest, merely nodded her head.

LATER THE SAME NIGHT, ASA RETURNED to Jerusalem, catching the bus for Western Jerusalem to Neve Shannan Street, in the vicinity of the Israel Museum. By using the Egged public transportation system, rather than his own car with the blue license plate from Ramallah, he felt it would prevent being stopped again by the Israeli police. Shortly before the museum, he descended the bus, walking down a well-lit path, past a small supermarket and several old villas until he came to a clearing with two high-rise towers belonging to the Hebrew University and housing faculty members and visiting staff.

He was looking for Neve Shaanan 18. When he found the building, he took the elevator to the seventh floor, searching the four apartments for a familiar name. Finally, he found it, and then knocked at the door. When no one answered, he leaned on the doorbell, waiting.

Opening the door dressed only in a white terrycloth robe with a matching white towel on her head, Beth Dumont looked stunned to see him.

"Did I catch you at a bad moment, Beth?" he smiled broadly.

"No, not at all," she admitted. "I always greet all my guests like this!" her green eyes sparkling with anticipation.

He closed the door, leaning against it, tracing his fingers over her cheekbones, sliding the towel off her head. Pulling her into his arms, he slowly kissed her, reveling in the softness of her lips. She moaned aloud when he plunged his tongue into her mouth. He untied her robe, feeling the heat of her naked body as he pulled her against him, exploding from desire. He felt her hand on his chest, moving down his legs. He lifted Beth in his arms, his mouth tight on hers, placing her on the carpet before the doors to the balcony. He turned off the overhead light, tearing at his shirt and jeans. He slipped beside her on the floor, running his hands from her ankles, to her thighs, to her stomach, lingering at her engorged nipples as she cried out:

"Don't stop—make me yours!"

Ten

THE FOLLOWING WEEK, ASA ARRANGED a meeting between the two families. The male members of both families entered the Sheikh's tent. Asa's mother was escorted to the tent reserved specifically for women—known as the harem—where she was entertained and feasted in an elaborate style of hospitality known exclusively in desert tribal society. The ordeal of attempting to converse with the mother of the bride, named Isawiyah, in a dialect different from Palestinian Arabic, was excruciating as the feast continued for several hours in the time-honored tradition of Bedouin hospitality. After partaking of the special feast prepared specifically for Asa's parents—sheep, roasted whole, stuffed with rice—a sweetened tea perfumed with mint leaves was served.

It was a Bedouin custom to continue eating until the honored guest stood up signifying complete satiation. Muni Ibrahimi stood up after an appropriate amount of time had elapsed, grateful to her son for his private coaching prior to their arrival in the desert. This permitted the other women in the family to desist from eating as well.

It was time to dispense with the gifts Muni brought with her. On the evening Asa had revealed his intention to marry into a Bedouin family, both Muni and Samil Ibrahimi stayed up half the night trying to solve their dilemma without compounding the situation by shaming Asa into giving up the idea of marriage or, worse yet, losing him in the process. They both concluded that in order to keep peace in the family, they would accept Asa's wishes to be married to his Bedouin bride.

Muni Ibrahimi turned to Shulha's mother, a woman with deeply wrinkled skin who looked old enough to be the bride's grandmother, handing her exquisite gold jewelry once belonging to a great-aunt, as a token of gratitude and acceptance of the betrothal between her son and the Sheikh's daughter. She turned to Shulha, wearing the traditional black Bedouin dress and beaded veil revealing lovely almond-shaped dark eyes shining with joy, bestowing her future daughter-in-law with a necklace, earrings, bracelet, and gold ring. The women who had crowded into the tent were all members of the Sheikh's family—married daughters with children or daughters-in-law. The excitement stirred by the presents, amid the babble of women's voices and the refrain of children, coupled with the enormous quantity of food Muni Ibrahimi was required to consume in order not to insult the hostess, left her in a state of gastrointestinal distress. Finally, she requested that Shulha go to her father's tent with a message to her future father-in-law:

"The time has come to return to Jerusalem!"

On the drive back to East Jerusalem, Asa Ibrahimi felt relieved about the first meeting between the two families. It had gone off well as far as he could observe. Neither of his parents had a negative comment about the whole meeting, and clearly, he could see they were taken by the beauty and exquisite nature of his bride-to-be.

Little did he know they were both filled with heartache, foreseeing a union of two incompatibles intellectually, culturally, and socially. Neither of them expected much happiness for their son, nor did they anticipate any personal joy themselves from the union of two people from such different worlds. By the time Asa left them off in Ramallah, continuing on his way to his own apartment in East Jerusalem, they remained in a quandary over their eldest son. How could he be so magnetized by the primitive enchantment of the desert, the Sheikh, and his daughter, barely sixteen years old? They felt none of the romanticism or euphoria of desert existence that so enraptured their son. All they knew was the blood-chilling realization they had spent one full day of their lives with a backward tribal leader and his clan in a remote part of the desert as isolated and anachronistic as a visit to a foreign planet.

The last thought on Muni Ibrahimi's mind before she fell into a troubled sleep was the dowry requested by the Sheikh before the marriage was to be consummated: it consisted of ten sheep, five goats, and three camels. Muni did not know whether to laugh or cry as she rolled over on her side, relieved to be back in Jerusalem and out of reach of the semi-nomadic Bedouin Ta'amireh tribe.

SHORTLY BEFORE 3:30 AM, the middle of October, a platoon of soldiers in the advanced paratroop training corps were in the process of completing field maneuvers in the Negev desert. The training exercise combined tanks, planes, and infantry in simulated battle conditions. The Battalion Commander, Colonel Neyri Ben-Ner, stood before his men in the moonlight and talked to his paratroopers:

"As you are all aware, we've been on field exercises for close to a month and a half. Each one of you has performed superbly in combined support of our air force and armored personnel. As your commanding officer, it has been a source of deep pride to watch your growth, to see you drive yourselves to your full potential, under duress doing extremely difficult maneuvers as well as arduous field exercises with little or no sleep, with relentless conditions and harsh weather. As the elite Paratroop Corps in Zahal, you personify the best within our military and our society. Persevere, for our country must be defended at all times. It has been my honor to lead you. You will be discharged officially from my command in only forty-eight hours. All drills, exercises, and maneuvers will continue to be performed in the next two days according to the highest standards set from the inception of your training under my command.

"Any questions? It's time to break up camp, to return to base. We'll be marching sixty-five miles, complete with light as well as full gear and weapons. You have less than twenty minutes to be ready to move out."

After their march back to their base, carrying stretchers and heavy gear, Colonel Ben-Ner announced:

"There will be a commander's review at 1900 hours this evening. Get moving, men."

At 7:00 PM sharp, the platoon was standing in formation, freshly showered, shaven, in clean uniforms and brown boots shining sufficiently to see one's reflection, and with their sleeping quarters in impeccable order.

Since the commander's review included weapons inspection as well, it was completed shortly before 2100 hours, or 9:00 PM. The platoon now thought they would be permitted to sleep. Those soldiers who refused to remove their boots in case they were awakened in the middle of the night ignored the warning of rotting feet. Fully clothed, the paratroopers collapsed on their cots; within seconds, they were fast asleep. Those who took the time to remove their boots felt as if the soles and heels of their bruised and battered feet were lit by a steady flame.

By 2300 hours, 11:00 PM, the platoon was awakened from a deep sleep, ordered to be ready to move out within the hour for another nighttime field exercise. The commanding officer led his troops, carrying out the same maneuvers as his men, never asking of them what he did not demand first of himself. Colonel Ben-Ner now had one hour in which to go through his mail and paperwork before the platoon carried out the required exercises.

Neyri looked briefly through the paperwork left piled on his desk by his secretary. Setting the file aside, he opened an aerogram from the States, a letter from a Harvard professor who once was his mentor. Over the years, a growing friendship had evolved with Arnie Davidovitz. Neyri read the letter quickly, hungry for news of his pending visit.

He pulled out a sheet of blank paper from his desk drawer, dating it with the day, the month, then the year, in typical Israeli fashion:

15/10/00

Dear Arnie:
I just returned to my base after a month and a half out in the field with the platoon. With luck, I'll be able to complete this letter to you without interruption, before a scheduled midnight exercise.

As you know, I am always eager for news from you. You sound as if you want to return to Israel, but it's almost 2001 and you have yet to confirm if you are coming during the winter semester. With little time to spare from my command, I have not spoken to my good friend and your colleague at the Hebrew University, David Ha-Levy, to ascertain if you have accepted his offer to do research on the Palestinian-Israeli conflict. I hope your next letter will confirm this, as well as the time of your arrival so we both can welcome you to our country with warmth and hospitality.

In your latest letter, you ask about the paratroops and what it takes to convert a raw recruit into a top-notch soldier. I train advanced paratroopers. By the time they are placed under my command, they have already completed seven months of basic training in Zahal.

The Paratroop Corps has, over the years, acquired the reputation of being not only an elite corps but a dangerous place to serve as well. In reality, it is no more dangerous than any other combat duty. However, the drills and the maneuvers are hard: running, marching, arms drills, shooting practice, obstacle courses, and physical fitness exercises. Field maneuvers can last anywhere from ten days to two months. It can be very challenging being away from the base in all kinds of weather, out of touch with family and friends in civilian life for any length of time, living in pup tents, sleeping on the ground—if they manage to sleep at all.

After parachute jumps (seven of them, two at night and one with full battle gear), they receive the red berets and their coveted parachute wings, pinned on the uniforms of the cadets in a military ceremony. Only the exceptional cadets (what in Zahal we refer to as the "cream of the crop") are selected to go on to a six-month officers' training course to hone the soldier's command and leadership skills.[14] Once they complete the Officers' Training Course, I command them in advanced paratroop training in combined exercises with all the other divisions of the IDF. The paratroopers also continue with sapper training, squadron training, mortar training, and continuous exposure to parachuting and other intensive courses.

As to what is going on in the country, the latest Intifada is doing sufficient damage to lives and to the economies of Jews and Arabs alike. Attitudes are hardening. The political process has come to a halt while the extremists on both sides are flaming the fires even higher. If ever we needed men of vision and courage, it is now. I'm off with my men. Am awaiting another letter from you shortly.

Warmest regards,
Neyri

By the time Ben-Ner's platoon arrived back at the base, the sun was rising on a new day. All hopes of sleep were removed from the paratroopers' minds the moment non-stop fitness drills commenced upon their return.

eleven

ON THE LAST DAY OF OCTOBER, the members of the Ta'amireh tribes gathered together, waiting impatiently for the caravan bringing the bride to the bridegroom.

Off in the distance, the bride was mounted atop a camel-litter, seated on an ornate marriage canopy. The camel was a handsome specimen lavishly decorated for the wedding ceremony about to begin. Accompanying the bride, on either side of the camel, were two of her unmarried female friends waving scarves. Shulha was attired in a gown of crimson red and forest green, one which her own mother had worn when she had been a maiden. Thrown over her slender shoulders was a shepherd's gold-laced cloak. Unveiled, her naked face was luminous, a flawless, breathtakingly beautiful portrait of a Bedouin princess of the desert. As the procession neared the tent of the bridegroom, she urged the camel into a kneeling position. With youthful agility, she descended between the slender horns of the camel. Outside the tent, a black slave belonging to her father held the reins of a white mare, a battle horse with noticeable scars from many raids. Due to the mare's courage and unsurpassed beauty, she was considered sacred by the tribe. Spreading a white lamb's-skin rug over the mare, known as "virgin fleece," Shulha bestowed a wedding present to her bridegroom, in accordance with Bedouin custom.

An old Bedouin man, carrying a baby lamb one week old in his arms, approached her. He placed the lamb at her feet. Expertly and swiftly, the old Bedouin slit the lamb's throat as a sacrificial offering. He grabbed hold of the mare's halter, steadying the horse agitated by the scent of freshly shed blood. Dipping his finger in the lamb's blood, he painted the tribal mark on the mare's white neck.

Sheikh Muhammad stood before his daughter, holding the hand of an eight-year-old boy, recently orphaned. In accordance with Bedouin custom since time immemorial, the slaughtered lamb was handed over to the child.

In the next instant, Shulha vaulted on the back of the white mare. At a walking pace, she guided the mare through the length and breadth of the camp. Behind her, the black slave was holding a great silver sword over her head, signifying to the tribe she was the virginal bride of Asa Ibrahimi. Members of the Ta'amireh tribe, lined up before black tents made of goat-skin, greeted the bride with joyous cries of happiness. When Shulha concluded this ritual, she turned back to the tent of the bridegroom. Alighting from the mare, she removed the white lamb-skin rug from the horse, spreading the rug on the nuptial couch. Retreating into the women's harem, she waited with great anticipation for the bridegroom to call her to him. The simple Bedouin wedding ceremony was now over.

When the bride was beckoned to return to the bridegroom, the first thing she did was to remove the middle pole of the tent, placing it on the ground. A noticeable droop in the roof of the tent was now apparent—a Bedouin sign to anyone who chanced by the tent that a bride and bridegroom were at last together as man and wife.[15]

Muni Ibrahimi, wearing a Western-styled blue silk dress, felt a tug on her sleeve. Turning, she saw it was Isawiyah, the mother of the bride, motioning for her to enter the women's tent for the festive wedding meal. Isawiyah was wearing a black gown elaborately embroidered in gold on the sleeves, collar, and waist. She also wore the traditional beaded veil, revealing a deeply wrinkled forehead and bloodshot, chocolate-brown eyes. Silver bracelets adorned her wrists, showing the gnarled hands and protruding veins of an old woman. Muni shuddered knowing Isawiyah was actually chronologically five years younger than she. In reality, the mother of the bride seemed to be a woman approaching her seventieth year, her ageing due to the harshness of the backbreaking physical work expected of Bedouin women.

"Come! Come!" she motioned to her. The festivities could now begin, including the lavish meal, dancing, singing, and the playing of the *rababa,* a one-stringed violin that is a favorite instrument in the desert.

Within the marriage tent, Asa Ibrahimi leaned on his left elbow, staring down at his wife. Then he threw the extra covers off, examining her from head to toe the way a mother examines a newborn baby. It was the first time he was seeing her face without the ubiquitous veil.

Shulha was more exquisite than he'd imagined. Her complexion was unblemished, smooth as silk to his fingertips. He traced the outline of her body from her elegant throat, down and around the curve of her young breasts held high and taut. Her breasts were tiny, as was her body and waist, more like a young girl than a full grown woman. Shulha was still a maiden he thought, not yet his woman. Moments ago, Asa had broken her hymen with the gentle prodding of his fingers. Now it was time to show his wife the ways of love between a man and a woman.

Shulha shivered as his hands glided softly and gently toward the warmth between her legs. Gently he massaged the mound of dark hair as he bent to tease her nipples with his mouth. As she arched her back, he rolled on top of her, entering as their eyes met. Plunging deep inside, he raised her small hips to meet the urgency of his explosion. When it was all over, he wondered how different it had been with Beth Dumont. When they had merged, it was unlike anything he had experienced before. They had both been on fire, lusting for each other like animals in heat. With his bride, he felt none of this fire. It was only now dawning on him how the sheer simplicity of his wife would erect a barrier to deep intimacy. She would merely serve as a mother to his children and be a conduit for physical enjoyment and release. He closed his eyes against the knowledge that no matter what he did, where he went, or whom he loved, emptiness and dissatisfaction was following him like a lunging shadow he could never lose.

A week after the wedding celebrations concluded in Ein Fashkha, Asa attended the ceremonies at the Hebrew University where he was awarded the doctor of philosophy degree. Seated in the audience were his proud parents, and his favorite aunt, uncle, and cousin. Absent were his wife and his brother Hassam, still on Israel's most-wanted list of terrorists, unable to show his face in so public a ceremony. Beth Dumont was in the audience, beaming a radiant smile. He had told her the truth; he had married a Bedouin woman. It didn't matter to Beth as long as when he returned to Jerusalem, he would return to her arms.

Twelve

IT WAS NOVEMBER 15, 2000. In the Palestinian city of Ramallah, the inhabitants were in the sixth week of the latest "Al-Aqsa Intifada," leading to deaths, curfews, destruction of property, detentions, and arrest of the male population under the age of twenty.

Seated at his desk, surrounded by books in his study, Samil Ibrahimi read over notes for a special lecture series by an outside faculty member at the Al-Quds University. He awakened, as usual, before sunrise to bask in the silence in order to read the daily newspaper or refresh his class notes without interruption. This morning, he appeared distracted. He ran a hand through his graying hair, finding it difficult to concentrate. Gathering his notes, he slid them inside his battered, black briefcase, snapping the lock. The springs on his marital bed creaked. He grimaced involuntarily in a momentary flash of guilt at having probably awakened his wife Muni from a desperately needed sleep. He listened for footsteps from his wife's bedroom. To his relief, the quiet of the early morning persisted. He slumped back against the chair, closing his eyes, trying to refocus his mind.

The events since the end of September had aged him. He no longer looked a youthful fifty-two; rather, he had become haggard, gaunt, and deeply disturbed by the death of his youngest boy. He had warned all three of his sons since they were old enough to understand that he was against any involvement with terrorism. To no avail. His son Mahmoud now lay in a grave for rioting against the occupation forces.

His middle son, Hassam, was now a high-ranking member of Hamas, and his eldest son, Asa, the most promising of the three boys, had become embittered by his detention at the Russian Compound and the interrogation by Shin Bet/Israel General Security Service. As if Asa were a militant by mere blood relations, he had been arrested because his two brothers were in the resistance movement. Were they crazy, he wondered, knowing that they were actually pushing Asa in the direction of becoming a martyr for the cause by their reprehensible treatment? They knew he was clean; they knew he was a student at the Hebrew University, among the elite Palestinians completing a Ph.D. Yet they treated all Arabs the same, no matter what they did to improve their lives.

This Intifada in the year 2000 was different from the last one, which began in 1987 and lasted until 1993. This time, the Arabs possessing Israeli citizenship, and living within the Green Line, joined in the Intifada, a decidedly chilling factor for the Israeli Jews to consider.

Since 1967, the Israelis were the occupiers of Arab land. For thirty-three years, this occupied territory was being expropriated for new Jewish settlements throughout the West Bank and Gaza to establish "facts" on the ground, to ensure that no Arab town, village, or city would be contiguous, necessitating the passing of Jewish checkpoints. All the pieces needed to ensure the strangulation of the Palestinian Arabs prior to the establishment of statehood was being put into place years in advance, ensuring the Palestinian Arabs' dependence on the Israeli Jews' economy, markets, and general infrastructure of roads, electricity, water, telecommunications, and every other aspect of daily living.

To the Palestinians and Israeli Arabs, this "benevolent occupation" resulted in no independence, no autonomy, continued roadblocks and humiliation at the time-consuming checkpoints to wear them down, creating inaccessibility to other Arab towns, jobs, schooling, family and friends. The Palestinian Authority run by Yasir Arafat was a lackey of the occupation, expected to round up Arab militants and hand them over to the Jews, while he, Arafat, continued to run his corrupt organization, which the majority of Arabs detested. Where did the 1993 Oslo Accords lead them? Samil wondered. Not to statehood and to a just peace but to the status quo, intolerable to each and every Arab. From his people's perspective, the Oslo Accord was not worth the paper it was written on, yet now the world was blaming them for the break-down of the peace process and faulting them for resorting to violence instead of accepting peace as offered by Barak.[16] Peace was an impossible entity. How could the Arabs ever consent to peace with the Israeli Zionists, a front for colonialism, imperialism, racism, fascism, and the brutal exploitation of his people?

Circles of hell, he thought; they were mired in circles of hell. Barring a miracle, they were all doomed to a life of hatred, frustration, humiliation, occupation, subordination, subservience, invisibility, exploitation, and inequality. How was he to prevent his beloved son Asa from becoming a member of Hamas, or the Islamic Jihad, or Fatah, or the Al-Aqsa Brigade, or any of the other factions under the umbrella of the Palestinian Liberation Organization?[17] Was he destined to lose everything—the land he loved and his three sons—to liberate the land?

IN THE ARAB CHRISTIAN TOWN OF BEIT JALA later that night, Israeli Apache helicopters swooped down on the unsuspecting villagers attempting to recover from the daytime tank fire and gunshots. The attack by the Israeli soldiers in Beit Jala and the nearby Beit Sahour was in retaliation for the continuous shelling of the nearby Jewish city of Gilo by armed Palestinians.

All day and all night, no one in Beit Jala slept from the relentless bombardment. Panic and fear of dying overwhelmed every man, woman, and child in the Christian town.

In the Western sector of Jerusalem, the crowded #18 Egged bus headed past the King David Hotel. A young man aged nineteen boarded the bus, wearing an oversized green parka worn by Israeli soldiers. He pushed his way to the middle of the accordion bus. From all appearances, he looked like a Sephardic Jew on his way to the Canyon, the largest mall in the city. In actuality, he was a Hamas volunteer suicide bomber from Gaza intent on avenging the death of his brother and brother-in-law, both killed in an Israeli raid in recent days.

As the driver braked to a stop before a red light a block past the supermarket in the trendy section of Emek Refaim, the dark-skinned man slowly moved his hand until it rested against his mid-section and pressed the device hidden beneath his khaki winter coat. In the next instant, the bus and all its occupants blew apart in all directions. People on the street screamed when body parts flew through the air. A young mother pushing her two-year-old daughter in a stroller went into shock at the sight of a bodyless head.

Within minutes, Magen David Adom ambulances were converging on the shell of the #18 bus. The police and Hevrah Kadishah—the units collecting body parts—came to the scene in a coordinated effort at rescuing the wounded and salvaging what remained of the dead. By nightfall, Hamas claimed responsibility for the suicide bombing attack, which initially left twenty-seven dead and eight seriously wounded. Two of the wounded—a ten-year-old boy and his thirty-four-year-old mother—died during the emergency surgery to save their lives.

THE ARAB NEIGHBORHOOD OF RAMALLAH was asleep at 4:00 AM when an Israeli officer and members of his unit stopped their jeep in front of the Ibrahimi apartment. Behind the officer was another jeep-load of soldiers and a demolition truck.

Colonel Neyri Ben-Ner switched on his communication system:

"Rafi, this is Ben-Ner. Proceed as planned, over."

"Rafi here. On our way, over."

Four of his paratroopers headed for the second-floor landing. Spilling out of the second jeep, paratroopers spread out along the parameter of the street.

On the second floor, soldiers pounded on the door to the apartment owned by the Ibrahimi family. Inside, Muni and Samil had been fast asleep in their bedroom. In another room, their son Asa—visiting them as he did once a month since his marriage—was fully dressed, ready to depart before sunrise back to the Ta'amireh tribe and his wife. Hearing the crashing of the front door, he jerked open his bedroom door, and found his way was barred by two paratroopers in red berets aiming their M-16 assault rifles at his chest.

His parents tumbled out of their room, dressed in pajamas and robes.

His father was rubbing the sleep out of his eyes, as if unable to believe whether he was having a nightmare or facing reality.

"What's going on here?" his father demanded.

Colonel Neyri Ben-Ner entered the living room. The terror in the room was palpable. He knew within moments it would increase. His orders were clear.

"You have twenty-four hours to pack your clothes and remove any of your valuables. Your apartment, and those of your neighbors in this building, will be completely demolished."

"There must be some mistake, officer. We are not terrorists. My wife and I are academics, as well as my son Asa. Why in the world are you doing this?" Samil Ibrahimi demanded, horror and incomprehension spread across his face.

Neyri Ben-Ner approached the family.

"By now you should know that harboring a terrorist or being connected with a suicide bomber will result in the destruction of property. A few hours ago, a suicide bomber from Hamas blew up the #18 bus, killing, maiming, and wounding Israeli men, women, and children in Jerusalem. The latest bombing was master-minded by your son, Hassam Ibrahimi, a terrorist who has been hiding underground for the past year-and-a-half. Get dressed, Mr. and Mrs. Ibrahimi, or you will find yourselves on the street in your pajamas."

His parents returned to their bedroom, accompanied by a soldier. Asa Ibrahimi took a step toward the commanding officer, stopped by the barrel of the rifle.

"Why are you carrying out orders to do collective punishment to my family? It's not fair!"

"I'm sure the survivors of the number 18 bus agree with you. It's not fair they have to dig graves and bury their dead today, now is it?"

"It is cruel and inhuman punishment to destroy my parents' home and all their possessions. They already lost their land and property in the 1948 debacle. Now you are doing this to us again?"

"At least you'll have your lives to live afterwards, unlike the dead Jews in Jerusalem."

Neyri Ben-Ner turned away from Asa Ibrahimi and his enraged countenance. He switched on his system:

"Rafi, get the rest of the residents out of the building and those residing on either side of this apartment complex. Warn residents to steer clear of the blasting and demolition crew to avoid unnecessary casualties in the area, over."

"Rafi here. Read you clear, over."

Without a glance at Asa Ibrahimi, Ben-Ner walked out of the apartment complex and down the stairs, to command the rest of the operation.

Colonel Ben-Ner knew what would follow. Within twenty-four hours, the dazed family would be evacuated from their apartment, carrying the last of their possessions to the street. As soon as the loudspeakers gave the orders to clear the building and those surrounding it, the entire neighborhood of Ramallah would be alerted that another home was being targeted for demolition. Eyes filled with hatred would appear on the street or on the balconies. Soon, wailing would fill the air, the wailing of the women and children whose homes and possessions were being wiped out—as if they never existed—while they themselves stood by helpless to stop the destruction.

This time, thought Ben-Ner, it would be worse. By this act of collective punishment, he knew deep in his heart he was helping to sow the seeds of the next terrorist, Asa Ibrahimi. They'd find his brother Hassam, and eventually assassinate him, triggering sufficient rage and lust for revenge to turn Asa Ibrahimi into a terrorist. It had happened before, on numerous occasions. Ben-Ner had no doubt it would occur again.

He was beginning to despise the work he was carrying out for the defense of Israel. It was no longer an army facing soldiers in battle on the frontlines. These were now the frontlines, except that the enemy was no longer a soldier like himself; rather, the enemy was the Arab people in the street, their stone-throwing children, their enraged women and vulnerable children being used as pawns by families and militants to die as "martyrs" for the cause of the resistance, against tanks, helicopters, and a lethal army. He could no longer stomach receiving or giving the orders. It was getting more and more difficult every day. He was fatigued all the time. Perhaps it was an accumulative fatigue from years of pushing himself too hard in a relentless race against time. Until recently, he had been proud to be a soldier of Israel, to be the frontline of defense, to wear the uniform of the Israel Defense Forces. Not anymore. The myth of the demonized enemy no longer worked for him. The myth that they had no alternative but to hold onto the occupied territory for security or for a future trump card to be played around the peace conference table was corroding the moral fabric of Israelis as a people. There had to be a solution to killing, violence, destruction, terror, fear and abnormal lives. There had to be, he thought.

Twenty-four hours later, the orders were given to demolish the apartment building. Moments before the crumbling of the building by the demolition crew, a silence pervaded the area as the neighbors and friends of the Ibrahimi family gathered around them to give comfort and support through their personal nightmare.[18]

When the job was completed, Neyri Ben-Ner's driver drove out of the area in haste. Shortly, the walls of the Old City loomed in front of them. Neyri Ben-Ner reminded himself that these orders to destroy the homes belonging to the families of suspected terrorists dated back to the British Mandate period. It was little consolation to him that the origin of this collective punishment was vintage British. It did not erase the fact that it was still heartbreakingly cruel to destroy what was irreplaceable for the average struggling Arab family, given the low per capita income in this part of the world. Moreover, he reasoned with bitterness, it did not deter terrorists from becoming volunteers or terrorism from escalating.

Neyri turned to his driver:

"Take me to Talbiyah, #12 Ahad Ha-am Street," he requested, leaning back in the seat, feeling more tired than he ever remembered in his life.

Thirteen

"THERE'S TOO MUCH HATRED HERE. We have to do something to change the hatred," Neyri was speaking, sprawled out in David Ha-Levy's study, drinking strong Turkish coffee, looking for answers to his dilemma.

David had grown up with Neyri. They had attended the same gymnasium high school together; they had entered the army as new recruits at the same time, and had been accepted into the paratroop brigade. Both had been married, divorced, and were childless. Each was attempting, in his own way, to come to terms with existence, searching for a solution to the dilemma of being surrounded by violence and retaliation, and their lethal effect of further violence without end.

"There's only one thing which can change what's happened to the Arab people and the Jewish people, do you know what I'm talking about?"

Neyri shook his head, feeling some of his exhaustion and depression lifting in David's presence.

"Attitudes are cast in cement here. They must change first before there are any solutions. In order to stop the violence between the Arabs and Jews for a century now, we have to stop demonizing each other as objects rather than people. It makes it easier to retain the cycle of violence since you can do anything you want to an object. If, on the other hand, we viewed each other as people with the same yearnings, desires, needs, goals and hopes, only then will there be a shift. What's preventing this from happening are the people who profit from keeping the violence going."

"You mean Arafat and the terrorist factions?"

"Yes, and the Israeli military machine is big business, Neyri, don't ever forget that. Personally, I don't believe either side wants peace. The Arabs don't want peace. They would have to give up their dream of getting all the land back taken from them in wars since 1948. We, Jews, in my opinion, really don't want peace either. We would have to give up the dream of Greater Israel including occupied land we have retained since 1967, and all the settlements built on this occupied land over the past thirty-four years."

"Is greed, then, perpetuating the violence on both sides?"

"One way of looking at it. Unless and until peace offers more to either side, killing is going to continue."

"I'm sick to my soul of all this violence."

"There just might be another explanation. Maybe David Shipler, the *New York Times* journalist who wrote the 1986 Pulitzer Prize-winning book *Arab and Jew: Wounded Spirits in a Promised Land,* was right in his contention that there was a close parallel between the two Semitic races. The conflict between the two people was necessitated by the fear on both sides that the hate would turn to love if the flames of hatred weren't stoked for an eternity.[19]

"As a historian, a thinker, and a researcher, I've had a chance to look closely at why nations or people go to war. Most of the time, war is promoted for inane reasons, like nationalism. Wars have been fought in the name of religion and nationalism ad nauseum, causing people to butcher each other for centuries. You know better than anyone, Neyri, what war is really all about on the battlefield. We both fought in the Lebanon War. The very first time you shoot another human being, it's something you never forget, no matter how long you live. It's imprinted on every cell in your body. Isn't this correct? I know it's imprinted on mine."

"I've never spoken to anyone about this. It's not something the average person in the street, or, for that matter, my family would understand.

Even my brother and I have not exchanged notes about our battles. It's not what soldiers do, anywhere in the world, I suppose."

"Do you know the reason?"

"Yes, since there are no words in the human vocabulary to describe what we see in war, we feel isolated from the rest of humanity. Organized, professional killing on the battlefield is barbaric, ugly, and disastrous to the victims and the perpetrators. It goes against every moral fiber of one's being. After the war is over, we keep it buried deeply in our subconscious," Neyri admitted.

"War is trauma. It never leaves those who have seen combat. Did you know that one-third of the soldiers who fought in the 1973 Yom Kippur War have remained psychological basket cases, unable to function in the real world? How many Israelis know these statistics? How many outside of these victims' families and friends honestly care?" David inquired.

"Everyone goes back to 'normal life' expecting these soldiers to do likewise. What they don't realize is there's no world to go back to that resembles normality after you have been exposed to the barbarity of seeing men dying on the battlefield. It's not heroic. It's not glamorous as it is often depicted. Once war begins, soldiers fight for the sake of the unit. It's not even for the country or nationalism. It's to protect one's unit, that's where the heroism comes in, that's where the selflessness evolves, each man watching out for the next man beside him in the trenches."

"David, why hasn't war been outlawed in the world, then, if it is fought for ulterior motives other than the defense of one's nation?"

"For the same reason war continues in our country. It's to someone's advantage to keep the war machinery oiled."

"Why isn't the myth of war blown to shreds, and the reality of war depicted as it really is, not like in the 1991 Gulf War, a sanitized war that didn't even seem real, yet 100,000 Iraqis were pulverized in their tanks?"[20]

"People seem to have short memories and they are brain-washed by propaganda pounded into their heads by politicians and the media. We're all involved in this hoax. We're all guilty. We're all to blame if we end up destroying this earth of ours. We have enough intercontinental ballistic missiles to wipe out the entire planet earth. Whenever we stockpile war machinery, we end up using it. The same applies to these nuclear warheads; the chances are quite high we'll find a pretext to use them in the foreseeable future. What have we done to stop the proliferation of such weapons? What are the chances of a rogue state or terrorists getting their hands on enriched uranium and centrifuges to make their own dirty bombs and deploy them in our lifetime?"

"Why are we sitting on our hands doing nothing?"

"I'm doing research; I plan to write a book to expose the myths. It's all I feel I can contribute at present. It's what each one of us can contribute individually that might make it possible, one day, to have peace in the world. It will take an epiphany to awaken people."

"I still don't know what I can do personally to stop what's going on in my country. So I'm back to zero."

"No, you're not, Neyri. You've come full circle. You're not back to zero. Now you have to decide how you want to proceed, where you want to spend your energy, and to what purpose you will devote the rest of your life," David stated solemnly.

fourteen

"WE HAD OUR LIFE'S SAVINGS VESTED in our Ramallah home, Asa. We don't have even a shekel to lay out on the purchase of another place to live," announced Asa Ibrahimi's father, looking stunned, shattered, defenseless, and exhausted after the ordeal of watching the destruction of his home.

"Stay here in my rented apartment until we can figure out what to do. Not all is lost. We are more than our possessions. We can fight this. We'll go to the Israeli Supreme Court to try to get justice done."

"You're wasting your time, Asa. We'll never be compensated. Your brother is a Hamas terrorist responsible for crimes against the State of Israel. The courts will never rule in our favor," exclaimed his distraught mother, who had remained silent since leaving Ramallah. Somehow, she did not seem as broken as his father. Anger burned in her dark brown eyes, so he knew she was fairing well. In his father's eyes, all he saw was a man dazed, unable to focus. It scared him. It made him realize just how much he loved his father, and how he feared losing him.

"Let's get something to eat. You must rest from your ordeal. Then we'll figure out what steps we should take, if any," suggested Asa Ibrahimi, feeling a deep burden of responsibility for his parents and their predicament.

AT THE TEL NOF AIR FORCE BASE, Colonel Neyri Ben-Ner walked across his base to the office of his commanding officer, who was nowhere to be found. He left a message with the secretary: "I need an appointment today with Brigadier-General Nachmani. Please tell him it cannot wait."

Two hours later, after a brief but difficult meeting with Brigadier-General Nachmani, Neyri retraced his steps through the large base, noting the difference in his stride and his own personal relief.

An enormous burden had lifted from his heart when he clarified out loud his expectations to his commanding officer.

"I want to step down from my command."

"Why?"

"For personal reasons."

"That's not good enough, Neyri. If you want another command, I need to know why."

"Perhaps I haven't made myself clear. I don't want another command. I want to give up my command because I plan to give up my career in the army to return to civilian life."

"To do what?"

"To return to school, to get a higher degree in a field that interests me."

"Then what?"

"Why, work, of course."

"In a nine-to-five job? You're not cut out for this, I know it, and so should you. After twenty years in the IDF, the adjustments to civilian life are extremely difficult for most of us."

"I'm ready. In fact, I've been ready for a long time. I didn't know it until only recently."

"What happened to change your mind?"

"I don't like what I'm becoming. I don't like confronting Palestinians throwing rocks at my patrol. I don't like hunting down Palestinian militants and assassinating them. I don't like demolishing Palestinian homes. I don't like the tit-for-tat responses, the violence, and the heavy retaliations. I've lost the spark necessary to continue in my command, to be an example to my men. I don't have it in me any more. I'm tired now most of the time. I need to get out. When may I be released from my command?"

"In June. This will give me enough time to find a suitable replacement for you. You've done a superb job until now, Neyri. I expect you to continue to do so until you are relieved on June 1."

"I'll do my best."

"I know you will. I think you're making a mistake. We all get burned out. Would you reconsider if I gave you a three-month leave of absence after June and then decide?"

"No, Brigadier-General Nachmani, nothing is going to change my mind."

THREE DAYS LATER, THE ISRAELI ARMY targeted the militant Hamas leader responsible for the latest series of suicide bombings in Jerusalem, Tel Aviv, and Afula. For the past year, he had managed to elude his enemies. He knew he was on Israel's most-wanted list. As a high-ranking member of Hamas, he had been personally instrumental in orchestrating "martyr" missions in Tel Aviv, Haifa, Afula, Hadera, Petach Tikvah, and Jerusalem, one after the other in unrelenting hits that kept Israeli Jews in a state of panic, never knowing when or where the next human bomb would detonate, taking the lives of Jewish civilians in the carnage.

Hassam Ibrahimi snapped off his car radio, concentrating on the road to the Jebalya refugee camp where he planned to enlist new volunteers to join Hamas as human fuses. Hassam Ibrahimi was a man in his early twenties who had spent his teens defying his parents and anyone else in authority, including his teachers. His parents had objected to his militancy, always pointing out his older brother, Asa, as a model he should follow. There was neither jealousy nor closeness with Asa. He considered Asa an idealistic dreamer who believed in the co-existence of Jews and Arabs on Palestinian land. He had long ago given up convincing Asa to join the cause; instead he had concentrated all his efforts on his younger brother, Mahmoud, who had met an untimely death, pelted by rubber bullets, arriving brain dead at the Ramallah hospital.

What a pity to lose his brother, who had been eager to join Fatah or Hamas, following in his own footsteps. His parents had been beyond consolation since his brother's death at the hands of the Israelis. Yet, they still begged him to get out of Hamas, to go into hiding before it was too late.

He glanced at his wristwatch. It was 4:00 PM. He had to accomplish his objective at Jebalya, and then head back to his home in Gaza before the curfew would go into effect. For over a week, ever since the suicide bombing in Jerusalem, no one in Gaza knew precisely when the curfew would be lifted. Until then, there was a shoot-to-kill command from the Israeli army for anyone found outside their homes after the evening curfew. His people were penned in like animals. He felt no remorse in treating his enemies in like manner by blowing them up as if they were of no value to anyone on earth.

He began to slow down his blue Fiat, noticing two stalled cars up ahead. One of the cars was a Peugeot with its hood up. He jammed his foot on the brakes, leaning his head out the car window at the droning of a helicopter within sight of the refugee camp. Instantly, Hassam realized it was a set-up. His heart began thudding wildly in his chest as he grabbed the door handle to flee from his car. In the next instant, Hassam Ibrahimi's car burst into an inferno as a missile directed with precision from the Apache helicopter pierced the hood of his vehicle, vaporizing him in the driver's seat, ridding Hamas of yet another leader who had caused so many devastating deaths among the Jewish people of Israel.

The same evening, when Samil Ibrahimi returned from Bir Zeit University to his son Asa's apartment on Saladin Street, he turned on the Arabic news to learn the following statistics: Since the outbreak of the Intifada at the end of September, 170 Palestinians had been killed, with over 6,000 wounded; 22 of those killed were young children under the age of fifteen, including his own son Mahmoud.

Before Dr. Ibrahimi had a chance to absorb this news, the announcer switched to the day's event at the entrance to the Jebalya refugee camp in Gaza. The assassination had targeted a Hamas militant described as twenty-five and a permanent resident in Ramallah, and identified as the second son of Professors Samil and Muni Ibrahimi to die within two months' time. A photo of Hassam Ibrahimi appeared on the screen as Samil Ibrahimi jumped off the sofa, beating on his chest and screaming out his pain. By the time his wife found him crumpled on the floor, he had been dead for over an hour, the result of a massive heart attack.

fifteen

HUNDREDS OF GAZANS MINGLED with Hamas militants carrying the body of Hassam Ibrahimi to his burial site. Amid the roaring anger of the crowds, black-hooded militants vowed revenge for the latest assassination of one of their leaders, pelleting the air with AK–47 machinegun fire to underscore their rage and desire for vengeance.

In the West Bank town of Ramallah, the funeral for Hassam Ibrahimi's father was in process. Mourners flocked from all over the city, as well as from East Jerusalem and the two campuses of Beir Zeit and Al-Quds. Samil Ibrahimi was well known, well-liked, and revered as a political science scholar with Marxist leaning.

Clustered around Muni and Asa Ibrahimi were relatives and close friends, colleagues and former students giving emotional support for the incomprehensible fate of a father and a son dying on the same day. In the forefront of their thoughts was the additional mourning over a beloved teenage son and brother, combined with the destruction of Muni and Samil's home, all within a brief span of time. For several days after the two funerals, Asa Ibrahimi's East Jerusalem apartment was lined with people paying condolence calls.

Asa remained beside his mother on his used, gray cloth sofa, smoking incessantly, barely speaking to anyone. None of his Bedouin family was present. It was by his own decree that his wife was not with him.

Upon learning of the death of his father and the assassination of his brother, Asa informed the Sheikh:

"It would be best if my wife remained with the Ta'amireh tribe, having no exposure whatsoever to life in the city away from the desert. I do not know how long I will have to remain with my mother in Jerusalem."

The Sheikh nodded his consent but pressed him further. "Is there something you are not telling me, Asa?" the Sheikh asked him in his customary way of speaking softly while piercingly staring into his eyes as if to see deep within his soul. "Nothing," he retorted a shade too sharp, "why would I hold anything back from you?" There was a more compelling reason Asa did not want Shulha with him. It had nothing to do with his daughter's humble origin, concluded his father-in-law.

Within twenty-four hours of his brother's funeral, two strangers showed up unannounced on Asa's doorstep, delivering a cryptic message to him:

"Sheikh Yassin, the leader of Hamas, sends his condolences to you and your mother."

"Please tell Sheikh Yassin my mother and I am humbled and comforted by his message," responded Asa with alacrity.

"We will convey your words to Sheikh Yassin," they nodded and departed shortly thereafter.

Long after the living room was emptied of people, Asa felt the lingering presence of the two Hamas emissaries. In the kitchen, Asa helped his mother clean dishes and cover leftover food brought by well-wishers. Muni turned to him asking:

"Who were those two strangers? I didn't like the looks of them. Are they personal friends of Hassam? Are they from Hamas?" she demanded.

"Hamas."

"What did they want from you?" she asked, fear showing in her dark, mournful eyes.

"They offered us condolences from Sheikh Yassin, the leader of Hamas."

"Is that all they came to convey? Merely a condolence message from their terrorist leader?"

"I do not believe, *Umm,* they were sent all the way from Gaza merely for words of consolation from the powerful Hamas leader. Encrypted in the message was, I believe, an invitation to join Hamas in order to take over my brother's former leadership position within the organization," Asa detailed.

"No! I forbid it!"

"That's what I told them ... so they left," he smiled only with his lips. His eyes remained cold and dead as if sightless, the way a blind person would stare into the void.

"Will they be back?"

"Probably."

"What do you intend to do about it?"

"Nothing. Hamas works through volunteers. You can't coerce someone into militancy or it won't work. They're not stupid. Lately they have changed their tactics, from what my brother told me before ... before he was murdered. They are seeking members more educated and trained. It better serves their needs."

"How long do you think you can hold out from this type of pressure? They might kill you if they think you are cooperating with our enemies."

"They might. Then again, they might not. It doesn't really matter one way or another," he admitted, returning dried dishes to the kitchen cupboard.

His mother stopped what she was doing, placing both hands on his shoulders, forcing him to look at her. "Asa, talk to me, tell me what's in your heart. Promise me you won't do anything as foolish as your brothers!"

"Promises? What do promises mean anymore? It's just empty, like all of our words!" he said bitterly.

"We must help one another live through this nightmare. You're all I have left, my son. You have a wife and her tribe for emotional support. I have only you. I'm afraid, afraid for both of us. We're two people adrift, as if we were clinging to one life raft in the middle of a rough sea. Although I have my students, I am an old woman. You are young with a whole life yet to live, building a new family with Shulha, and one day children, *Insha Allah*. Nothing else is more important than that."

"I don't know what to tell you, Umm, except how I really feel at this moment. Nothing means anything to me anymore. Whatever hopes and dreams I had have been buried along with my father and both of my brothers."

"Our pain and agony are so raw. We both require time to heal from our wounds. No one can give you a reason to live, Asa, not even your own mother. I've never known you to give up, you of all people!" she sounded frightened by the bitterness of his words as well as the knowledge, within the deepest recesses of her soul, that she felt precisely as he did. Now they would be living under the twin umbrella of terror: the one created by the occupation, and the other born of hopelessness and helplessness, creating victims of them both.

ISRAELI JEWS WERE BEING SLAUGHTERED with impunity by Arab terrorists during the month of October and November 2000:

October 2 – Wichiav Zalesevky, 24, of Ashdod was shot to death in his head in the Masha village on the Samaria highway.

October 2 – Sgt. Max Hazan, 20, of Dimona was shot near Beit Sahur and died of his wounds.

October 8 – Hillel Lieberman, 36, of Elon Moreh received multiple bullet wounds as he entered southern Nablus.

October 12 – Two IDF reserve soldiers, Yosef Avrahami and Vadim Novesche, 33, drove in error into Ramallah, were lynched by an enraged Palestinian mob, shot, and flung to their deaths from the police building while the perpetrators raised their blood-stained hands in victory.

October 19 – Binyamin Herling, 64, a rabbi from Kedumim, sustained fatal injuries on a Mt. Ebal trip with Israeli men, women, and children near Nablus when Fatah and Palestinian security forces opened fire.

October 28 – Marik Gavrilov, 25, of Benei Aysh was found dead in his charred car on the outskirts of Bitunia and Ramallah.

October 30 – Eish Kodesh Gilmor, 25, of Mevo Modi'in was shot to death during his security watch at the National Insurance Institute, East Jerusalem branch.

October 30 – Amos Machiouf, 30, of Gilo/Jerusalem was murdered in a ravine near Beit Jala refugee camp.

November 1 – Lt. David-Hen Cohen, 21, of Karmiel together with Sgt. Shlomo Adshina, 20, of Kibbutz Ze'elim were shot to death in Al-Hader, near Bethlehem.

November 1 – Reservist Major Amir Zohar, 34, of Jerusalem, on active reserve duty in the Jordan Valley was killed in the Nahal Elisha settlement.

November 2 – Ayelet S. Levy, 28, and Hanan Levy, 33, were blown up in a car bomb explosion at the Mahane Yehuda open market in Jerusalem; among the injured were ten Jerusalemites. Islamic Jihad accepted responsibility for the bloody attack.

November 8 – Noa Dahan, 35, of Moshav Mivtahim was shot to death driving to her job at the Arab Rafah border crossing into Gaza.

November 10 – Sgt. Shahar Vekret, 20, of Lod, was shot to death by Palestinians near Rachel's Tomb, Bethlehem.

November 11 – Sgt. Avner Shalom, 28, of Eilat died in a shooting attack at the Gush Katif junction in Gaza.

November 13 – Sarah Leisha, 42, of Neveh Tzuf, traveling near Ofra died from fatal gunshot wounds from a passing car.

November 13 – Cpl. Elad Wallenstein, 18, of Ashkelon and Cpl. Amit Zaana, 19, of Netanya died of gunshot wounds from a passing car while in a military bus headed in the direction of Ofra.

November 13 – Gabi Zaghouri, 36, of Netivot, while driving a truck near Kissufim junction, was shot to death as he approached the southern section of the Gaza Strip.

November 18 – Staff Sgt. Baruch Flum, 21, of Tel Aviv was shot and killed by a senior Palestinian Preventive Security Service officer in Kfar Darom.

November 18 – Staff Sgt. Sharon Shitoubi, 21, of Ramle, was seriously wounded in the Kfar Darom shooting attack. He subsequently died of his wounds on November 20.

November 20 – Miriam Amitai, 35, and Gavriel Biton, 34, both from Kfar Darom fell victim of a roadside bomb explosion of a bus loaded with children from Kfar Darom headed for school in Gush Katif. Injured were nine, including five children.

November 21 – Itamar Yefet, 18, of Netzer Hazani died from a gunshot wound to the head by a Palestinian sniper at the Gush Katif junction.

November 22 – Shoshana Reis, 21, of Hadera, and Meir Bahrame, 35, of Givat Olga were killed when a passing bus on Hadera's main street was detonated. The area was filled with shoppers and people driving home from work. Sixty people were wounded.

November 23 – Lt. Edward Matchnik, 21, of Beersheba died in an explosion near Gush Katif in the Gaza Strip at the District Coordination Office.

November 23 – Sgt. Samar Hussein, 19, of Hurfeish was shot and killed by Palestinian snipers who opened fire at soldiers on patrol near the Erez crossing.

November 24 – Major Sharon Arameh, 25, of Ashkelon was fatally wounded by Palestinian fire near Neve Kekalim in the Gaza Strip.

November 24 – Ariel Jeraffi, 40, of Petah Tikva was killed near Otzarin by Palestinian fire in the West Bank.[21]

November . . .

sixteen

NEYRI BEN-NER HAD NOT BEEN HOME in months. The uprising and suicide bombings were taxing not only the soldiers of Israel but the border police as well, with no end in sight.

On Thursday evening, December 21, on the first night of Chanukah, Neyri called his parents and his brother's house, telling them he was unable to make it back to Jerusalem for their annual party. Later the same night, he returned to his office to write a letter to his former teacher and friend from Harvard University, Arnie Davidovitz.

21/12/00

Dear Arnie:

This letter is long overdue by several months by my calculations. From the news you have been seeing in the U.S., I'm assuming you have correctly assessed that the riots on the West Bank and in the Gaza Strip are still blazing out of control. It underscores the basic premise of my former teacher in international relations, Yehoshofat Harkabi, who maintained since the late eighties that our de facto annexation of occupied territory is an error and if we continue in this misguided policy, the territories will become an albatross.[22] As the years go by, I agree with Harkabi more and more vociferously that our government is leading us toward disaster. I want to quote you something from his book, which has never left me since I first read it: "If the State of Israel comes to grief (God forbid), it will not be because of a lack of weaponry or money, but because of skewed political thinking and because Jews who understood the situation did not exert themselves to convince the Israelis to change that thinking. What are at stake are the survival of Israel and the status of Judaism. Israel will soon face its moment of truth. The crisis that faces the nation will be all-consuming."[23]

I see decline in Israeli society everywhere—the disastrous decline in our quality of life, quality of leadership, and the lingering effects of mistakes since the 1982 Lebanon War. We have "progressed" from a nation of sacred Zionism to a nation that scoffs at Zionism as passé; from a nation that considered labor redemptive to a nation who abhors physical labor, looking down on it as "Arabusque" (a derogatory term for "dirty" Arab work); from austerity in the fifties and sixties to the mind-numbing greed and materialism of the eighties, nineties, and into the twenty-first century; from a unified nation—particularly during wartime—to the importance of the individual in our society; from a moral nation to one with eyes averted from rampant corruption in government officials as well as in our civilians; from a compassionate nation whose soldiers believed always in the "purity of arms," acting morally on the battlefield to protect civilians and remove Israeli dead or wounded left on enemy territory, to turning one's backs on the slaughter of eight hundred Palestinian women, children, and the elderly in the infamous Lebanese Phalangist atrocities in the Sabra and Shatilla refugee camps in Damur, Lebanon; from belief in our intelligentsia and the written word, to becoming untouched by the outpouring of the press on the moral decay seeping into the fabric of our lives—these are the things that torment me lately. In the depth of my being, I believe Amos Oz is right in maintaining that the conflict between Israel and the Palestinians is a collision between right and right.[24]

I feel a sense of despair that unless there is a voice of reason—like Rabin's—to return the occupied territory won in the 1967 War for peace with the Palestinians, we will be drawn into a quagmire untenable for either side. The only hope I have is the following: both sides are aware that if a war of no return were unleashed (God help us), there will be no winners, only losers.

It seems all I have been doing lately whenever I have a minute to myself, which is rare, is to think about the two miracles—the establishment of the State of Israel in 1948, and the miraculous reunification of Jerusalem in the 1967 Six-Day War. We are a people who believe wholeheartedly in miracles, even our secular soldiers concluded this after fighting for, and winning, Jerusalem. Now, let's you and I reflect on these miracles. Since the 1967 War when we became an occupation force over occupied territory, how have we treated this miraculous occurrence? We have essentially relied only on military force as an answer and we have a de facto annexation of Palestinian territory in the West Bank and in Gaza. We have turned this miracle into a nightmare for us—as conquerors and occupiers—as well as making the lives of the Palestinians into a hell on earth by controlling their lives under our military occupation. Hence, the riots that flared from 1987 to 1993, and the current, ongoing Intifada, leaving dead and wounded on both sides, instability to our economies, and a sense of bone-weary hopelessness as we futilely await a political solution to eradicate the status quo and finally lift the burden off the shoulders of the soldiers of Israel.

Since 1973 when we were caught with our pants down, not believing the Arabs would "dare" fight us again, what did we do but "trip" into our next war in Lebanon—a personal war of two leaders in Israel who steered Israel into a dark tunnel. The only light shining in the 1982 Lebanon offensive was the light from the courageous officers and soldiers who refused to serve this war, who could not stomach the atrocities they were witnessing to get to the PLO by whatever means it took. So the seeds of hatred were planted once more against the Jewish people.

I will leave you with this thought, Arnie. The Six-Day War and the territory captured were like diamonds sparkling tantalizingly before our eyes. Since the Arabs refused land for peace after this war, we held tenaciously to the territory in the West Bank and Gaza, never admitting how our lives were being affected, how each year we held tighter to the land until the diamonds were so dulled, it is as if it has lost all its luster. This is how I see our lives today—lusterless.

Are you still considering coming in February 2001 for research pur-poses? I do hope so because we need people like you here, eager to seek solutions to our intractable problems. Besides, it's been too long already, and you are missed deeply.

Wishing you a happy New Year, with 2001 almost here—

> Warm regards,
> Neyri

It was only after mailing the letter to the States did Neyri realize he never mentioned stepping down from his command in June. There would be sufficient opportunity to tell Arnie once he arrived in the country.

Somehow, Neyri managed to find time in his busy schedule to fill out applications to graduate schools in the U.S. He planned to inform his family once he had been accepted by a school of his choice.

PART II

January 2001

seventeen

BY THE END OF JANUARY 2001, within the State of Israel, anyone who had previously held a left-wing political position favoring a peaceful co-existence with the Arabs was left in a state of complete despair, seeing the platform decimated by the explosive Intifada now in its fourth month of continuous rioting. The uprising was far more virulent and costly than the previous one.

The dreaded "fifth column" Ben Gurion had warned about in 1948 seemed to have grown like a wild mushroom. The 760,000 refugees fleeing before, during, and after the British Mandate was handed over, now numbered five million Arabs, all demanding their "right of return" under United Nations Resolution 194. If Israel were to accept five million antagonistic Palestinians within its midst, it would be tantamount to willful self-destruction. After months of suicide bombings, drive-by shootings of civilians in their automobiles, as well as the knifing of people in the streets, Israeli Jews were in a state of unrelenting watchfulness over their children, family, friends, and neighbors. Their lives were now reduced to a surreal existence. There appeared to be no way to move forward, or to live normal lives. For all intents and purposes, the terrorists were winning.

The world hardly reacted to their plight, giving Israeli Jews the distinct impression that no one cared how terrorism was destroying Israeli

Jewish society, underscoring their feelings of deep isolation. Consequently, the Israeli Defense Forces attacked the terrorist infrastructure in their cells, cars, and on the streets of Gaza to deter them from inflicting further harm on innocent Jewish civilians and soldiers. These retaliatory raids enraged the Arab militants and the Arab civilian population, ensuring the violence would be stoked endlessly. Israel was castigated for its lethal missile strikes against Hamas leadership, creating the impression that the real victims in this conflict were the suffering Palestinian Arabs being subdued by the military might of the occupation forces. It was another public relations coup of the Palestinian Arabs. To Arab satisfaction, the world continued to be duped by lies, distortions, and misconceptions, as if they were stringed instruments played by experts in Middle Eastern duplicity. For Israeli Jews, there was no escape from reality. Their only alternative was to stand firm in the face of a deepseated hatred reminiscent of the anti-Semitic genocidal Germanic rage. It was a racist hatred inculcated into the minds of Arab children from birth, ensuring that the seeds of destruction would be transplanted to succeeding generations.

What few people in Israel questioned was the causal root of Palestinian rage and hatred. It was not hatred per se against the Jews as much as it was against the Zionist political machinery which at first denied there were any Arabs in the "wasteland" that constituted Palestinian territory prior to 1948. Next, it was denied that 760,000 to 1 million Arabs were driven out of the land according to "Tokhnit Daled, Plan D," approved by Prime Minister Ben Gurion and carried out by the Haganah despite protestations to the contrary. Eventually, these same "invisible Arabs" were not permitted to return to their villages within the Green Line in 1949, including the token 100,000 initially granted the status to return.

Despite the Israeli Declaration of Independence granting equality to all citizens as a democratic State of Israel, this equality and democracy in essence extended only to Jewish citizens, relegating Israeli-Arabs to second-class citizenship and all that implied. The "benevolent occupation" of the Israeli military authorities since 1967 over Palestinian Arabs who lived in the occupied territories of the West Bank and Gaza eventually evolved into a brutal subjugation of the Palestinian people after the 1987 Intifada, a revolt of Palestinian men, women, and children against Israeli occupation. Living ghettoized lives; experiencing curfews for days, weeks, and months at a time; faced with the demolition of their homes and property, with diminished access to water, food, electricity, and transportation; subjected to roadblocks, arrests and interrogations, the Palestinian people confronted bitter circumstances on a daily basis. All these measures of occupation prevented facility of movement, self-determination and, residually, the abolishment of democratic principles of freedom by the occupation forces. For the Palestinian people, the nightmare was all-encompassing, dating back to the initial 1948 disaster, when they became refugees and stateless people up to and including the present moment.[25]

If the reasons for Palestinian hatred were dissected, digested, and fully comprehended from the daily perspective of Palestinian lives truncated, segregated, and isolated, perhaps then the Israeli people—whether they be doves or hawks, proponents of settlements and a Greater Israel or zealous advocates of "transfer" (expulsion to another Arab state)—could fully comprehend what actually was happening in their very midst. Israeli Jewish citizens were too caught up in sheer survival mode to give more than a cursory glance at their own suffering and that of the Palestinian people, and stop the political machinations grinding both people into oblivion.[26]

Whenever the suicide attacks were directed at the heart and soul of the country—targeting Israeli youths drinking coffee at cafes; dancing with lovers at discos; celebrating a joyous occasion at restaurants—the Jews of Israel turned inward, burying their dead, bleeding with open wounds, ravaged by despair, helplessness, and the hopelessness that neither a political nor a military solution would be found to combat the problems endemic to the conflict between two people living on the same sacred land. The fundamentalists on both sides ruled categorically: if either side were to voluntarily relinquish its hold on this holy land, he did not deserve to possess the land ... or to live.

On the evening of February 5, the phone rang in David Ha-Levy's apartment. It was an overseas call from Harvard University's eminent historian, Arnie Davidovitz, confirming his arrival within the next two days for a six-month sabbatical at the Hebrew University.

"Why Arnie, are you choosing Israel, of all places, with the ongoing Intifada?"

"I believe it is possible to draw up a blueprint for peace. I want both of us to work together to search for a solution to the Arab-Israeli conflict," Arnie Davidovitz disclosed.

"I've never known you to be a hopeless dreamer, Arnie. What you are asking is an impossibility given the reality of our situation here. I've come to the dreary conclusion the Palestinian Arabs will broker no peace deal."

"I've never known you to be so rightist in your thinking, David. What in the world has happened to you since you left the States?" Arnie demanded.

"My eyes have been opened since Arafat killed any possibility of a peace agreement, igniting a series of vicious, unrelenting attacks in my land. Are you still sure you want to come here?" inquired a puzzled David.

"I told you before we're going to find a solution to the Middle East crisis. If the Catholics and the Protestants in Ireland can work out their differences, surely there is a glimmer of hope and light in the Middle East as well."

"Have you always been a perennial optimist, Arnie?"

"Always!"

"When does your flight arrive in Israel?"

IN THE DESERT'S VAST ISOLATION from all civilization (with the exception of the Ta'amireh tribe, his wife, and her immediate family), Asa Ibrahimi discovered solace. After the official mourning for his father and brother, he remained with his mother in Ramallah for a few weeks to be a source of comfort and help to her. As a widow mourning the loss of a husband and two sons as well as a home of her own—with her identity now in tatters—his mother appeared adrift like a boat without a sail. Leaving her to return to Ein Fashkha was traumatic for both of them, but it had to be done.

On the first evening alone in the tent with his wife, Asa allowed the gentleness of Shulha's voice and hands to soothe him after a slow process of lovemaking, leaving him physically sated but emotionally yearning for the arms of another woman. Shulha continued to whisper endearments in his ears. She shifted her position, raising herself on her elbow in order to see the expression on his face.

"What is it, Shulha?"

"Asa, give me your hand," she said placing it over her stomach. It felt more taut than usual. He recalled that during their lovemaking, when he had suckled her breasts, she had involuntarily cried out. Had he hurt her, he wondered with concern, rather than bringing her pleasure as he had intended?

"What are you trying to tell me, Shulha?"

"We are going to have a baby."

"A baby? You are pregnant? Are you okay? When will it be born?" he questioned her, stunned by the knowledge that his own progeny was now growing inside her womb.

"July, *Insha Allah*. It will be a boy. He will be as handsome as you."

"How do you know?" he teased.

"I'm a woman. You must trust, Asa, and be patient. Soon you will have a son to name after your father. You are not the same without him. You do not speak to me or play with me like before. So I know you are crying inside. Your son will take sadness from your heart. Then we can be happy again. Like before," she told him simply.

The eloquent simplicity of this woman who was his wife touched him. It surprised him in ways he had not understood before. Perhaps creating this child would bring him in tune with her spirit, the way he had hoped when they were in the throes of love, before marriage and reality cast a shadow over their romance. He would make an effort to regain those feelings for her, he thought, as he took his wife in his arms, watching her fall into a blissful sleep.

But it was not easy for him. The moment he fell into a deep sleep, he dreamed of Beth, awakening in the dark, longing for the touch, shape, and heat of her body. He became hard and pulsating. He awakened his wife, not waiting for her to be aroused, sliding deep within her as he plunged into her depth, searching for his release.

eighteen

ON THE EVENING OF FEBRUARY 15, snow fell in Jerusalem, continuing unabated until the early hours of morning. Jerusalemites awakened to the startling sight of the entire city blanketed in a soft white mantle. Driving was hazardous in a city of hills without provision for snow removal. All schools, municipalities, and government offices remained closed while inhabitants delighted in a day away from routine.

In the southern section of Jerusalem, on Klausner Street, Professor Arnie Davidovitz sat in the study of David Ha-Levy's deceased father, reviewing the Palestinian National Charter. From time to time, he would glance up at the snowdrifts, bite down on his pipe, and then returned to his research.

Over a week since his arrival in the holy city of Jerusalem, he was grateful to David Ha-Levy for opening his parents' home to him. "This house needed the warmth you can provide. Now I won't dread coming back to my home anymore, with you in it," David openly admitted to him.

Arnie Davidovitz relit his pipe. He walked over to the glass balcony door, with a partial view of the walled Old City of Jerusalem. The city of David, he thought solemnly, as he admired the beauty of the most hotly contested city in the world, wondering if, perhaps, he had been too optimistic that a conflict of this duration and intensity was resolvable.

Having read the Palestinian National Charter all morning, he found the disturbing language of the PNC chilling and difficult to digest. He returned to his desk, summarizing the Charter, which was initially set down at the Palestinian Liberation Organization's National Congress, held in Cairo from July 1 to July 17, 1968. At that Congress, the following decisions and declarations were made:

It is a national duty to bring up Palestinians in a revolutionary manner, working for the liberation of Palestine through armed struggle. The nucleus of the Palestinian liberation war is commando action, with Arab unity and liberation as its primary objective in the overthrow of Zionism and its elimination from Palestine. The armed revolution will not cease until the homeland is liberated from imperialist aggression (i.e., Zionism).

Regardless of the passage of time, the partitioning of Palestine in 1947 and the establishment of the state of Israel is entirely illegal. It is contrary to the will of the Palestinian people; the Balfour Declaration and the Palestinian mandate are deemed null and void. Jewish historical and/or religious ties with Palestine conflict with historical facts. Judaism is a religion, not an independent nationality; they do not constitute a single nation with their own identity.

The Palestinian people reject all solutions substituting for the total liberation of Palestine. Zionism, as a political movement, is racist, fanatic, aggressive, expansionist, and colonial in aim, and its methods are fascist. Israel is a geographical base for world imperialism and hence a constant threat to peace in the Middle East and the world. The liberation of Palestine will destroy the illegitimate movement known as Zionism, and outlaw its very existence. The Palestinian people possess the genuine legal right to liberate and retrieve their homeland.[27]

It was apparent to Arnie that the Charter spelled out the clear intentions of the Palestinian Liberation Movement: no cessation of violence or the armed revolution until the homeland (referred to as Palestine) is liberated from imperialist aggression (that is, Zionism and the Jews).

Arnie opened another document signed on Sabbath eve, on May 14, 1948, Fifth Day of Iyar 5708, Proclamation of the Provisional Council of State the Declaration of the Establishment of the State of Israel in the City of Tel Aviv, and summarized its contents:

The birthplace of the Jewish people: Eretz-Israel (the Land of Israel). On November 2, 1917 the Balfour Declaration re-affirmed the League of Nations' Mandate sanctioning internationally the Jewish people's right to rebuild its national home in the land of Israel. On November 29, 1947, the United Nations General Assembly passed a resolution for the establishment of a Jewish State in Eretz-Israel, open for Jewish immigration, based on freedom, justice, peace, and complete equality of social and political rights to all its inhabitants irrespective of religion, race, or sex, safeguarding holy places of all religions and adhering faithfully to the principles of the United Nations Charter.[28]

Arnie remained disturbed by the virulent language of the PNC Charter. He pulled a pad of legal-sized paper toward him and lifted a pen to scribble notes in his illegible scrawl:

What is the Arab-Israeli conflict? It is not only a fight over the land, but over modernization, scientific and technological advances, a culture that fears coming out of the Dark Ages; in fact, it is a culture preferring stagnation to growth in order not to be threatened, overwhelmed, taken over by modernity, by secularism, and the eradication of a carefully protected "divine" way of life.

Anything opposing the Koranic posture is to be avoided or smashed. It is a gigantic clash of two cultures—not only two divergent religions. In the seventh century Muhammad, aged forty received a "call" or "vision" to carry a divine message to the Arab people—"There is no God but God and Muhammad is his Prophet." His purpose was to unite the tribes and communities. In 622 AD Muhammad fled from Mecca to Hathrib, better known as Medina, carrying the message to the entire Arab world through Islam. Muhammad's vision of a universal community spread to all parts of the world after his death in 632 AD. The Islamic movement evolved into a vast empire. Initially it was carried on by Abu Bakr, Muhammad's father-in-law, and Umar, a relative who became the Khalifa (Caliph) after Muhammad. Jordan, Syria, Persia, Byzantia, Iraq, and Iran were conquered and ruled under the Omayyads Dynasty until it was overthrown in 747 AD by the Abbasid Dynasty.

For the next five centuries, Islam ruled over a mighty empire, even though the nomadic Bedouins never changed, always moving in circles around their grazing grounds praying five times a day: at dawn, at noon, in the afternoon, at sunset (known as the "Maghrib prayer"), and finally in the evening, after dinner. The life of the Bedouin consisted of "an eye for an eye," as they attempted to raise camels and sheep, and to raid caravans for subsistence on desolate stretches of sand, ever seeking the blade of *hamdh,* salt grass, for their animals under a cruel sun that baked skin to leather, brutally exhausting their bodies. Inherent in the soul of the Bedouin is a deep pride that stems from the belief in a superior faith and manhood, with a deep fear of dishonor. A proud race of people, the Bedouin are hospitable, courteous, and generous, considering it a sacred duty to treat all strangers in the desert with respect. It is to be noted that Bedouins live and die by the sword; in many respects, they can be said to have a split personality known as *izdiwaj*—from their quiet, kind personality can erupt a murderously brutal rage, if provoked.[29]

From the Mongol invasion of the thirteenth century through the Black Death and second Mongol invasion in the fourteenth century, to the nineteenth century, Arab stagnation set in. The search for knowledge and the freedom of thought that typified the golden period of the Arab Renaissance from the seventh to the thirteenth centuries shriveled, replaced by dogmatism and fundamentalism.

The decline from a golden past to a dismal present of poverty, ignorance, and passivity, created a pathological preoccupation with this past, to the point of a chronic illness through end of the eighteenth century. To the horror of Arabia, Napoleon descended on the Arabian lands between 1789 and 1801, bringing in his wake Western culture and civilization.

Arab stagnation culminated in a loss of power, and apathy. It was not to awaken again until the period after World War II when Arab nationalism arose on the scene in the attempt at a united Arab front. The rude awakening resulting from a series of defeat at the hands of Israel in 1948, 1956, 1967, and 1973 led to soul-searching and introspection to comprehend this catastrophe. They blamed it on a turning away from Islam; they blamed it on Arab weakness, backwardness, and stagnation. Others blamed it on a chronic need to live in the faded past rather than acknowledge reality in the present. Finally, other Arabic intellectuals attributed their failure to a gross inferiority complex due to their lack of modernization in comparison to the Western world.

Arnie Davidovitz hunted for a fresh pen in the desk drawer after running out of ink. Then he underscored the following note: *The Arab people will remain a defeated people whose anger, hatred, and jealousy is a direct result of a decaying society. Unless and until it develops along the lines of science and technology, it will remain a backward nation in the twenty-first century.*

The phone rang. When he lifted the receiver, he heard David's deep, calm voice on the line:

"Arnie, thought I'd come over this afternoon to discuss a proposal for our joint research project on the Middle East. Unless, of course, you have other plans, like cross-country skiing to Jaffa Gate?" he laughed, feeling more lighthearted with his former advisor and good friend living in his family home. It somehow made the absence of his parents easier to bear, knowing there was life in the home despite their untimely death.

"Love nothing better, David, my boy. I've already begun taking notes on some historical points I needed to clarify for myself. Come by for an early dinner. Bring a change of clothes with you to stay over. Wouldn't want you to drive back in the evening when the ground might start to freeze. There is some wicked hilly terrain in this city."

"It will give us the whole evening to work on our proposal. Don't worry about dinner. I'll order some take-out food from my favorite restaurant downtown. See you later, Arnie."

He hung up the phone, glanced at his wristwatch, and then headed for the kitchen to prepare a hearty breakfast, grateful for such a profitable morning. After breakfast, Arnie showered, wondering how Israelis managed to keep the water from the shower running into their bedroom, a nasty occurrence since his arrival over a week ago. Reminding himself to ask David why modern Israeli apartments still retained plumbing from the dark ages, he dressed casually in dark slacks and a thick mohair sweater knitted by his deceased wife.

He adjusted his blue shirt collar over the neck of the charcoal grey sweater, glancing at his image in the mirror. Clearly, he was far too overweight, noticing how his potbelly aged him. Apparently he had gone to seed, being a widower for the past three years. Miriam had been his right arm throughout their difficult but loving marriage. Once it was clear she was infertile, his wife had devoted herself to her own career as a biologist at Wellesley College until an aggressively growing cancer killed her at the age of fifty-eight.

They had been so devoted to each other, yet he didn't realize until living alone in their Cambridge home that she had also been his best friend. Now he remorsefully felt the pangs of bereavement as he peered at his face in the mirror, seeing lines never seen before, especially around his blue eyes and forehead. The only thing going for him, he thought derisively, was his thick head of salt-and-pepper hair. Things could be worse, he could be bald, he laughed, returning to his desk to call Jacqueline Cohen, a Harvard colleague scheduled to fly shortly to Israel for a sabbatical.

nineteen

IT WAS SNOWING HEAVILY OUTSIDE the Brattle Street apartment in Cambridge as the taxi driver loaded Jacky Cohen's suitcases into the trunk of his cab.

She was relieved to see traffic was light and that highway crews were treating the main roads. With any luck, they would make it to Logan Airport with time to spare before her flight to the Middle East.

"Where are you headed on a night like this?" the cab driver inquired as he slowed down at the Callahan Tunnel.

"I'm flying to Tel Aviv," she replied, nonplussed.

"You're a brave lady, with all the violence over there and all. The Arabs are still in an uprising I hear. Both sides are burying their dead. Visiting relatives over there, are you?"

"Actually I'll be doing research."

"Good luck to you, lady, you're sure going to need it."

The driver stopped talking, concentrating on the slick road conditions. Jacky Cohen rested her tense shoulders against the cold leather seats in the back of the cab, grateful for the silence.

In the past few years, she would have given anything to relinquish the "normalcy" of her teaching job at Harvard for the "abnormal" intensity of Israeli society. She had lived in Israel as a student. It seemed so long ago. She knew Israel was a changed society since the eighties. Yet her conversation a short while ago with Arnie Davidovitz evoked only a sense of delight at being in Jerusalem, as he described the beauty of the landscape covered in the first snow of the year. He had leased a small, clean apartment for her in the Kiryat Shemuel section of town on Rehov Palmach with the help of his colleague, David Ha-Levy. She knew the area around Palmach and was pleased to be so well situated.

Despite the weather in Boston, the cab driver dropped her off in front of El Al without delay. After the routine search and questions by the El Al security team, she was relieved of her luggage and handed a boarding pass. Feeling unburdened for the first time in weeks, she went through the security check for her carry-on luggage and laptop computer. When she arrived at the gate, she noticed the area was already filling up with passengers waiting to board. She found a seat near the glass windows. Slipping out of her black wool, maxi-length coat, Jacky reached inside her handbag for her cellular phone. After a brief conversation with her aunt, she settled back, reflecting on how stressful the last few weeks had been as she had attempted to tie up loose ends in the department, and in her private life. It was as if she were racing against time in the hope that things would not unravel like a loose thread in a hem.

Shortly before midnight, all passengers were boarded. Delayed for takeoff a full hour while the wings of the 777 Boeing jet were being deiced, she finally heard the captain's voice over the loud speaker:

"Ladies and gentlemen, please fasten your seat belts as we taxi to the runway for takeoff."

The lift-off on any flight always thrilled her. Tonight, her adrenaline was racing overtime due to the excitement of journeying to Israel. It brought back memories of her previous trip to Jerusalem years ago when she had been a young girl, meeting the man whom she eventually married while studying as an undergraduate in the Overseas Program at the Hebrew University. He seemed exceptionally bright and interesting to her. She had been young, innocent, and naïve, excusing his cynical approach to life as part of his personality and not to be taken seriously. It was only years later that she came to the realization that a person's character is his fate. Even before her marriage, she had deeply disquieting feelings. She had brushed away her instinctual reaction, the way one brushes crumbs off a table, sweeping all warnings into the dustbin.

It took her ten, long, difficult years of questioning his behavior toward her to comprehend why she felt buried alive in this loveless, cold marriage. Shortly after the divorce, she received the doctoral degree in psychology. Grounded in her own career, she was able to let go of years of pain, replacing it with light and joyous moments with friends and family. Yet, she never quite trusted enough in long-term relationships to try one again.

Once the pilot reached cruising altitude, Jacky's thoughts were interrupted by the stewardess inquiring:

"Would you care for a bottle of wine, compliments of El Al?"

"Yes, thank you. Dry red wine, please," responded Jacky, removing her seatbelt and reclining the window seat, hoping the ten-hour flight would go by speedily.

After dinner, when the lights were lowered in the cabin, she slept for a few hours. When she awakened, the sun was rising and the religious Jews along with the Hasidim on the packed plane were lining up for the morning prayers on each side of the aisle. Enwrapped in phylactery and *talitot,* fringed prayer shawls, she observed the ancient Judaic tradition of turning to God to offer the morning *Shaharit* prayer. Touched deeply by the sight of this devotion—recalling a childhood with a devout father and mother—tears spurted from her huge, brown eyes as she felt the returning sadness of being orphaned as a teen. Except for her devoted aunt and uncle in Harvard, Massachusetts, she was without kin.

Grateful to be offered a hot towel, Jacky edged down the aisle to the lavatory. Within the narrow confines of the toilet facilities, she glanced in the mirror at her large brown eyes, straight nose, and full lips, noticing for the first time how much younger and fresher she appeared without a trace of makeup. She brushed her teeth, reapplied natural gloss to her lips, and ran a brush over the thick chestnut brown hair she wore straight to the shoulders. The black pantsuit and white turtleneck sweater looked stylish and unwrinkled. Satisfied with her appearance after the long flight, she returned to her seat just as the captain was making an announcement:

"Please fasten your seatbelts for our descent. We will be landing shortly at the Ben Gurion Airport. On behalf of the captain and the crew, we thank you for flying El Al flight 027. Local time is 2:30 PM. The weather in Tel Aviv is warmer than usual for February, nine degrees Celsius. All stewards, please return to your seats for landing."

The landing gear locked into place. Jacky peered out the window. They were still flying above the clouds, which reminded her of soft, billowing cotton. In the next instant, the wings cleared the clouds, and the skyline of Tel Aviv emerged.

As the 777 Boeing's wheels touched down on the runway, spontaneous applause erupted among the passengers.

Home at last, she thought. The excitement of arriving and being met by Arnie Davidovitz erased all signs of fatigue from her face and body.

Twenty

THE FOLLOWING MORNING JACKY STOOD in a white terry-cloth robe, watching the sun rising off her bedroom balcony on Rehov Palmach. It was a beautiful February morning, crisp and clear. All signs of the recent snowfall had vanished. Occasionally the silence was broken by the sound of a delivery truck or the start of a car engine by a reserve soldier returning to his base. Sipping coffee on her first morning back in the holy city, she felt grateful to Arnie and his friend David Ha-Levy for renting the lovely small apartment for her. They made sure to amply stock the refrigerator with fresh milk, cheese, eggs, and bread.

By 6:00 AM, she was showered and casually dressed in a pair of jeans and a black turtleneck sweater. Once she unpacked her belongings in the furnished apartment, she headed toward Gaza Street to locate the fruit and vegetable market she had frequented years ago as a student. Shortly before 8:00 AM, she returned with her purchases just as the phone was ringing.

It was Arnie, suggesting a drive to Tel Aviv to the Respite Center for disabled soldiers from previous wars, to arrange with the staff in-depth interviews with the veterans. After collecting enough data, she planned to write a text on the psychological wounds of war decades after the event of the Six-Day War in 1967 and the Yom Kippur War in 1973.

"I'm all ready, Arnie. Meet you downstairs in fifteen minutes."

They spent the morning at the Respite Center. Afterwards, Arnie parked near Dizengoff Square, taking her to lunch at an outdoor café.

"Espresso coffee, please, for the two of us," ordered Arnie. "We're waiting for a friend. After he arrives, we'll place our food order."

"Who's the friend, Arnie? I've never seen you this impatient before. All you've been doing for the past ten minutes is check your wristwatch. Must be someone important?"

"He is. I'm impatient because Ben-Ner is late as usual."

"Ben-Ner?"

"Don't you recall my telling you in the States about a former Israeli student of mine, Neyri Ben-Ner?"

"Ah, yes, of course I do. The Israeli colonel of yours?"

"The same. He's joining us for lunch. By the way, are you jet lagged? You look radiant as always so it's hard for me to tell."

"Thank you, Arnie, and no I'm not jet-lagged, at least not at the moment. When was the last time you and Ben-Ner were together in the States?"

"About a dozen years ago. You know, Jacky, a man can change quite a bit in twelve years, especially when he's a career office in Zahal."

"Zahal?"

"That's Hebrew for the Israel Defense Forces or the IDF."

"Have you both kept in touch with each other over the years?"

"Usually we corresponded by letters or a quick note from Ben-Ner written in the field."

"No e-mail in the IDF?"

"Neyri doesn't have a desk job. In between training troops, he's always out on assignments."

"What unit is he in?"

"*Sayeret Tzanhanim,* Paratroop Reconnaissance."

"What's so special about this officer, may I ask?"

"I'll let you decide for yourself. From the looks of the stride of the man coming toward us, I'd say you won't have long to wait."

Jacky turned around, observing a tall figure in an army uniform walking swiftly, confidently, and assuredly toward their table. From his rank insignia and medals, the colonel made an impressive appearance. She noticed the red beret tucked snugly under his epaulettes, and the brown boots of the Paratroop Brigade. Ben-Ner was shockingly good-looking, she thought, creating tension by his mere presence. As he glanced in her direction, his chiseled face and aquiline nose offset by sparkling brown eyes caught her completely off guard.

Arnie stood up to receive a bear hug from the strapping officer who towered over him.

"Ben-Ner, you're late, as you always were to all of my classes!"

"Some things never change, Arnie. Good to see you."

Turning to gaze at Jacky Cohen, Neyri's eyes lingered on her face, hair, and figure a moment longer than he had anticipated. Then he extended a firm handshake, saying in Hebrew as he sat down next to her:

"*Na'im m'od.* Pleased to meet you."

"*Shalom,* Colonel Ben-Ner."

"Jacky, you'll soon find out we're a very relaxed and informal country. So call me Neyri," he said as he motioned for the waiter to approach their table.

"Have you ordered yet, Arnie?"

"No, actually, we were waiting for you."

"Okay, this restaurant has the best hummus and tehina in town," he suggested, explaining to Jacky that a platter of ground chick-peas and pita would be an excellent choice.

"Sounds good to me. I'm ravenous as always," rejoined a jovial Arnie Davidovitz as he appraised the face and features of the colonel.

Neyri Ben-Ner was better looking than in his youth, if that were possible, Arnie reflected, noting how powerful a figure he cut. What he saw in Neyri's eyes belied the exterior. They were the eyes of a burnt-out man who had not aged chronologically as much as by the nature of what he had been forced to witness from youth until maturity.

Neyri spoke to the waiter in rapid Hebrew, placing their order and including coffee refills for everyone. Then he turned his full attention to the two Americans.

Addressing Arnie, he asked: "What brings you back to Israel at this time?"

"The first reason is the stalled peace process. The second is linking up with you again, my friend," Arnie admitted.

"We're no closer to peace than we were when I was your student at Harvard University. Glad you're back, Arnie, so we can pick up where we left off. Do you remember how we used to argue endlessly on how to motivate peace in a country that has known only warfare and violence for over half a century?"

"How could I ever forget those midnight brunches in my Cambridge home? Tell us the truth, Neyri. How bad is the situation in the country?"

Neyri Ben-Ner shrugged his shoulders as he warmed his fingers on the steaming cup of coffee. The weather had dropped to minus one degree Celsius overnight, cooler than Tel Avivians liked it at this time of year. Jacky wore a black leather jacket over her turtleneck sweater, enjoying the relatively balmy weather after the sub-freezing temperature in Cambridge.

"Here we like to say, *yiyeh tov,*" he replied as he looked into Jacky's unusually large eyes, noticing sensitivity and alertness. Then he explained: "That means, it'll be okay. How is your Hebrew, by the way, Jacky?"

"Practically non-existent," she admitted.

"Before you're here six months, you'll be talking like one of us."

He raised the coffee cup to his lips. She noticed the shape of his mouth, soft and sensuous. He lowered the cup to the saucer, gazing at her for a moment as if reading her thoughts. A warm liquid feeling edged up from the soles of her feet to her throat. It was as if a fire were raging through her body, disconcerting her. She glanced in Arnie's direction, grateful to discover his eyes were glued on his platter rather than on her face.

"The Intifada is not new to us, I'm afraid," Neyri attempted to answer Arnie's question about the latest uprising in Israel. "You see that the first Palestinian revolt erupted in December 1987. It lasted until 1993. Both sides suffered. We lost people. They lost people. With this second uprising since the end of September, we're losing jobs and our economy is in trouble. The Arabs are hurting as well. We're too interconnected not to be affected. This time the tourist industry has been severely damaged. The hotels, normally packed to capacity, are empty. As you know, it has a snowball effect on the food industry, stores, restaurants, tour guides, and so on and so forth. I'm afraid we're in for the long haul. It won't be pleasant for any of us," he admitted.

"Are you personally involved in fighting the Intifada?" Jacky asked, dipping her pita bread in the plate of humus.

"I'm in the paratroops. I have my own command where I'm training paratroop officers who are always in demand for difficult missions on our borders or in the interior of the country. The Reserves are called up thirty to forty days a year and lately sent to places like Gaza. It's not a pretty picture," he admitted, the light going out of his eyes.

She noticed he had deep lines around his eyes and alongside his mouth. As he bent toward her, his golden brown hair fell over his forehead, making him appear vulnerable. For a brief moment she felt a premonition of danger. It momentarily startled her. Shaking off the vision, she moved her head, loosening a lock of her hair and inadvertently brushing his cheek. Their eyes met and held. It was as if she were seeing the scene outside the context of reality, as if time had stopped, granting them all the time in the world to gaze at each other. He moved his shoulders back, causing her heart to lurch. It brought her back to her senses.

"What brings you to Israel, Jacky?"

"I'll be doing research at the Hebrew University."

"You're on sabbatical from Harvard?"

"Yes, I am."

"What's your field?"

"Psychology."

"What kind of research will you be doing?"

"I plan to interview veteran soldiers from the 1967 and 1973 wars for a book on the long-term implications of war."

"Good luck on your topic. You certainly came to the right country for your research."

Turning to Arnie, he told him: "By the way, you should know I applied to several graduate schools in America to complete a degree in international relations. I should know by April or thereabouts if I've been accepted."

"Good to hear, Neyri. Will the Israeli army release you for any length of time?" Arnie asked as he drained his coffee cup.

"In my case, it doesn't matter any longer. I plan to step down from my command this June," he informed both of them, smiling directly at Jacky. She smiled back at him, feeling perfectly relaxed now, finding it easier to talk to him than expected.

"How does your family feel about you leaving Israel?" Arnie inquired as he wiped his plate clean.

"They'll get used to the idea. Besides, I'm only a flight away from home. Arnie, are you headed back to Jerusalem after lunch?"

"Yes, I have an appointment with David Ha-Levy on a research proposal we are doing together. Why?"

"I'm headed for the Golan Heights. Thought Jacky would be interested in accompanying me to the Nafah army base so I could show her the sites of the battles on the Golan during the Yom Kippur War. Unless you have other plans?" he inquired, turning to her.

"I'd like nothing better. It would be invaluable for my research. Are you sure I wouldn't be in the way if you have business on the base?"

"Not at all. It would be my pleasure. Afterwards, I plan to return to Jerusalem. If there's enough time, I want to show you Giv-at Ha-Tahmoshet, Ammunition Hill, where the major battle for Jerusalem took place in 1967 as well."

Shortly thereafter they parted from Arnie Davidovitz. All along the drive to the Golan Heights, Neyri Ben-Ner brought her up-to-date on the two wars she was researching. After hearing how the Nafah army base played a pivotal role in the Yom Kippur War, serving as headquarters for Northern Command in 1973, she was bombarded by acute visualization as he described the scenes of the initial aerial attack on the headquarters by Syrian MIGs strafing the area, something that none of the soldiers or tank commanders of the war ever forgot once the tide of war changed in Israel's favor after three weeks of slaughter between Israel, Syria, and Egypt. At the "Valley of Tears" where the final onslaught between Syria and Israel took place, the relics of burnt-out tanks from over twenty-eight years ago lay in a twisted hulk of metal forever reminding the nation that over twenty-five hundred Israeli soldiers were annihilated in the Yom Kippur War, a war never to be forgotten by the soldiers who survived or by the nation that stood behind them.

By late afternoon, after a three-hour drive from the Golan, Neyri escorted Jacky to the memorial at Ammunition Hill in Jerusalem where she saw the tunnels dug by Jordanian soldiers. He described the hand-to-hand combat that took place in 1967 between Israeli paratroops and the Jordanian soldiers who held tenaciously to the Old City until the Israelis won, reuniting East and West Jerusalem for the first time since the 1948 War of Independence.

At the end of the day, Jacky rode back to Palmach Street in a sobered state of mind.

"I'll get in touch with you when I can," Neyri promised as he escorted her to the front door. In the next moment he was gone, heading back to the Tel Nof Air Force base.

Twenty-one

THE SOUND OF THE *MUEZZIN* emanating from the loudspeaker in the minaret on the Temple Mount awakened Shulha from a deep sleep. Slowly she opened her eyes, listening to the soft breathing of her husband, as he laid cupped to her back, shoulders, and thighs. She felt a sense of contentment and inner peace envelop her as if she were enwrapped luxuriously in a silken garment of exquisite warmth. A demure smile of fulfillment spread over her face.

It was more than a week since they had traversed the desert to Jericho, onward to Jerusalem for a prenatal examination by a practiced obstetrician in the city. Neither of them had anticipated the warning they received from the Ramallah physician. The obstetrician insisted— for the sake of the baby and the mother—Shulha remain in East Jerusalem rather than return to the desert. A Caesarean section would be required. A message was hurriedly sent to her parents in Ein Fashkha not to expect them back until after the birth of their baby in mid-July.

For the most part, there were no difficulties in the new living arrangement in the city with Asa's mother. Shulha remained quiet and docile, keeping to herself, and looking radiant at the beginning of her second trimester. Her mother-in-law was subdued as well, keeping the same academic load in the winter session as usual. It was obvious that some spark within the older woman had diminished, and she was obviously carrying burdens that would have overwhelmed a weaker person. When Muni returned in the late afternoons from the Bir Zeit campus, Shulha thought she looked fatigued and drained.

In order to help his mother pay the bills and save for the pending delivery charges, her husband worked eight hours a day tutoring students in the late afternoon or early evenings. In his spare time, Asa started revisions on his thesis in an attempt to publish it, leaving her alone many nights when he went to the Hebrew University library.

At first, Shulha had been overwhelmed by the noise of city life, the teeming number of people crowded into East Jerusalem, the rush of cars and foot traffic everywhere she went, the strange sight of young Christian Arab women abandoning the modest chador for Western attire. In jeans or tight-fighting clothing, there seemed no difference between them and the Israeli Jews she had seen in the Jewish sector. Shulha's initial reaction to the city was fear. The strangeness, the noise, the close juxtaposition of apartment buildings and stores so appalled her spirit that she fled back to her husband's apartment, longing for the silence of the desert that was broken only by the sound of the sheep as she grazed them on the fertile field near their encampment.

Shulha heard her husband stirring beside her, the magic of the moment interrupted by the return to reality. It was 4:00 AM, time for the first morning prayer to begin at the Al-Aqsa Mosque.

She turned her body to face her husband. Asa reached out a hand, placing it on her belly and cradling her in his arms, reluctant to leave the warmth of his marital bed to hastily dress and walk the short distance to the *Haram al-Sharif,* the Temple Mount.

"Asa, it is Friday. Your mother has promised to take me to the Haram al-Sharif this morning where women and children gather to wait for the prayers to be completed. We will bring a basket of food to picnic next to the *Qubbat as-Sakhra,* the Dome of the Rock. You will meet us there after the morning prayer, please?"

"Whatever you desire, my little dove," he whispered, breathing in her warmth and the pungent smell of her body, then forcing himself to stand on the Persian carpet beside the bed, chilled by the cold morning air permeating his raw, damp apartment. Within moments he was dressed in loose-fitting black pants, ready to prostrate himself at the mosque. He struggled into an old black sweatshirt from the university. Now fully awake after washing his face and brushing his teeth, he ran a comb through his black hair.

The first rays of sunrise showed in the east as he headed toward the Al-Aqsa Mosque on foot, enveloped in the silence of Jerusalem and its solemn beauty, while most of its inhabitants were still asleep. At the approach to Damascus Gate, he heard the first braying of a goat as several Muslim men hurried toward the mosque. Momentarily, he was at peace with himself. In the desert, he reflected, this sense of peace was a daily encounter. Here in the city, these moments of contentment were reduced to the handful of minutes when he was walking to morning prayer.

Traversing the Temple Mount area between the Dome of the Rock and the Al-Aqsa Mosque (known in Arabic as *Masjid al-Aqsa*), he blocked all thoughts from his perception, in an attempt to discipline himself to open his heart fully in prayer. He washed his hands at the ablution area located several meters from the entrance to Al-Aqsa. Within the mosque hundreds of worshippers were already kneeling on multi-colored Persian rugs of all hues and sizes. At the rear of the mosque, Asa lowered himself on the ground, in the ritual prostration known as *sajdah*.

When the prayers were completed, he returned to his daily routine, often functioning as if he were a robot wound up to perform perfunctorily. Each day he had a renewed fight within him to ward off the inevitable feelings of frustration, pent-up anger, and depression over a life gone awry. He had been filled with ambivalence since his return to East Jerusalem with his wife. It was bad enough that he was tainted by the looks of his neighbors, acquaintances, and so-called "friends" because he had deigned to live as a nomad in the desert with a Bedouin wife; now he had to protect his wife from learning the bitter truth that his status had been reduced another notch by marrying her and living among her tribesmen. It was not something he learned after the fact; as a Palestinian, he was well-steeped in the ways of his people, knowing full well how the majority looked down upon Bedouins as illiterates lacking education, whose gypsy-like mode of living as semi-nomads was beneath the sophistication of city-dwellers. It hadn't bothered him at all while he remained cloistered in Ein Fashkha. It tormented him ever since his return to Saladin Street. He recalled with bitterness how his parents had tried, unsuccessfully, to talk him out of marrying a Bedouin and living in Ein Fashkha.

He walked through the Muslim *suk,* sat down in his favorite restaurant outside Jaffa Gate ordering freshly baked bread with Turkish coffee, and opened the morning paper.

Two hours later, Asa Ibrahimi left the newspaper on the table. He descended the steps into the Muslim marketplace, oblivious that his waiter was observing him. As the waiter cleared off the table, he noticed the newspaper left behind: the East Jerusalem newspaper *Al-Fajr.* Momentarily puzzled, the waiter stared at the disappearing back of Asa Ibrahimi as he became further and further lost in the cavernous turns of the marketplace whose open storefronts bore very little business. Ibrahimi was a steady customer. Everyone knew he came from a highly educated family, with both of his deceased brothers once militant members of Fatah and Hamas since their early teens. It had always been hard to believe how Asa Ibrahimi resisted becoming a freedom fighter like his younger brothers. It had been rumored his parents would have been pushed over the edge had their eldest son rebelled and disobeyed them too.

As the waiter wiped the table clean of crumbs, he placed the newspaper under his arm, whistling softly, a slow smile of recognition appearing on his face. The daily Arabic newspaper *Al-Fajr* was a staunch supporter of Arafat's Fatah, the terrorist unit serving as an umbrella for all other factions. The waiter wondered about Asa Ibrahimi; all the pieces of the puzzle did not fit together—a son of elite Palestinian parents, an advanced degree from the enemy's university, married to a Bedouin, clashing head-on with Palestinian values on education and fierce pride. He merits careful watching, the waiter thought as he entered the kitchen and dropped the dirty dishes into the sudsy water.

AS THE EARLY MORNING RAYS of the sun enveloped Shulha and Muni Ibrahimi on their walk to the walled Old City, Asa's mother escorted her daughter-in-law to an octagonal-shaped outdoor temple adjacent to the golden Dome of the Rock. Shortly before 8:00 AM, the area was already filled with other Muslim women, spread out on multi-colored blankets on the stone floor, picnicking with their children.

Shulha was in the beginning of her fourth month of pregnancy. She took a pillow out of the basket filled with food, placing it against a pillar to prop up her aching back. Instead of the usual fear that assailed her since leaving the strict, parochial confines of her father's tent, she was filled with excitement and joy, feeling the child flutter within her womb. The Temple Mount area—massive in size and carved in stone floors, and ornate, massive Roman columns leading to either of the mosques—enveloped her being with stark solemnity and sacredness of the area. In this most holy of all places for Arabs and Jews alike, Shulha fully comprehended for the first time the yearning of her people to possess this area in the same way the Jews yearned for the rebuilding of the ancient splendor of King Solomon's majestic Jewish Temple, destroyed in 70 AD by the Romans. Never before in her life could she recall a moment such as this where she felt in tune with the magnificence of her own people and culture despite being so far from the familiarity and comforting way of life of the desert.

Tears formed at the corners of her eyes as she thought of the fragility of life. Allah had blessed her with the love she felt toward her husband as well as the child she was carrying in her womb—Asa's child. It was a pure, innocent love requiring little in return except for the gift to be perceived, received, and honored in the way it was intended: with the fullness of her heart and soul. When she opened her lovely eyes, clouded with tears, she noticed her mother-in-law staring at her face with concern.

"Are you alright, Shulha? Why are you crying, my child?"

"I am weeping from joy, waiting for your son to return to us in peace, health, and fulfillment."

"It is good and right that you are here with us. Soon, very soon, your child—and my grandchild—will be born, *Insha Allah,* God willing. Until the birth, know you are loved, and how much more so after you bring life into this world."

"Am I?" responded a startled Shulha, not quite certain that giving love fully would result in love being returned to her three-fold.

LONG AFTER THE RETURN from the picnic on the Temple Mount, Muni Ibrahimi reflected how she had misjudged her Bedouin daughter-in-law based on her own preconceptions and prejudices of Bedouin society. After living under the same roof with Shulha for the last several weeks, she was surprised to detect a side to the young woman she had not believed possible: Shulha was an astute observer, and blessed with innate intelligence. Forced into close proximity, particularly in the evenings after Asa left for the library, the two women sat together in the living room mending, crocheting, or knitting baby blankets and sweaters. It was on one such evening, when the wind was howling outside and torrents of rain was beating on the window panes, that Muni felt a sense of deep comfort and warmth beside this gentle, beautiful woman. How she had changed, she noted with surprise, since Shulha moved to Jerusalem. No longer was she clinging to her mourning the way one held on to treasured memories as if what was left of her life was already passé. The deep loneliness and bitterness she had been feeling for the company of her deceased husband and sons was lifting; settling in its place was a wise comprehension that one's life included wrenching losses as well as joyous moments. Continuing to reject the cards she had been dealt in life as cruel, harsh, unjust, or unfair would be tantamount to castigating Allah for her fate, something she considered abhorrent and sinful.

Several weeks after her daughter-in-law's arrival, toward the end of February, she had been seated in her husband's study attempting to reread a book of poetry by the Lebanese poet Kahlil Gibran when Shulha entered the room.

"May I disturb you, Umm?"

"Of course, Shulha, please be seated. You are not disturbing me."

Shulha sat down opposite her mother-in-law, looking demure and thoughtful. She folded both her small hands on her protruding lap, raised her exquisite eyes, holding her mother-in-law's kindly gaze. Speaking in a breathless tone of voice, as if anxious to be fully heard without being interrupted, she stated:

"Long before I ever met your son, when I was approaching my twelfth year, I requested of my father to be taught how to read and write. Within the Ta'amireh tribe, we had several outstanding people who had been self-taught. In the tradition of our tribe, this knowledge was handed down to whoever wanted to learn. My father arranged for daily lessons with an elder who taught me to write in Arabic script and to speak in the dialect of the Palestinian people. I wish to be a perfect wife to your son, to make him love me, and to be proud of me the way you are proud of him. If you would be kind enough to continue to teach me so I could read the books you and Asa read, I will be grateful to you for the rest of my life. I hope I am not asking too much from you, Umm. If I am, then please forgive me, since my thirst for knowledge and my eagerness to proceed forward has made me set aside my bashfulness and has perhaps made me too bold?"

"What makes you think my son doesn't love you at this moment, Shulha?"

"He seems changed to me."

"Since when?"

"Ever since the wedding ceremony."

"There's always an initial adjustment after marriage."

"I don't feel Asa's closeness to me. He seems filled with mourning. The light has gone out of his eyes when he looks at me."

"Perhaps the problem has nothing to do with you at all. Do not be so quick, my child, to blame yourself. Asa has not been happy with himself for a long time before he met you. This society—the occupation, and the lack of freedom, and lack of independence it entails for a stateless people—marks each one of us. Consequently, Asa is very angry with himself. This doesn't necessarily mean he is angry with you, or with me, or that he doesn't love you."

"He will be less angry and will love me more if you teach me."

"I promise you, I will teach you anything you want to learn."

"Thank you, Umm. Now I am very happy to be with you in Jerusalem."

"It is so good to have you here, my daughter. You have brought light to my heart and have taken the darkness away for me. Do you realize, Shulha, what a gift you have given me with your presence?"

This encounter with her lovely daughter-in-law was so touching, Muni thought of it often with immense happiness. That same night she began to teach Shulha the exquisite poetry of Gibran, known throughout Arabia as the quintessential poet, philosopher, and artist who touched the heart and soul of his people.

Before the two women parted, they embraced. Muni Ibrahimi promised her daughter-in-law the lessons would remain a secret until Shulha chose to disclose it to her husband.

Twenty-Two

ON A COLD, RAINY EVENING the first Saturday night in March, Arnie Davidovitz invited several Israeli friends to his apartment to meet Jacky Cohen. As the living room started filling up with guests, he glanced around the room with satisfaction. Jacky was seated on the sofa engaged in conversation with David Ha-Levy. Opposite them were a lawyer and his wife speaking in Hebrew to a political scientist recently returned from abroad. In the back of the room, standing near the drinks, was the historian Beth Dumont, speaking to Asa Ibrahimi who had been brought to the party by David Ha-Levy. The Palestinian had made quite an impression on him. He found him articulate, sharp, and sensitive. Arnie was looking forward to a lengthy discussion with him before the evening was over.

The living room, filled with old furniture seemingly well-worn yet comfortable, was inviting and cozy in contrast to the rain and wind slashing the shutters. The white walls were hung with oil portraits of well-known Israeli artists. Pictures and collection of gifts from all parts of the world filled an étagère, as did porcelain tea cups from England. A large Persian rug in deep mauve brought the room together, lending it warmth and coziness. From what David indicated about his deceased parents, his father had been a successful businessman in security systems. He had traveled all over the world with his wife and, apparently, she ran his office for him until they were killed in an airplane crash while en route to Mozambique.

Arnie was carrying a tray of barekas, a light French pastry filled with cheese, potato, and spinach, heated to perfection for his guests. He placed the tray on the coffee table, and then glanced with admiration at Jacky Cohen. She looked lovely in a full-length dress in a deep wine color, offset by a strand of cultured pearls; her thick chestnut hair was piled loosely on top of her head, soft tendrils flowing past her ears adorned with pearl earrings. He had always thought her above-average in looks, with natural color highlighting her cheek bones, and a complexion that seemed flawless to him. The most arresting feature on her face was her eyes—wide, open, perceptive. They had first met at the chancellor's home in Cambridge when she was newly hired at Harvard in the psychology department. They became quick friends and colleagues. She had been the youngest assistant professor ever hired by the university, making quite a stir among the faculty. After publishing well-received books, her tenure was all but ensured within a ten-year period. At the age of thirty-eight, an aura of a youthful persona and sharpened perception combined to heighten one's awareness that she was a product of a fine American education. From the little Jacky revealed about her private life, he had gathered that she had endured a marriage to a man with an autocratic personality. Ironic, wasn't it, he thought, as he turned to answer the door bell, that a psychologist had been unable to penetrate such a persona and avoid a marital ordeal of some magnitude. From what his own wife attempted to convey to him over the years, women were suckers for men who needed them.

After the last guest departed, Arnie suggested to his close friends lingering in the living room:

"If no one plans to rush off, I'll prepare a midnight brunch for us."

The doorbell rang before anyone was able to respond. Standing in the foyer, dripping wet in a green army coat, was Colonel Ben-Ner.

"You're just in time to help us prepare some hot food, Neyri. So pleased you could get away from your base!" Arnie announced as he relieved Neyri of his drenched garments, hanging the wet army jacket over a kitchen chair.

"My pleasure, Arnie, I assure you."

Neyri Ben-Ner stepped into the living room, arrested by Jacky's breathtaking presence.

"Good to see you again, Neyri."

"Likewise," he responded, dazzling her with white teeth and a shapely mouth curved into a suggestion of a smile, as if he could read all her thoughts, and would, if they were not in public. It was the first time in her life that any man made her feel as if she were being undressed only with his eyes. She felt the rush of blood to her face.

With everyone more than pleased to assist, they shortly sat down to piping hot food, freshly brewed coffee, and engaging conversation. Arnie lit his pipe, looking around the room in pleasure. Turning to Neyri, he inquired,

"What time do you have to return to your base?"

"Between 4:00 and 5:00 AM at the latest, why?"

"Just want to pick your brain," he admitted.

Looking at the people gathered around the table, Arnie said: "This is the first time I have in one room an Israeli Jewish historian, an Israeli officer, an Israeli-Palestinian, and two foreign research scholars. Now, perhaps, I can get some answers to why peace is so elusive in the Middle East. Any one of you care to jump into the fire first, so to speak?" he chuckled, knowing it was payback time now that he had their undivided attention, or so he hoped. He leaned back in the dining-room chair, relighting his pipe, waiting to see how this discussion would hold up.

"Do you intend to solve the Arab-Israeli conflict between now and 4:00 AM, Arnie?" inquired a dubious David Ha-Levy, knowing full-well how Arnie would capitalize on his captive audience.

"Of course. Shall we begin with you, then, David? What's your take on the conflict?"

"First of all, Arnie, to do this topic justice, we should break down the issues so it's more workable. We should first look at why there is a conflict, then look at whether there are resolutions to the conflict, and thirdly, if there are no resolutions, what are the alternatives."

"Sounds reasonable to me. Why don't we hear the conflict from a Palestinian perspective, please," he urged Asa to begin.

"I believe that we must all be aware that the conflict started way before Israel became a state in 1948. Let me remind you that as far back as 1899, a former mayor of Jerusalem, Yussef Ziah el-Khaldi, urged the chief rabbi of Paris that Zionists should find another place for a homeland and . . . "

"Except that El-Khaldi conceded, did he not, the historical right of the Jews to be in Palestine?" interrupted Arnie Davidovitz.[30]

"True," retorted Asa, "however, if Herzl had paid attention to this letter which was passed on to him, then perhaps this catastrophe could have been avoided."

"You're missing the point, Asa," indicated David. "There was no other land for the Jews. This is the land promised to Israel by God, and only this land is holy to the Jews. There is no other place in the entire world we could have established a homeland except here, you know this as well as I," he said with animation.

"Another solution should have been found by the Zionists," Asa insisted. "We were an integral part of this land with only a small number of Jews before 1948. To have our land granted to Zionists by imperialist Britain with the 1917 Balfour Declaration, and subsequently partitioned by the United Nations in November 1947, were illegal acts of colonialism which the Arab people condemn and deplore. How can you justify something that was, and is still, illegal and suddenly make it legal and okay?" he demanded.

"Can't we use the same argument of illegality of the Arabic response to the Balfour Declaration and the partitioning of the land; that is, you cannot turn something considered legal by the whole world, and turn it into an illegal issue because the Arabic people do not like the facts on the ground," interjected Jacky, following the conversation closely.

"Look, many assumptions were made by the world and particularly by Zionists that we would accept this partitioning of our land. Many Jews believed erroneously that we would welcome any material progress made once the Zionists were firmly established in our land at the expense of our own nationalism," Asa attempted to explain.

"Let me see if I understand you correctly, Asa," Jacky said. "Are you claiming the Zionists totally misread Arab psychology, that the Jews were unable to comprehend that Arabs did not have the same desires for progress as they aspired to as a people?"

"Precisely. I believe it is a profound failing. In fact, this type of thinking continues until today, as our economies are intertwined and every time either side gives a hiccup, we're at a standstill," he concluded, looking around the room to see how this was being perceived.

Neyri poured another cup of coffee and then said:

"It was never the intention of Zionists to oust the Arabs who were already living on this land in order to establish a sovereign nation of Israel. In fact, Ben Gurion stated unequivocally that under no circumstances are the rights of the inhabitants to be infringed upon. Zionism was not to conquer what has already been conquered by other inhabitants, but to settle where the present inhabitants of the land have not been established and to work the land."[31]

"For a minute, here, I was thinking I'm right back in Northern Ireland," said Beth Dumont, looking austere in a black outfit that made her complexion appear whiter than usual. "Seems like there is a collision between two peoples who are both right, but neither is willing to bend one iota. In Ireland the fight for one hundred years has been over religion between the Catholics and the Protestants, both maintaining the other is wrong. Same thing here. Do you want the same results? A fight to the death with one hundred years of bloodshed? Sounds to me like you'll all be losers, just like we have been in my country, with lives destroyed and no normalcy possible when both sides exist to hate and destroy each other," countered Beth, her face flushed with tension as she relived some of the horror in her country, which had exacted an enormous price throughout her childhood.

"Are there any solutions?" queried Arnie, emptying his tobacco in a nearby ashtray, and then filling his pouch with fresh tobacco.

"Maybe there will never be peace here," suggested Beth, her eyes glazing with tears. "Maybe conflict and bloodshed is all this country knows."

"If that's the case, there is no future. I for one don't feel this way," admitted David, "and now I'm talking as an Israeli Jew. Both sides have to be willing to pay the price for peace. Both sides will have to compromise over the land that will or will not be returned—and here I'm talking about land won in wars, not the partitioned land of 1948. Again, compromise must be made, including the legality of the partitioning to begin with. Otherwise, we're not even talking the same language. Concessions will also have to be made over the right of return of Arab refugees from the 1948 war. As you know there were about 760,000 refugees after the 1948 war. Five million Arabs have been born since 1948. To accept all these refugees back into Israel proper is demographic and democratic suicide. We should not be held accountable for repatriating five million refugees. We will compensate the Arab refugees only after thousands of Jewish refugees fleeing from Yemen, Morocco, Tunisia, Egypt, Iran, and Iraq between 1948 and today are compensated by these Arab regimes. Furthermore, concessions will also have to be made on both sides over the sovereignty of Jerusalem, with both sides claiming it as the capital."

"How would a Palestinian respond?"

"From a Palestinian perspective," Asa explained, "I can tell you that you are deluding yourself if you believe there is a solution to the Arab-Israeli conflict. The only solution from a Palestinian perspective, backed by the Palestinian National Charter, is a *jihad,* a holy war, against Israel. All the land is being illegally occupied, not just the West Bank and Gaza. This means there will be no rest until the Palestinians end the occupation of our land, not just from 1967 but from 1948 as well. Compromise is totally unacceptable. Even if the occupation and the annexation of our land continue, we believe Israel will be destroyed. The Intifada is tearing Israel apart, tearing Israel down—it's the perennial thorn in Israel's side. We will not allow Israel to live as long as Palestinians are not living. Don't you see what's being done to Israel? With whom will we make peace when there is no one who wants peace with us? By the same token, why would we want peace with occupiers? Did we not rid ourselves of the Ottoman Turks and the British? One day, it is our fervent belief, we will rid ourselves of Zionism and the Israeli Jews as well. Time is on our side, not Israel's, because we pride ourselves on our patience and our ability to persevere," Asa Ibrahimi declared, summarizing the position upheld by the majority of radical Palestinians.

"Are you saying there is only one solution—a forceful one that will involve the wholesale slaughter of a people? Is this what I hear you saying?" Jacky asked for clarification.

"David?" Arnie deferred to him.

"Up until now, the Palestinian people have been against Arafat, because Arafat has been posturing for peace. For the Palestinians, peace is not possible for another reason we have not mentioned. There is hate here in this region. Maybe at first the Palestinians only feared us. But now they hate what's been done to them. The occupation since 1967 has pushed them into this hatred. You see, everything has been taken from the Palestinians. What remains are the living dead.[32] They no longer care, you see, because the only thing that fills them is hatred and their need to restore the dignity we have supposedly taken from them," he said softly, but to all the people in the room it sounded as if he were shouting.

Arnie Davidovitz sucked on his pipe, looking at the people gathered around the table.

"Neyri, you've been silent all evening. What are you thinking?"

"About all the missed chances for peace, Arnie."

"You're absolutely right, Neyri. I think this is a critical point. For those of you who are unaware of these missed opportunities, let me first enumerate them. Afterwards, let's figure out why this happened.

"After 1967, not only were the Arabs and the PLO rejectionists, so were the United States and Israel. However, starting February 1970, Egyptian president Gamal Abdel-Nasser indicated peace would be possible between Israel and the Arab States under the following conditions: Israel would have to evacuate the occupied territories and accept a settlement of the Palestinian refugee problem. Next, in February 1971, Nasser's successor, Anwar Sadat, offered Israel a full peace treaty on the pre-June 1967 borders, with security guarantees and recognized borders. It was promptly rejected by Israel. Jordan also was ready to recognize Israel if it returned to the pre-June 1967 border. Again, no response from Israel. The United States backed Israel's rejection of Sadat's 1971 peace offer because it began to view Israel as a strategic asset and it was more in its favor to continue to block peace efforts until the Arabs would recognize Washington as a better benefactor than Moscow. In late 1970, both the Arab states and the PLO pushed for a two-state solution while Israel continued to reject it with great alarm. Again, in

October 1977, the Soviet-American peace proposal was accepted by the PLO, but when Israel protested, the U.S. backed away from the plan.

"Significantly in August 1981 there was a Saudi—a Fahd—peace plan. According to journalist and author Amos Elon, this produced panic among Israeli leaders. Again in February 1982, Uri Avnery, the editor of *Ha-Olam Hazeh* newspaper who dared to contact the PLO before it became fashionable here and in America, indicated a similar reaction to a Syrian proposal calling for the end of the war between the Arabs and Israel, along with the confirmation of the right of Palestinians to an independent state alongside Israel in the occupied territories.'[33] There were other missed chances. Why am I elaborating on these missed chances? Precisely to point out to all of you that the record confirms that the United States and Israel are the rejectionists, not the Palestinians or the Arab states. In fact, the Arab states and the PLO since the 1970s have joined the international accommodationists' consensus.[34] What both David and Asa have indicated about this conflict does not go beyond what is generally known by mainstream civilians here and abroad. I want to raise this discussion a notch. We need to delve deeper," he suggested.

"It was my understanding that Israel offered to return the occupied territories to Egypt, Syria, and Jordan after the 1967 Six-Day War, and their proposals were rejected," Jacky stated.

"Correct, on June 19, 1967, Israel proposed a peace agreement with Egypt based on the international borders and the security needs of Israel," Arnie stated. "A few days later, Egypt and Syria rejected it outright. They demanded that Israel's withdrawal be based on an unconditional withdrawal without stipulations of borders and security needs. Once Israel received this rejection, they reversed their own policy of returning the territories, deciding to annex the land instead. When Israel proposed returning between ninety and ninety-eight percent of the West Bank to King Hussein of Jordan, he also rejected this. It was all or nothing. The Arab Khartoum conference in September 1967 decided on no recognition, no negotiation, and no peace with Israel. Since 1967, Israel has depended on the status quo, preferring to sit tight, to wait for a peace offer from the Arabs. Instead of peace, Israel was surprised by an unanticipated war in 1973, conferring frightening losses as well as the outbreak of two Intifadas.[35]

"Who controlled the territories before 1967?" interjected Neyri. "It was Jordan, Syria, and Egypt, was it not? These same leaders refused to give the West Bank and Gaza Strip with Jerusalem as the capital to the Palestinians. Yet this is what is being proposed that Israel agree to now. If these Arab leaders had accepted Israel's offer to return the territories on June 19, 1967 in return for peace and security, so much bloodshed would have been avoided. What about the missed chance of the Palestinians—the 1947 partition into a two-state solution proposed by the U.N.? It was rejected outright by the Arabs. It was a better solution than what's being offered today."[36]

"I have always been led to believe that the Arabs wanted to ultimately destroy the State of Israel," Jacky indicated. "Now you are stating here that they once did but now they are reaching out for peace? I also thought the establishment of a Palestinian state next to Israel meant the first step toward Israel's destruction. How are we to know really what the Arabs want if they are dancing to two different tunes? First, they want to utterly destroy Israel. Now they are willing to let Israel live if they just get their own state? What if they are resorting to propaganda rhetoric merely to get their state, and then they will turn on Israel?

"I don't blame you for being skeptical, Jacky," Arnie concluded. "The evidence from the past is overwhelming that the Arabs were opposed to a two-state solution under the Peel Commission in 1937 and again under the U.N. in 1947. In 1920, Arab terrorism was directed against Jewish civilians; in the 1930s and 1940s, the Arabs openly supported Hitler and the Nazis against the Jewish people. I am also aware that Professor Edward Said of Columbia University has stated for the record that Palestinian nationalism has been based on driving all Israeli Jews out. Moreover, Said, as well as Noam Chomsky from MIT, both harsh critics of Israel, have rejected a two-state solution in preference to a binational secular state. Such a notion would destroy Israel as a sovereign Jewish state and would be a ploy for its destruction. However, there is a consensus of opinion that when the Palestinians want their own state more than they want to destroy Israel, most Israelis will welcome this. I believe the Palestinians have reached this point and that a two-state solution is the only viable option for peace in the Middle East.[37]

"Since 1982 I've also noticed that the media have become blatantly anti-Israel with a slant toward the Palestinians, with distortions and glaring omissions both in the press and on television often portraying Israel in a harsh light. What do you make of this?" Jacky inquired.

"I believe there is a double standard as well as unfairness when it comes to portraying Israel to the world. But this is only a recent phenomenon. Up to the late seventies and early eighties, Jewish support of Israel was practically unanimous and the non-Jews treaded lightly as well, since Israel was erected on the ashes of the Holocaust. I'm afraid the honeymoon is over," he admitted.[38]

"I believe it is not only hatred between the Palestinians and the Israelis that continues to stoke the fires—it is also fear. We already know the Arabs fear Westernization, particularly its ideology, which conflicts with Arab culture. I'm talking about Israeli fear of the Palestinians. What's the underlying reason?" Jacky queried.

"Israel fears having its legitimacy challenged," answered Arnie. "Israel also views the Palestinians as *Amalek,* the eternal enemy that must be blotted out for all time, so it can live in peace. It fears the bitter, racist, anti-Semitic tones in the press and in Palestinian textbooks. It fears that the real intention of the Palestinians is the gradual destruction of Israel."

"It's true, we do fear this," admitted Neyri. "Do you know what the best-selling book was in Ramallah as recently as 1999? It was Hitler's *Mein Kampf.* Do you know how we are depicted in the Arabic press? We're presented as ugly Jews with hooked noses. We are called vile names in these daily presses and often it is written that Hitler failed to complete the job so the Arabs will do it for him. Is it any wonder that even among those of us in Israel who desire a two-state solution to settle this conflict, we prefer to remain a people apart, with no contact, no reciprocity, no integration or assimilation?"[39]

"What does Israel want?" Jacky insisted. "Isn't this rejectionist policy of Israel contributing to further conflict? All along we've heard in the States that there is no one for Israel to talk to. Yet, you are saying the exact opposite," declared Jacky, taken aback by the way the discussion was heading under Arnie's historical analysis, whose facts were difficult to refute.

"I'll defer to David. As an Israeli historian, it would be best to hear it from him or else you might feel I am bashing Israel," concluded Arnie as he refilled his pipe with fresh tobacco, waiting for David Ha-Levy to clarify what has been occurring in Israel since 1977, when the right-wing political party, the Likud, and Menachem Begin came to power.

"Many analysts in Israel—including historians like myself, sociologists like Baruch Kimmerling and Joel Migdal, the reknowned Arabist Yehoshafat Harkabi, and well-known Israeli journalists—have come to the following conclusions: since 1967, when Israel became an occupation force, it set itself on a course of oppression and military conflict. As Arnie just pointed out correctly, Israel retains a military dependency with the United States, which has led to Israel maintaining the position of fourth largest military power in the world. However, the day may come when Israel will face military defeat as it almost did in October 1973, in the first few days of that sudden, unexpected war. If Israel was ready to roll out nuclear missiles in 1973, why would anyone think it wouldn't resort to this threat at some future time? It is the feeling of many analysts that Israel is drifting toward social, moral, and political degeneration, or as Harkabi succinctly put it in his 1988 book *Israel's Fateful Hour,* Israel is heading toward national suicide. One of our journalists, Amos Elon, believes irrationalism has already overtaken Israeli existence.[40] The Palestinians are cornered, penned in ghettos, relying on an undying faith that if they only hold on with a tenaciousness to the land and to their homes, they will endure and the Israeli occupation will wither away by the decay that's eating away at the fabric of Israeli society," concluded David Ha-Levy. Asa Ibrahimi, whose life had been made a hell by the policies established since 1967, felt vindicated by his former advisor.

"With this shift toward right-wing extremism in national policy since 1977, can either you, Arnie, or David predict what direction Israel is now moving toward?" inquired a thoughtful Neyri as he attempted to absorb the sobering conversation.

Arnie deferred to David, in order that an Israeli researcher-historian like Ha-Levy, with an impeccable reputation as a scholar, make the Israeli position believable.

"International isolation will continue," explained David, "as well as continuing dependence on the United States, with its concomitant pressure for Israel to serve U.S. interests. There will be continued militarization of Israeli society, a continued rise in religious fanaticism, and an ongoing sense that permanent conflict is inevitable, along with the perpetual disruption and destabilization of the region. What I am describing is Israel's reach for hegemony over the region, with U.S. blessings. Hegemony will now replace co-existence with the Arabs because Israel will no longer believe in obtaining peace with her neighbors since it no longer fits in with its political agenda of dominance. In a word, Israel wants to create the 'new reality' that it endeavored and failed to create with the 1982 invasion of Lebanon and its attempt to destroy the Palestinian national movement. Israel has always held out hope for a Jordanian solution whereby all the Palestinians would be absorbed under the Hashemite kingdom. However, given the fighting between Jordan's King Hussein and the Palestinians during the 1970 Black September massacre in his country, where three thousand Palestinians were killed by the King's Bedouin army, that concept has to go. A more likely scenario will be the eventual overthrow of the Hashemite state. If this scenario does take place, Israel could then more easily slip into the occupied territories and absorb it under its complete sovereignty."[41]

"Isn't this merely conjecture on your part, David?" inquired Neyri, clearly disturbed to have Israel viewed in such a poor light by his own countrymen.

"Actually, Neyri, it gets worse. No, this is not conjecture, nor was the fiasco in Lebanon with the death of twenty-five thousand Lebanese and Palestinian Arabs and nine hundred Israeli soldiers. The only consolation of this dreadful war was the knowledge there were men like Colonel Eli Geva and others like him who refused to lead his troops into West Beirut. The other heroes are the Israeli journalists who have been telling the bald truth for years now, whether anyone here or abroad cares to take heed that Israel is in self-destruction mode. Let me tell you what a former adviser to Prime Minister Rabin fears. His article appeared recently in the journal *Davar*. His name is Yoram Peri. He

fears that if Israel is forced to sign a peace settlement with the PLO, giving up territories and having the establishment of a Palestinian state on
its doorstep, there could be a military coup in Israel. I believe he's right
in his assessment.[42] In fact, I believe that since Ben Gurion was prime
minister, Israel has not deviated one iota from his blueprint and his
political and military objectives, which he summarized for one of his
aides at the 1949 Armistice Agreement in Rhodes: 'Before the founding of the state ... our main interest was self-defense ... but now the
issue at hand is conquest, not self-defense....' [43] 'Peace is vital—but
not at any price,' he subsequently wrote in his diary.[44]

"Why is there no peace movement among the Palestinians, like there
is among the Israelis?" Jacky demanded. "Why do the Palestinians maintain hideous racist statements against Israel in their textbooks, depicting Israeli Jews as monsters? By the same token, why do Palestinians
and Arabs from all walks of life continue to believe and perpetuate conspiracy theories about the Jews? You talk here, Arnie and David, about
the new revisionist historians both in Israel and throughout the world
ferreting out myths from facts and attempting to write a more accurate, historical accounting of 1948 and beyond. Why isn't there a com-
parable undertaking in the Arab and Palestinian world? Let's call a spade
a spade shall we? Neither Israel nor the Palestinians are innocents in
this conflict. Neither has come out of this conflict with clean hands.
Both have shed blood. Both are guilty in maintaining the protracted
battle over the land. Both have been naysayers when offered peace terms.
Both have dug their heels in the sand, preferring the status quo and
intractable positions over peaceful co-existence. It wears me out to hear
anyone denouncing Israel as fully culpable while maintaining the Palestinians as the poor, suffering refugees being crushed under the heels of
the Goliath Israel. It doesn't matter who's right or who's wrong anymore. What matters is that someone put a stop to this madness, the
madness of the Israeli leaders and Palestinian leaders who don't give a
damn how much pain and suffering they are inflicting on their own
people for sheer political gain!"

Long after the discussion broke up at the table and everyone went
their separate ways, Jacky Cohen was unable to sleep. She was upset to
realize that after fifty-three years of statehood, the best a Jewish Israeli

could expect was a burning hatred that seemed to have no end. The longer it burned, the hotter the embers. The best a Palestinian Arab could expect was stagnation, a stagnation of such immense proportions that it distorted time, reality, the present, the past, and the future. And now, according to David and Arnie's assessment, Israel was on the road to Armeggedon. The mitigating factor propelling Israel down this self-destructive path was a historic fear for its own survival arising from the experience of the Holocaust and leading to intransigence in reaching out for a peaceful accord.

She needed to think long and hard over the present situation in Israel—the stoning of Arab children; the civil uprising by adult Arabs, including Israeli Arabs identifying with the Palestinian cause; the retaliation by the Israeli soldiers using rubber pellets that often left victims blinded, resorting to live ammunition and helicopter gun ships to assassinate leaders, triggering further avenging suicide bombers throughout the length and breadth of the country. There had to be a solution to this senseless violence, which bred only more violence and more hatred, a hatred turning into an uncontrollable and all-consuming rage.

Who would be the conduit for peace, Jacky wondered, as sleep eluded her. Had not Rabin offered to be such a conduit? The price he paid for pursuing peace in the Middle East was his own life, taken on November 4, 1995 by a young Israeli Yemenite Jew and religious extremist law student at Bar-Ilan University, Yigal Amir, an assassin bent on the Jewish fundamentalist position that all the land was holy and forbidden to be relinquished to one's enemy. With such intractable positions taken by both the Arabs and the Jews, were they headed for an Armageddon? If there would be a final and conclusive battle between the forces of good and evil, who would be the victor in this vast, decisive conflict? What if there would be no victor—what then?

Shuddering from the cold permeating her bedroom, Jacky finally crawled under the sheets, pulling the down comforter over her head, remembering Neyri's parting words.

"I'm due back at my base shortly. Depending on my schedule, I'll look you up on campus," he offered.

"I'd like that."

"*L'hitraot*, see you again, Jacky."

Then he vanished from the room before she could get her bearings. Surely it was just a strong feeling of chemistry between them, nothing more, she told herself. If it just involved a chemical attraction, then she was on safe ground, she argued. Lust she could deal with. It was love and surrendering to such feelings that frightened her, after having been exposed to a man who trampled on feelings and emotions. She forced herself to push away all thoughts of negative feelings from the past, not wanting to lose the intensity of the aura she felt tonight. Jacky finally fell into a deep sleep as the sunshine bathed her room in its golden light.

On the drive back to his base, Neyri Ben-Ner was deeply disturbed by a brief conversation he had had with the Palestinian Asa Ibrahimi before he left the apartment:

"It seems as though we have met before, Asa. Yet, I don't remember where," he admitted.

"Yes, we met on November 12, in Ramallah. It was the night you gave the orders to demolish my parents' home. Now do you recall under what circumstances we met?"

He could not put this conversation out of his mind. Like a broken record, he heard Asa Ibrahimi's voice breaking with pain. By the time he reached his base, he felt heavy with despair and remorse.

Twenty-Three

ON A COLD, CRISP DAY THE MIDDLE OF MARCH, Shulha Ibrahimi decided to venture into West Jerusalem, in search of a birthday present for her husband.

Beneath a battered trench coat once belonging to Asa's father, she wore a long, black Bedouin dress embroidered with appliqué at the neck and along the sleeves. A white muslin scarf covered long hair thickly braided coiled down her back.

For the past several weeks, she had discarded the custom of wearing the black veil and matching headdress. At first she felt naked revealing her face to men, women and children, wondering if she had made the right decision to abandon the Bedouin custom. Initially, when passing one of the mirrors in the East Jerusalem apartment, she was startled to see her own face completely open, visible and vulnerable for all to observe. As the days turned to weeks, Shulha grew accustomed to the feel of the sun, wind, and rain on her face. It felt remarkably refreshing, exquisitely wholesome, and completely liberating. On some level, she was reluctant to return eventually to Ein Fashkha. It would be mandatory, once again, to don the cloth that ostensibly hid her from the world, making her not only inaccessible but invisible as well to the prying eyes of other males while ensuring proper modesty among the Ta'amireh tribe.

Walking unhurriedly along the streets of the Israeli Jews, she stopped from time to time to glance at the window displays. On Ben Yehuda Street, she eyed the assortment of leather handbags in the storefront of Ha-Atik. Then she headed for the Bell Tower's mall located on King George Street. Half an hour later, clutching a plastic bag containing her husband's birthday present, she walked elatedly toward Jaffa Road.

At the main intersection of Jaffa Road and King George, she casually glanced toward the glass-enclosed Sbarro pizzeria while waiting for the traffic lights to change. A man and a woman were seated alongside the glass window. The angle of the man's head caught her attention; there was something strikingly familiar about it. She appraised the woman openly: her long, cascading blond curls swirling around her beautiful face gave the woman an angelic appearance.

The moment the lights changed, Shulha felt the surging of the crowd as she crossed safely to the other side of Jaffa Road. Fixated on the Sbarro restaurant, she remained standing beneath a store awning, staring across the street at the profile of the man. It was none other than her own husband.

Oblivious to everything happening in the vicinity—pedestrians in the street, cars on the road, the shivering of her body—she stood staring at the scene across the street. With disbelief etched on her face drained of natural color, she watched as Asa bent his head toward the woman, as if paying close attention to her every word, in sharp contrast to the manner in which he reluctantly engaged in conversation with his own wife.

As if to solace herself, she subconsciously placed a hand on her abdomen, as if she needed to remind herself that it was his child she was carrying in her womb. Suddenly overcome with emotion, she felt shame, humiliation, and betrayal engulf her in a paroxysm of violent emotion threatening to overwhelm her senses.

Later she would feel the intense anger turning to rage, a rage propelling her to action. At this moment in time, as she stared in agony at the scene before her—one that she could neither evade, deny, nor rationalize out of existence—she felt as if her limbs were paralyzed. "There is another woman in my husband's life," she thought in despair.

"Who is she? Has he known her as long as he has known me? What difference does it make!" she finally cried out, biting down on her lower lip to prevent from crying in public. Involuntarily, her hands were shaking, causing the plastic bag containing a leather wallet to create a rustling sound against her stomach. Placing a free hand on her own heart, she needed to ascertain whether it had been severed from her chest by a blunt instrument, making her wonder why she was not bleeding to death on the sidewalk for all to witness.

In the next instant, when she fully comprehended for the first time that Asa Ibrahimi did not love her as he claimed, her abdomen started heaving with uncontrollable sobs rising from the depth of her being. Mortified lest Asa discover his wife witnessing his betrayal of her, Shulha bowed her head, hurrying away, pounding her feet into the pavement of West Jerusalem in a desperate attempt to escape the scene on Jaffa Road.

Once within the safety of the Saladin apartment, she headed for the privacy of the bedroom, thankful that Muni Ibrahimi was still on campus. Shulha shoved a chair against the bedroom door to ensure no one would find her in this state of agitation before she figured out what she must do to preserve what was left of her dignity as a woman whose love had been trampled as surely as if she were one of her father's sheep being led to the slaughter for the *Eid-al-Fitr*, the Feast of Ramadan.

Prostrating herself on the Persian rug beside the bed, she prayed to be shown the way to resolution. It was exceedingly difficult for her to swallow or breathe naturally. She alternated between supplication and sobs of wrenching loss, betrayal, and abandonment by a man who once made the sun shine when he chanced to smile at her.

Despite being sore in body and soul, she forced herself to a prone position, dragging herself to the bathroom where she stripped naked. She turned the water full force allowing it to cascade over her hair, face, and body as if seeking a cleansing and a relief from an intolerable sorrow burrowing its way to her soul. After towel drying her body, she carefully removed from the closet the most elegantly embroidered black Bedouin dress she possessed in her trousseau. In a homemade basket with a lid used to carry the few treasured belongings from her father's tent, she folded the rest of her dresses, underwear, and nightgowns carefully into the basket, closing the lid securely.

Then she sat down on the bed, waiting for her husband to return home to her.

Twenty-four

THE HEBREW UNIVERSITY'S MOUNT SCOPUS CAMPUS was bustling with students and faculty as Jacky walked from her office to the cafeteria. In the back of the crowded room, she saw Arnie Davidovitz motioning to her. Over soup and salad, they talked about their current work projects.

"How's your research going, Jacky?"

"Better than expected, really. I've found all the resources I've needed available in the library. More importantly, I've been to Tel Aviv a few times and held interviews with veterans from the '67 Six-Day War as well as the '73 Yom Kippur battle. Apparently, both wars were extremely difficult for Israeli soldiers."

"All the wars have been traumatic, some more than others. The '73 war was too close for comfort. It caught Israel off guard. In some instances, it took forty-eight to seventy-two hours to become fully mobilized due to Yom Kippur, when all communications are shut down throughout the country. Too many lives were lost because someone was asleep at the helm. Ask anyone who lived through that bitter war or fought in it and you'll see it's a war that never seems to be part of the past. It's like weeds in your garden that crop up time and again no matter how hard you attempt to control the growth."

"The interesting finding is that both sets of veterans—those who fought twenty-seven years ago in '73 as well as thirty-three years ago in the 1967 War—still talk about how incredibly old they felt after their first war. They were nineteen, twenty, or twenty-one when they faced war, yet they recalled feeling old in a young man's body, along with the sadness and melancholy which war produces in warriors."

"You'd be hard-pressed to get any soldier in active duty in Israel or even among the reserves to ever admit such a thing in public."

"Why?"

"There are certain things forbidden to be discussed outside the army, within civilian life. I believe such a topic would fall under the category considered *sodi,* secret."

"What a burden of silence to place on the shoulders of young men and women! I've noticed from personal observation that a country constantly under siege has to deal with residual effects. The tempo of life is so different, didn't you notice? The few days I spent in Tel Aviv made Jerusalem appear almost tranquil in comparison. It's so intense in both cities, actually. I wouldn't know how to describe it to people back home. Israel is a nation always on the edge, waiting for the next blow."

"Hell of a price to pay for survival," Arnie observed. "The irony of all this is that Israel came into existence to provide a sanctuary for Jews, ostensibly to be a safe haven."

"How long will this violence continue, do you think?"

"Until a form of parity evolves and the balance of power is more equalized. Only then will the Palestinians be able to agree to talking peace. If one of the parties is strong and the other weak, it doesn't make for a reliable partner for conflict resolution."

"How's the book coming along, the one you and David Ha-Levy are writing on the conflict?"

"We're interviewing Arabs from all walks of life—Palestinians living in Israel within the Green Line, those in refugee camps on the West Bank and in the Gaza Strip. Then we'll begin gathering interviews from Israeli Jews. We have a long road to go, especially with both sides hardening their attitudes. Every time there is a suicide bombing or a raid, one or the other retaliates and the hatred sinks deeper."

"What if Israel stopped retaliating for any length of time, no matter the provocation? What, in your opinion, would occur?"

"The Arabs would view it as a decisive weakness. They would undoubtedly strike out with impunity. They would conclude that Israel has gone soft and weak. They would kill and plunder without a stop."

The color drained from Jacky's face. He reached out to pat her hand. "The truth is rather ugly, isn't it?"

"How do Israeli Jews live such normal lives in spite of all the fear, terror, violence, and death all around them, day after day, year after year?"

"Lots of defense mechanisms are in place, I believe."

"You mean denial, repression, suppression?"

"Yes, as well as a coarse outer shell that many people from abroad call arrogance, hubris, impatience. Inside there's a lot of compassion. There are many Israeli Jews who still want to believe that if we only show respect, sensitivity, and dignity to the Arabs, they will stop wanting to liquidate the sovereign state of Israel."

"Do you actually believe this?"

"We'll never know, will we, until they try it. My take on this whole conflict is that the type of violence found in this country can be very addictive; it's like a narcotic. Over time it can be very intoxicating."[45]

"As a psychologist, I concur. It can also be a distraction from the boredom of everyday existence."

"It can also provide meaning to life if one believes the myth of war enough."[46]

"What do you mean?"

"We're all looking for a purpose to our lives, how to make life more meaningful. War is a high; it allows us to feel we have a noble purpose, and our soldiers are courageous, willing to die for the love of country. Ask any soldier if the reality of war is noble, and they will tell you the truth: war is dehumanizing to those in battle. One rages in order to kill or be killed, but when it is over, the survivors of war—the soldiers— are the biggest victims of them all. They are discarded after the battle, after the professional job is done. No one wants to hear the truth from them. Hence, their perennial silence. This is why the myth of war persists. We have a way of shutting up our soldiers so the lie is intact from one generation to another. The enemy is always portrayed as absolutely evil. If we didn't demonize our enemy, no government or military could enable soldiers to kill. Here the demonizing is so complete on both sides of the conflict."

"What's going to break the pattern of killing and retaliation?"

"Wiser leaders or a miracle," he offered.

Jacky dug the fork into her salad. "Tell me something about Neyri Ben-Ner, will you, Arnie? What do you think of him?"

"As a soldier, a man, or a former student?"

"All of the above."

"You're attracted to him, I gather?"

"I'm reluctant to admit it, but yes, I guess I am."

"He's an exceptional person—a rare leader, a blend of capability, strength, intelligence, education, and depth. When I first met him over a dozen years ago, he was dealing with the loss of his brother. He was still in his shadow, so much so that Neyri couldn't locate his own. It came very close to shattering him. You know yourself from your own losses that there comes a time when you've loved someone deeply, with your entire being, and you lose the person through illness, death, or divorce. It takes every ounce of your strength not to cave in, to give up, and to pray for death to overtake you because it's preferable to living with such immense pain. Well, that's the way Neyri felt about Gideon. They were the best of friends, you know, and he emulated Gidi. Neyri was at Harvard with his bride, Ayelet. So when he wrote me several years later that they had separated and were getting a divorce, I was stunned."

"Why?"

"I remember them very much in love with each other."

"I see."

"Do you really? Neyri is not the kind of person who is half way with anyone or anything. It's either all the way with him or nothing at all."

"Do you know the reasons for the divorce?"

"No, I suggest you ask him the next time you see him."

"If I have the opportunity, I will. He said he would contact me. He hasn't yet."

"Officers in the Israeli army are kept rather busy, from what I've been told. In fact, the commitment and responsibilities of career officers are contributing factors for divorce rates to go sky high. Be patient. I happen to know he's very attracted to you."

"How do you know that?"

"He told me so, actually."

"Really? When?" she asked in disbelief.

"Neyri called me from his base a few days after he met you, to get your office and home number. While he had the opportunity, he wanted to know if there was a man in your life back in the States. So I told him there wasn't a man, but rather men, lined up at your door."

"Stop, Arnie! What a disastrous cupid you'd make!"

"Here I thought I was doing a marvelous job with the two of you! By the way, you've been blushing for the past few minutes, you know. What should I make of this, my dear Jacky?"

"Nothing, since I never blush. Shall we return our trays and go for a stroll around campus, unless you're tied up with other commitments?"

Twenty-five

AFTER CONFERRING ALL AFTERNOON with students on campus, Muni Ibrahimi returned later than usual to her son's apartment. The first thing she noticed was the latched front door, normally left open since Shulha was always home in the late afternoons preparing a vegetarian meal for the family. Often her son was absent from the dinner meal, which conflicted with his tutoring schedule. The two women looked forward to sharing this time together. Shulha was eager to learn what was happening on the highly politicized campus. Muni had even extended her an invitation to attend one of her lectures, which Shulha declined for myriad reasons.

The silence within the apartment was the next thing to accost the senses. She removed her black winter coat, hanging it in the living room closet, surprised by the absence of the kitchen smells accompanied by the lovely voice of her daughter-in-law. It didn't take long to discover that Shulha was nowhere to be found.

From the pantry door, she removed an apron, ready to prepare a light dinner sufficient for the entire family. By 6:00 PM, when neither her daughter-in-law nor her son appeared, she sat down alone at the table to eat couscous topped with sautéed vegetables, goat cheese, and Turkish coffee.

After the light dinner, Muni retreated to her study as she did every evening, to review lecture notes for the next day. By the time she glanced up from her preparations, she realized it was nearly 8:00 PM and clearly now there was reason to be concerned about the whereabouts of her daughter-in-law.

Muni walked directly to her son's bedroom, now shared with his wife. When she stepped inside the room, she noticed that the brushes Shulha used daily to brush out her long, thick braids were missing from the bedside table. An inner voice challenged her to fling open the one closet used by the young couple. Only her son's modest wardrobe appeared in the small space, empty of Shulha's personal belongings.

She sat down on the edge of the bed, attempting to comprehend what meaning this might have. Something must have happened with her family or the tribe, requiring her presence in Ein Fashkha, Muni reasoned, knowing full well she would stay up all night, if need be, to wait for her son and his explanation for the disappearance of his wife.

⠀⟨⟩⠀

WHEN ASA IBRAHIMI FINALLY OPENED the front door at 1:45 AM, he found the lights in his apartment blazing.

"What happened? Where is Shulha?" his mother demanded.

"She insisted on returning to Ein Fashkha for a while."

"Why?"

He shrugged in answer, wearily dragging himself to his bedroom and closing the door softly behind him.

Muni's whole demeanor changed after this brief, unsatisfactory encounter with her taciturn son. Knowing it was futile to pursue a conversation with her adult son if he was unwilling to communicate, she finally retired, falling into a troubled sleep. It disturbed her deeply to learn belatedly, despite living under the same roof as her son and his wife, of the trouble brewing between them like a boiling teapot ready to overflow.

Within the confines of his bedroom, Asa wept tears of sorrow for the second time in his life, recalling the bitter argument with his wife in this very room:

"You do not love me," she repeated after hurling accusations at him of his deceitfulness and his betrayal, a side to her that he had never witnessed before.

"What in the world are you talking about? What makes you think I don't love you?"

"If a man truly loves a woman, he has no need for another."

"Another woman? Are you delirious, Shulha? Is your pregnancy making you nuts? Are your hormones raging out of control, because if they are, you'd better get yourself back under control or else..."

"Or else, what? Are you threatening me? If you are, Asa Ibrahimi, be my guest, threaten as much as you want. All you have to do to divorce a Bedouin woman is to say 'Aley et talak. I divorce you,' three times, and you will be rid of me. Do you know it is so simple, and it cannot be revoked?" she flung back at him, her head held high in proud disobedience, anathema to tribal code and the strict patriarchal authoritarian laws enacted since time immemorial.

"I am not threatening you! I am not divorcing you! I am simply trying to understand what's gotten into you," he demanded, aware Shulha never appeared more beautiful than she did at this moment flushed with anger and rage.

"There's nothing wrong with me. There is something wrong with our relationship," she flung back at him with eyes blazing and a smoldering, wounded heart.

"What, be specific, before you drive me mad with your accusations!"

"I saw you. I saw you and another woman. Today. Seated in the Sbarro Restaurant on Jaffa Road. She was blond. Very beautiful. You couldn't take your eyes off her for even a moment to notice that I, your wife, was observing you, because you see, my dear Asa, you were enthralled with her so completely, there was no room in your world for any other observation or reality to intrude."

"Yes, I was with another woman today. But she means nothing to me. She is a colleague of mine from the Hebrew University, a research scholar whom I have known for several months."

"She means nothing to you? Really? You expect me to believe this when I saw with my own eyes how dazzled you were by her?"

"She means nothing to me, I repeat, nothing. I am not even attracted to her. She is a colleague. Besides, I love you."

"You are a liar as well as a betrayer. You twist everything so you appear innocent. You are not innocent. You have betrayed our marriage. I no longer trust you."

"What can I do to convince you I love only you?"

"A woman always knows if she is genuinely loved. Take me back to Ein Fashkha, now, at once!"

"Impossible! The obstetrician has warned us we must remain in the city until the baby is born."

"The baby will not be born for four-and-a-half months. Take me back to my father's tent. If not, I will find a way to go back on my own."

"You cannot leave here. The baby could be born premature, then what?"

"I will leave here. I need to be alone, in the desert, to sort things out in my heart and mind. Then I will return to Jerusalem to give birth to our child."

"You are making a serious mistake, Shulha."

"I would be making a mistake by remaining and listening to your lies."

He spread his hands in an imploring fashion. She lifted her eyes, staring at his face, revealing the agony in her soul. Wordlessly, he lifted the basket filled with her possessions, driving his wife back to Ein Fashkha before nightfall. After he had escorted Shulha to her father's tent, he attempted to gather her into his arms.

Recoiling from him as if a snake had touched her, she flung off his arm. He felt the sting of her wrath on the long, lonely journey back to East Jerusalem.

"What have I done?" he wept in the darkness of his room, knowing he had broken more than his vows to his wife. He had betrayed himself as much as he had betrayed Shulha and he didn't know how to redress the wrong.

Longing for what was no longer attainable, he thought of his father and brothers in his parents' former home in Ramallah, with all the memories of his childhood and youth. He reflected over his changing feelings for his wife—from the initial lust for her at first encounter, to disillusionment after their marriage, to a brotherly love and protectiveness when learning she was carrying his child. His passion had evaporated quickly, like a kindling fire dying shortly after a blazing start. For all his other emotional needs and physical cravings, he had turned to Beth Dumont as a pacifier.

"Why? Why?" he cried out into the lonely night, tortured by what he had done to his wife and his marriage.

Twenty-six

A FEW DAYS LATER, JACKY WAS SEATED in her office, with research notes spread all over her desk. Since it was Friday, it would be a half-day for her on campus, along with the country's businesses, schools, transportation, and the army, giving everyone a chance to run errands and travel home before the Sabbath started at sunset.

Gathering the notes she was working on, she shut down her computer, deciding to call it quits. Perching her dark sunglasses on top of her head, she swung open the office door, nearly colliding into the arms of Neyri Ben-Ner, looking handsome and amused as he smiled at her. He was close enough to touch, totally disarming her. Both were silent, but their eyes spoke volumes. He was the first to break the spell.

"How've you been, Jacky?"

"Okay, but I hardly expected to see you again."

"I always keep my word. Do you have any plans this afternoon?"

"Plans? No, why?"

"I thought we'd go downtown for lunch. Afterwards, I'd like very much to show you around Jerusalem."

"I'd love to"

"Good. Let's go."

DOWNTOWN JERUSALEM WAS BUSTLING with shoppers doing last-minute errands before the Sabbath. The streets were crowded with pedestrians. Egged buses were competing with automobiles snarling their way through traffic. It was the usual congestion in the busy downtown area. Neyri grabbed her hand, guiding her across King George Street to Melech Ha-Falafel, his favorite eating kiosk on Agrippas Street. Perched on a stool, they ate falafel, hummus, and tehina in a pita wrap, loaded down with salad.

With her back to the traffic, Jacky heard the Egged bus drivers grinding their gears as they waited impatiently for the lights to change. All around her swirled a pattern of life so different from America. In the short span of time since her arrival, she was re-intoxicated by life in Jerusalem—the sounds, smells, sights, and air of a city so arrestingly different, so intensely alive and meaningful to her. Seated beside Neyri, she was acutely aware of every nuance, especially the radiance she felt. Was it Jerusalem or Neyri having this effect on her, she wondered?

"I owe you a real dinner in a restaurant next time," he promised as he paid the bill.

When they reached his car parked on Hillel Street, he slipped behind the wheel of his Honda, heading in the direction of Talpiot. From time to time, she found herself glancing at his profile, realizing how little she actually knew about him.

"Tell me what it's like being an officer in Israel."

"I don't get more than two hours of sleep on a given night," he admitted, braking for a light on Derek Hebron. "We all feel the heavy burden and responsibilities of being commanding officers. There is no time for reflection, no time for much of a personal life. You get used to it, like anything else," he admitted. "Career officers have tunnel vision. It doesn't permit a healthy home environment for most of us. A high rate of divorce is one of the casualties, even though I swore it would never happen to me," he shrugged, wishing he had not brought up the topic. Comparing divorce notes was something he never indulged in if he could help it.

"Do you have any children?"

"No, though we did try. In fact, it became the primary reason for the divorce. Ayelet wanted children desperately. When she found out she was infertile, I couldn't convince her we should adopt. Ironically, she left me for another man who had three children. It gave her a reason for living, I suppose. I simply wasn't able to give her the attention she needed. What about you?"

"Same, no children from my marriage."

"To me there is no such thing as a failed relationship," explained Neyri. "It seems to me every relationship goes as far as it can go and then it's time to say goodbye. What I mean is every relationship teaches us about ourselves and life. Sometimes, it ends when it is time to learn from others."

"You seem so self-contained to me."

"Not really. I have my family and close friends who have given me lots of support. It keeps me going when things get rough. I'm very close to my younger brother, Omri. He's in the permanent army like I am."

"Is he your only sibling?" she asked, wondering if it was wise to bring up this topic.

"No, I had an older brother." He said nothing further, as he concentrated on his driving, taking a left into an area called the Haas Promenade. Once he parked the car, he reached out for her hand. They strolled casually along the promenade overlooking a panoramic view of the city of Jerusalem. He stopped to lean over a banister, pointing out the prominent areas well known to all Jerusalemites. Off to her left a group of Arab boys were playing soccer in a grassy field. To her right, people were walking or pushing strollers. She glanced at the skyline, noticing the way the shadows clung to the hillside, casting a golden light over the city, that created an irresistible aura of solemnity and peace. For several moments they both remained silent, absorbing the beauty of Jerusalem.

When Neyri turned to look directly at her, he admitted: "I haven't spoken about my brother for a very long time. He was killed during training, all too prevalent in the army," he told her, his eyes clouding with an irreconcilable loss.

"I'm so sorry."

"It's okay. It's time I talked about Gideon. In this country, we've had so many casualties. You never get used to it, especially if it's in your own family. It nearly destroyed us. We called him Gidi for short; he was two years older than me. He would have been forty-one this June, had he lived. He was everything I aspired to be—enormously accomplished, in an elite fighting unit, a commando, who loved being challenged by the army, no matter the price. He was twenty-one when a member of his own unit accidentally shot him in the throat. They were using live ammunition. A training exercise, you see. Gidi was killed instantaneously."

He stopped talking, his voice breaking with emotion and memories. The hurt was so deep it didn't matter how many years had elapsed, it still felt raw to him as if it had happened yesterday.

"My parents were crushed by his death, particularly my mother. She was never the same. None of us were. Yet, she never tried to stop Omri or me from following in our brother's footsteps. Omri became a tank commander, making quite a name for himself. He's thirty-five and has just been handed a new command, in armor. Omri has also managed, somehow, to keep his family life intact, with three daughters and a lovely wife. I'm proud of him," he admitted with justifiable pride.

"What about you, Jacky? You've said so little about yourself and your family."

She didn't answer immediately since it was difficult to share her own past with him without feeling vulnerable. Yet, on some level, she felt the compulsion to share a deep part of herself, feeling irresistibly magnetized by his own warmth. "My parents were killed ... it was an accident ... automobile ... head-on collision. I was in my early teens. My mother's sister and her husband in Harvard, Massachusetts, took over the role of my missing parents. I'm an only child and have always felt more alone than I care to admit. I've also learned to depend on friends or myself for comfort. Their unexpected death—and the horrible way they died—profoundly affected me. The first year after it happened, I often wished I had died with them, the legacy of survivor's guilt. Instead, I met a man who promised me the world. What he didn't tell me was that it came with a huge price."

She took a deep breath and then continued.

"He took freedom away from me—the freedom to think my own thoughts, to make my own decisions, choices, or to fall flat on my face in failure. He controlled everything, even the friends I could or could not have. He was overly critical, overly judgmental. I lasted ten years with him. Each day I felt my heart constricting more. Whatever feelings I once had for him simply vanished.

"I called a lawyer, finally, then packed my belongings and rented my own apartment. He didn't even show up at the civil divorce proceedings, sent his proxy instead—his own lawyer. It left me fearful that I would attract other men just like him. It made me wary. It also made me doubt myself, my own judgment of people and why I didn't see through him before I committed myself," she confessed.

"You shouldn't blame yourself, Jacky. Things like this happen all the time to others."

"I should have known better, should have listened to my inner voice warning me."

"Sometimes when we're so close to a problem we're unable to see the problem clearly or the person for any number of reasons. It sounds like he was so busy putting you down, it was very hurtful and confusing to you. Probably you couldn't even think straight."

"I couldn't. I also keep telling myself I didn't deserve the put-downs. Such treatment wears away at a person's self-esteem. I've spent the last seven years building it up again by doing challenging things in my research and publications and other interests I have."

"Have you permitted love in your life?"

"I've dated. I find American men too absorbed in accumulating money, status, and power to interest me beyond a date. Frankly, it has been a huge turn-off."

"What do you look for in a man?"

"I look for character in a man, since I believe one's fate is based on character. Underlying your own is a desire to protect and defend the Jewish people from destruction. This is not only noble and courageous professionally, it also means that your personal life with friends, and family, and lovers benefit from such special characteristics. I'm drawn to you for this reason. You're different. You inspire confidence in others with your self-assurance and self-direction. I like this immensely. It's something to emulate and to learn from you."

"Most women wouldn't describe me quite the way you have, you realize?"

"No, what do you mean?"

"My former wife claimed I was selfish to put Zahal before her and our personal life. She thought I was foolish, allowing myself to be used like a puppet, whenever or whatever I was called upon to do for the army, I was being used and manipulated. We had endless arguments on this all the time. She also was filled with intense anxiety and fear every time I either went on a mission or accepted a new command. She simply couldn't or wouldn't deal with the issues of being a soldier's wife. I never faulted her for this, only myself. I should have seen before I married her that she didn't have the stamina needed. The pressures on a family are rather intense. The disappointments are many. I loved my work because it was challenging and necessary from my perspective. After a while her attitude wore me out. Our marriage went downhill fast. It was heartbreaking to me to let her go, at first. You see, I always wanted a family and children just like my parents. It just wasn't meant to be. So we parted, she to build a future with another man who could offer her what I couldn't, and me, well, I just put all my energy into my work."

"Has it been enough to sustain you all these years?"

"No, not really. Now as I reflect, in many ways it was a substitute. By not standing still, I could be in denial and not permit myself to see or feel all I was missing out of life. Even my love affairs were empty of meaning. I kept turning to a new affair to fill the void. Not surprisingly, I felt more alone, not less, afterwards. So I stopped that too."

"Soon you'll be out of the army. Perhaps you'll be able to open yourself to a new, more fulfilling way of life."

"We all hope, don't we, for a better life than what we have?"

"Of course."

"Jacky, there's so much I like about you. I want to get to know you on a deep level," he admitted, all the while scrutinizing her face, realizing how attracted he was to her beauty and intelligence. "We've only just met, yet something seems to be pulling me toward you. I don't mean merely a physical attraction; it's far more than this. Do you remember the first time we met in Tel Aviv? I felt it then. I seem moved by your unusual spirit and sensitivity—the sensitivity to this land, my country, and my people. I'm hoping you feel as I do."

Jacky was silenced by the intensity of feelings. Something seemed to be squeezing her heart. She recognized it as immobilizing fear. Trembling, Jacky forced herself to breathe deeply. When he finally took her in his arms, he softly brushed his lips on her waiting mouth. A smoldering heat traveled throughout her body. She found herself returning the velvety softness of his kisses until it created a driving need to press her mouth and body against his in the primal act of merging. When they pulled apart for a moment, she stared searchingly into his eyes, seeing tenderness and gentleness along with a passion rivaling her own.

They walked back to the car, enveloped by the mysterious aura of love and its all-embracing magnetism, which seemed to have lit a torch in both of them.

Twenty-seven

TOWARD THE END OF MARCH, Jacky was sitting in her Palmach apartment reviewing recent interview notes with Israeli veteran soldiers. The raw data she was gathering was to be used in writing a text on the psychology of violence among war veterans and civilian populations exposed to traumatic events.

The quiet of a Jerusalem day was suddenly shattered by the sounds of police and ambulance sirens racing across the city. Jacky pushed back her desk chair. She flung open the balcony door overlooking the city of Jerusalem, wondering what section of the city was under direct attack. She knew with utter certainty it was another terrorist attack, most likely the latest target, the Egged city buses crowded with students, housewives, and the rest of the populace on errands. Nervously she ran a hand through her hair, recalling the daily chronicle of events since arriving in the country: March 1, in Mei Ami, one dead in a taxi; in Shalhevet Pass, in Hebron, the tragic death of a ten-month-old baby killed by Palestinian sniper fire while she was pushed in her carriage by her father, seriously wounded in the attack; March 4, in Netanya, three dead; and today, March 27, she wondered, as she paced nervously on the wide porch, how many Israeli lives would be claimed?

At moments such as this, uncertainty, caution, and fear permeated

Israel. Jerusalem, in particular, was a capital that never slept. The intensity of civilian life was disturbing. It felt frenzied, as if a clock had been wound too tight, ready to explode. Like an Israeli-born citizen, Jacky found herself turning on the news every hour on the hour, as if she needed to take the pulse of the nation.

In any other capital of the world, she would have been envisioning a medical emergency for a heart attack, stroke, or road accident. This was not just any capital; it was Jewish Jerusalem, a city extolling peace in the midst of bloody violence for centuries. Not only did the Romans destroy the Jewish Temple of Solomon in 70 AD, the Romans also made the streets, alleys, and roads flow with the blood of millions of murdered inhabitants, blacking out the skyline with the crucified bodies of Jews who had revolted against Roman rule and cruel occupation. In the twentieth and twenty-first centuries, war, terrorism, and stabbings had been relegated to a subculture, part and parcel of this land where Zionist Jews arrived as new immigrants in myriad waves of *Aliyah,* on their return to Zion.

When Jacky was a student in the overseas program at the Hebrew University in 1982, and she had just turned nineteen, Menachem Begin was the Prime Minister of Israel, and the Israeli offensive into Lebanon was in full swing. The major newspapers—*Ma'ariv, Ha'aretz,* and *Yediot Ah-ronot*—provided photos and names of the fallen soldiers in the war, creating a nation torn between their anguish over their losses, the necessity to protect their northern borders, as well as crush the Palestinians who were creating havoc for Israel and in the Lebanese capital of Beirut.

Despite the tension in 1982 due to the ongoing war—the first time in Israel's history that it was conducting an offensive campaign—she had managed to carve out quiet moments of leisure, taking long walks throughout the city of Jerusalem and hiking in the rest of the country to get a feel for the land. It didn't take long before she had fallen under the spell of Jerusalem, discovering an irresistible urge to view the city not only as the holy domain of three prominent religions, but also as a city of contrast, a city of brooding melancholy and pulsating energy, intensely alive, and compelling allegiance to its immortal fame.

Leaving it for the first time after a year's residency, it felt as if she had been torn from the arms of her mother when she had been most dependent on her as a child. Returning to the city after nineteen years, she was overwhelmed by the changes in neighborhoods and the expansion of settlements on the outskirts of Jerusalem, including Gilo, Efrat, Har Homah, Ma'ale Adumim, Pisgat Ziav, and other areas. Her senses were bombarded by the stimulus of densely populated areas, noise, and dirt. The open areas, wild fields as far as the eye could see, and unpaved paths in pastoral Talpiot had been obliterated, replaced by apartment buildings or the industrial section.

Whenever time permitted from her research and writing, she found herself wandering throughout the artist colony of Yemin Moshe, where unobstructed views of the walled Old City remained. In her two decades of absence from Israel, she had been transformed from a young, innocent girl to a woman prizing her ability to see, comprehend, and grow and change. Israel—Jerusalem in particular—had changed from a youthful nation where everything seemed possible, to its mid-point, where reflection and introspection were required in order to proceed to the next stage of maturity. The changes she was witnessing were cosmetic changes, all exterior changes in urban designs. Instead of freshness in insight, courageously seeking a healthier, less rigid and inflexible stance vis-à-vis the Arab population both within and outside the Green Line, she was witnessing a five-decade-old policy of hitting the enemy hard because this was the only language it understood. Hardness instilled a closed path and constricted hearts, offering little in the way of hope for the future. The longing on both sides of the divide for a better world necessitated a willingness to take the first steps toward embracing peace. The only embrace she was witnessing in the two months since her return was the dance of death. Given the reality, would she consider, under the circumstances, remaining in the country permanently? It was a question she could no more answer than if she were to ask herself whether she had fallen in love with a soldier of Israel. It was too soon to know the answer to either question. Yet, these questions remained in the back of her mind as something she would have to deal with sooner or later.

She was now in constant communication with Neyri Ben-Ner. Cellular phones had revolutionized Zahal, or so he told her. No longer were there long queues around army bases where reserve and career officers had to fight for a minute to call home. He called her day or night, whenever he had a spare moment from his command and all the duties connected with it.

He invited her to join his family for the Passover *seder* at his parents' home in the Katamon section of Jerusalem. Until then, they remained connected by phone and an occasional note hastily written from the field, like the one she had received the other day. In return, she wrote him back, hoping he could read between the lines that she missed him.

She left the porch, switching on the radio to the *Reshet Bet* station: "This is Danny Alon with the news: a suicide bomber has detonated a bomb on an Egged bus in the neighborhood of French Hill..."

The blast of police sirens and ambulances rushing to the latest bomb scare in French Hill sent fear through her. They were on a precipice, the Jewish people of Israel, a precipice afflicting every inhabitant in the land, and from which no one was exempt. Nothing short of a miracle, she knew, could alter the landscape, a landscape mired in blood, violence, and revenge.

She lifted the receiver, dialing Neyri's base, hoping she would hear his comforting voice at the other end of the line. A voice message was all she heard, indicating he was out in the field or out of communication. Leaving him a brief message, she entered the kitchen to prepare a fresh pot of coffee, knowing it would be a long time before she could unwind.

The next day, another suicide bomber detonated himself at a gas station near Sedeh Hemed, killing two more Israelis.

As the country prepared for the week-long Passover holiday, Jerusalem hotels geared up for the influx of visitors. There were few tourists from abroad, except for Christians on Easter pilgrimage in the holy city. Along Israel's borders and within the Israeli Defense Forces there was a high state of alert, to ward off any attacks on civilians during the spring festival commemorating Israel's exodus from Egyptian slavery and the freedom of a nation wandering in the desert toward the Promised Land.

At the Tel Nof Air Force Base, on the eve of Passover, Neyri Ben-Ner sat behind the wheel of his white Honda Civic, heading in the direction of Tel Aviv's Tel Hashomer Hospital to visit several members of his unit recently wounded in a shootout in Jenin. Two of the more seriously wounded soldiers had died the night before. After visiting the wounded, he drove first to Petach Tikvah, then onto Modi'in to pay condolence calls to the parents of the two paratroopers who had died in the raid. It was late afternoon by the time he parked his car outside his parents' home on Kav-Tet B'Novembre Street in Katamon.

Even the holiday aromas and the beautiful dining-room table set with his mother's finest dishes, glasses, and silverware could not lift the heaviness in his heart after seeing the wounded and the bereaved families in despair. Despite spending the last twenty years of his life in the IDF, he was not inured to their losses. No one could adjust completely to the reality of a hundred years of bloodshed between Arabs and Jews. After greeting his parents, Neyri headed for the shower, hoping the water would revive his lagging spirits, washing away his fatigue and sorrow.

Shortly before sunset, he drove the four blocks to Palmach Street to bring Jacky back to his home to meet his family. Seated around the Passover table were Neyri's parents, brother, sister-in-law, their three daughters, and Jacky. They were a secular Israeli family, but certain traditions—such as lighting the candles, sharing the Passover seder together with the entire family—were unifying factors in keeping them close, especially since the death of his grandfather.

Jacky was wearing a black sheath dress with black high heels. Her hair was worn straight to her shoulders, giving her a youthful and alluring appearance.

Neyri's father was seated at the head of the table. Jacob Ben-Ner was in his early sixties, working as a manager for the Soleh Boneh construction company. Aside from a full head of white hair and leathery skin from years of exposure working on building projects supervising Arab laborers from the Gaza Strip, he had the appearance of a strong and determined man with a deep sense of pride in his family. Neyri's mother, Miriam, was a jovial, warm, and inviting woman. Short, dark hair framed her unlined, attractive face. His younger brother, Omri, was a handsome replica of Neyri, she thought, except for his ash blond hair and hazel eyes. Omri's wife, Tali, a vivacious woman with short blond curls cascading around her face, appeared to be proud and sensitive to the needs of their three daughters aged nine, five, and 18 months.

Jacky glanced across the table, meeting Neyri's eyes over the two candelabras lit for the holiday. Her lovely smile took his breath away. It was all he could do to concentrate on the conversation with his family.

"Uncle Neyri, can we sing the whole *Haggadah* like we did last year?" begged his nine-year-old niece, a lovely golden-haired child.

"Certainly, Ronit, just pass the *Haggadot* to everyone and you can lead us."

It was customary that the segment of the *"Mah Nish-Ta-nah"* be recited by the youngest child at the seder table. Ronit coached her five-year-old sister to sing in unison:

"Mah nish ta-nah... Why is this night different from all other nights?"

Everyone applauded the children's recitation and then proceeded to sing aloud the entire Haggadah. Jacky joined in the uplifting singing of the Haggadah, finding it a lovely ritual, adding to the beauty, solemnity, and biblical connection to an ancient ritual practiced by Jews for thousands of years. After drinking two cups of wine, they stopped the singing to serve the long-awaited four-course dinner, an elaborate meal of chicken soup with matzoh balls, gefilte fish served with horseradish, broiled chicken, an old European dish of baked carrots and prunes known as *tzimmes,* fresh vegetables, and other side dishes prepared with the unleavened bread called matzoh. The food seemed endless, as did the conversation around the dinner table.

Jacky was grateful when the men switched from Hebrew to English, to make her more comfortable. She noticed Miriam struggling self-consciously to speak English, wanting to make her feel at home. Tali spoke English fluently. When Jacob Ben-Ner overheard the two women discussing the research project on the Yom Kippur War veterans, he told her:

"Jacky, I fought in the Yom Kippur War under Brigadier General Avigdor Kahalani. At the time he was a twenty-nine-year-old Lieutenant Colonel in the Seventh Armored Brigade, a brigade that my son Omri now commands. One night during the Yom Kippur War, our battalion took out four advancing Syrian T-62 tanks in thirty seconds."

"Thirty seconds?"

"We did it. I'm alive to tell you we did it. For this and other reasons, Kahalani received the *Ot Hagevura,* the highest medal of valor in the IDF.

"I still see Kahalani regularly, as do the remaining members of his former unit," Jacob informed her.

"Isn't this the key to Israel's survival, the closeness among its own people, particularly in time of war?" she asked.

"It's one of several. The other component is Zahal's ability to respond spontaneously and to improvise under battle conditions. The crucial composite is Israel's basic premise: when attacked, immediately bring the battle back to the enemy's turf," explained Jacob Ben-Ner.

"What are the chances of a seventh war? I understand there seems to be a rhythm to wars in this country," Jacky observed.

"Yes, they break out, on average, once every seven to ten years," Neyri concurred.

"As to another war, I doubt if Syria will want another round with us even to get the Golan back. The Palestinians do not have the military capability to war with us and win. So my take is no war, no peace," Mr. Ben-Ner explained."What about you, Omri, do you agree with this?"

"I'm more inclined to pessimism, as you know, *Aba.* I believe if there is no solution to be found, Jerusalem may soon be another Hebron, a violent and dangerous place for all of us in this city."[47]

"You can't mean this, Omri?" Tali interjected, creasing her forehead with frown lines, trying to dispel her fears. Since the outbreak of the Intifada at the end of September, life had become a hell again, with bombings, and intermittent stabbings a way of life once more. It was an intolerable way to live, but did they have any choice, she wondered as she spoon fed her youngest daughter seated in the high chair beside her?

"Tali, you know the Arabs aren't willing to recognize Israel's right to exist in peace within secure and recognized boundaries, even if we gave back occupied land captured in 1967," countered Omri Ben-Ner.

"The moment we do, they will demand we open the 1948 file when we accepted the partitioning of the land and the Arabs refused. There's no way to satisfy the Arabs' conditions because every time we accept one of their conditions, they will institute another condition, and then another, until we do what they want," Omri explained.

"Which is what?" Jacky wanted to know.

"To commit suicide. There are a number of ways they want to help us do this," explained Omri as he picked up his knife and fork to cut into the succulent chicken.

"One way is what they are attempting to do now—to cause so much instability in the country economically, politically, militarily, and psychologically that we will eventually do them a favor and wither away. They are hoping we will get so worn down by terrorism we will flee from this country. Do you notice anyone fleeing? I don't," he answered as he washed his food down with dry red wine.

"You just told your father the conflict is complicated. I'm having a hard time trying to understand why the two sides have been locked in conflict for over fifty years. What are the issues?" she asked, eating slowly and thoughtfully, grateful to everyone for speaking in English so she could follow the conversation, which deeply interested her.

"Actually, Jacky, the conflict is more than fifty years old. It didn't begin in 1947 or in the Arab rebellion from 1936 to 1939, or in the 1929 and 1921 outbreaks of Arab violence against the Jews living in this country. It was even before the 1917 Balfour Declaration and the British Mandate promising a portion of the land to Zionists. No, the conflict actually began in 1882, during the immigration of Jews from Europe to Palestine under the Ottoman Turks," Omri answered, rattling off these dates in history with ease.

"You mean to tell me this conflict between the Jews and Arabs is what, close to 120 years old?"

"Precisely," reiterated Omri as he helped himself to seconds.

"The conflict for many years was between Israel and the Arab world," Neyri expanded. "Only recently has it been between Israel and the Palestinians who have until the late sixties been kept on the back-burner by Arab intransigence. None of the Arab countries, with the exception of Jordan, attempted to incorporate into their country the 760,000 refugees from the 1948 war. They have been using the Palestinians as a political pawn for over fifty years, but the rage is against us, no matter what."

"They want a full peace only with the full restoration of Palestinian rights, which includes the return of all the refugees who now number in the millions," Neyri underscored. "They also want compensation for lost land, lost homes, lost property," he added. "As you know, Jacky, Israel cannot absorb millions of Arabs and still retain a Jewish state.[48]

"What are Israel's basic concerns?" Jacky queried.

"Security, in a word," Neyri told her, as his mother brought to the table a tray filled with a chocolate cinnamon cake and a fresh pot of coffee.

"What my brother means by security, Jacky, is that the Arab countries and the Palestinians have made it perfectly clear that the only way they will be at peace is when they liquidate us and rid the area of the sovereign nation called Israel. Hence, Israel can never feel secure enough, especially when the Holocaust is such a recent bitter reminder of our near extinction as a people."

"But I thought the Palestinian National Charter removed that type of language from their charter, or am I mistaken?" Jacky inquired, seeking clarification.

"You're under the same illusion as the rest of the world, Jacky, I'm afraid," Omri countered. "The same wording remains in their charter, and the same objective remains, which is to rectify the injustice, their perceived injustice that we not only won the first round with them in 1948 against all odds, but we also have won every war since 1948 and created a residual problem: they are now intensely humiliated. There is to be no compromise with Israel. If they did so and did not attempt to restore this historic wrong from their perspective, and therefore legitimate Israel's existence, then they would lose their raison d'être."

"What exactly do you mean by the term 'liquidation'?" she wanted to know.

"The extinction of our people, the massacre of all Israeli Jews, the confiscation of all the land given to us legally during the partition as well as all the land we have occupied since we won the 1967 war, taking over our homes and our property," he explained, as he got up from the table to pour her a second cup of coffee.

"How can they justify something so horrific?"

"You should know the Arabs consider themselves to not be aggressors by liquidating Israel, but consider Israelis aggressors for living on this land and defending it," Omri explained. "The Arabs believe Israel is evil and deserves to be destroyed because Israel was created illegally, so they claim, and this illegality is a crime against the Arab people. Therefore, by such reasoning, Israel is an evil state, there should be no mercy to the Israeli people, and they must be liquidated by any means possible. As long as Israel continues to exist, there will be no stability or peace in the Middle East. The rest of the world will continue to be in a quandary over the conflict in the Middle East."[49]

"Neyri, you have been very quiet. Is there a solution to this conflict, from your point of view?" inquired his father.

"If there were a solution, Aba, we would have found one already," Neyri concluded soberly. "I don't think either side truly wants peace. There have been so many missed opportunities for peace in the past fifty years. If we had peace, the IDF would be out of business as would the many terrorist factions in the Islamic Resistance Movement. Many people are aware that if peace were to occur between Arabs and Jews, internecine warfare would descend with a vengeance among Palestinians. By the same token, many feel the only thing keeping Israel intact is all her energy directed at the conflict with the Arab people.[50] Take this off the agenda, and Israel too would tear itself apart with internal problems of 'who's a Jew?' or 'should the country be a theocracy or a democracy?' Personally, I believe we're treading water, both sides waiting and hoping to wear the other side down, like in a war of attrition, where from sheer exhaustion the Arabs will give up their fight to get all the land back or the Jews will get so exhausted by the inability to live a normal life here in Israel that they'll emigrate. Also, the Arabs are hoping to collapse Israel's economy and its entire infrastructure in order to hasten the destruction along."

"What a nice topic for the holiday," Tali observed, and then laughingly she turned to Jacky to explain:

"We've all become experts politically because militarily we can't seem to find a solution to our conflict. For every Jew and Arab in the street, there will be ten different opinions on our problems and solutions or no solutions. I suggest we have our dessert and discuss the weather instead. Otherwise, I for one will be too depressed to eat the chocolate cinnamon coffee cake," admitted Tali as she quartered the round cake, placing the thick slices on a cake platter.

"Best suggestion I've heard all night," echoed her husband Omri.

Twenty-eight

LATER IN THE EVENING, AFTER THE WOMEN cleaned the dishes and put the remainder of the food away, Neyri drove in the direction of the Old City, parking near Dung Gate. The stars glittered in the sky like diamonds sparkling in a burst of shooting fireworks as Jacky and Neyri walked hand in hand to the *Kotel,* the Western Wall, and the holiest site of the Jews since the destruction of the Temple. For the first time in her life, Jacky didn't care about tomorrow or whether she had a future with this man beyond tonight. All she cared about was the pressure of his hand in hers.

There were a few men praying at the wall, even though it was close to midnight. On top of the wall, she noticed the ubiquitous Israeli soldier guarding the area where people had been attacked with stones thrown over the wall while in prayer. All through the long political discussion at dinner, she had been eager to comprehend all sides of the issues. She noticed that the one thing the family had omitted was the obvious: a key component to the conflict was the level of hatred fermenting between the Israeli Jews, the Palestinians, and other Arabs for fifty-three years. By far it was the most difficult obstacle to overcome. If they could just view each other as humans, without demonizing each other, without adhering to the propaganda spewed ad nauseum by both sides, only then could the other issues be tackled. Was she being naïve, she wondered, not to be convinced that the Arabs wanted to utterly destroy the people of Israel? Her brain was unable to go there, she told herself, as she peered down at the lights bouncing off the Western Wall, feeling at home in the country and at peace with the man beside her, holding her hand in his, tracing his fingers gently over her left palm and causing sensations through her body that she had long since forgotten were possible.

"Thank you for sharing your family. It means a lot to me," she admitted, feeling the old hunger for a family unit.

"Everyone loved you, including my mother and father," he admitted with pride.

"How do you know, Neyri?"

"If not, they would have continued to speak only in Hebrew rather than struggling to talk to you in English."

"I'm so glad we were able to communicate on some level."

"You made quite an impression on my family," he told her with evident pride. "My mother, in fact, wants me to bring you back for *Shabbat* the next time I get time off from the army. Would you like that?"

"Very much."

"Good. One of these days, I'll also take you to Mahane Julius, my brother's tank base."

"How does your brother react to your leaving the IDF in June?"

"Omri thinks I'll find life in America too bland, uniform, and boring. Besides, if a war breaks out in Israel, he knows I'll return immediately to rejoin my unit."

"What's the likelihood of this happening?"

"In this country, Jacky, it's always a possibility. We'll never repeat the errors made in the Yom Kippur War, ruling out the probability of war when intelligence factors and our instincts told a different story."

"What caused Israel to be so complaisant in 1973, thinking the Arabs wouldn't dare start a war after the lightning victory in the 1967 war?"

"Hubris."

"Is hubris a factor in the no-win situation between Arabs and Jews today?

"No, not at all."

"What is, then?"

"Stupidity, blindness, insecurity, I'd say. We haven't learned a thing from Rabin's assassination. The road to peace requires painful concessions that neither side is willing to pay."

"It's apparent you and Omri take completely divergent views politically—he's extreme right-wing Likud, and you sound like a left-wing Laborite."

"We never let our different political views and ideologies interfere with our relationship. It's been this way ever since we were kids. Gidi and I were alike in just about every way," he admitted.

"By the way, Jacky, I forgot to mention you need to be up at the break of dawn tomorrow morning," he said as he smiled a crooked smile that she was beginning to love. "Let's go, shall we?"

Outside her apartment, he opened the door, standing aside as she walked in first. He did not follow. Instead, he stood in the doorway, unmoving, until he suddenly pulled her into his arms, restraining himself as he slowly brought his mouth down, tasting her soft lips, feeling the heat of Jacky's body against his own.

"Until tomorrow," he whispered, and in an instant he closed the door behind him before he would change his mind.

✧⟨⟩✧

EARLY IN THE MORNING, THEY ARRIVED at their destination along the Dead Sea. They hastily stripped down to their bathing suits, walked to the water's edge, and shortly were floating in the lowest spot in the world. Sunlight sparkled on the water and on Jacky's body clad in a yellow bikini that off set her newly acquired tan. Neyri packed her in the medicinal mud from head to foot. She luxuriated in the feel of his hands on her body. He looked slim, toned, and muscled in tight black swimming trunks. She wanted to touch him with an ache that left her limp with longing.

Toward noon, they showered off the mud bath and headed to the nearby spring, where they swam beneath the falls of Ein Gedi. They played like teenagers under the waterfall, teasing, taunting, and splashing water at each other. She loved seeing this carefree side of him. He seemed so youthful, unburdened, and relaxed.

"Let's swim to the other side and dry off on the grass," she suggested.

He followed her to the embankment, lifting her up to a grassy area where they left their clothes and shoes. He reached for a towel, drying her arms and shoulders, and wrapping her wet hair. Then he pulled her into his arms. When his lips touched hers, she felt a molten liquid course through her body, as he explored the fullness of her mouth. It was a long, sensuous exploration, teasing her mouth with his lips and tongue, leaving them both craving more after they finally pulled apart. She wrapped her arms around his neck, pulling his mouth down in an urgent demand, leaving them both breathless as their bodies strained toward each other, heating both of them with desire.

Reluctantly, he untangled his body from hers, running his hand through his wet hair. He glanced toward the setting sun, frowning.

"We'd better be heading back to Jerusalem. We can grab the fruit and cheese we brought with us. That'll keep us until we get to a restaurant. I'd prefer not to hang around here, if that's okay with you?"

"Anything the matter, Neyri?"

"No, not at all. Let's get dressed, shall we?"

He didn't want to worry her. The shortest way home was past an Arab area where cars had been stoned several weeks back, and in the Wadi Kelt area several Jewish teenagers had been stabbed by Arab youths.

It was only after he began shifting gears to ascend the back road to Jerusalem that he began to breathe easier. They should not have lingered as long as they did in Ein Gedi. What was he thinking, he remonstrated, putting caution to the wind? The time had flown. It felt incredible being alone with her. He wished he could stop the hands of the clock. He wanted to have all the time in the world to be with her. He felt the desperate need to love Jacky unlike any woman he had ever known in his life.

He dropped Jacky off at her apartment, and then drove to his own home to shower. When he returned to pick her up later, he was wearing a casual pair of black slacks, a white short-sleeved shirt, open at the neck revealing a golden tan from the day's outing. Jacky was also bronzed to a lovely tan and wearing a long, white silk skirt and matching sleeveless blouse. Her face glowed with color and youth. She wore her hair simply pulled back in a pony tail.

They dined in a nearby restaurant on halibut steaks, baked potatoes, asparagus spears, wine, and matzoh.

"*L'chaim,*" he toasted, appearing relaxed and contented.

"To life," she said delighting in the moment and in the hours spent
with him. "Neyri, I want you to know I feel content to hold the moment
close to me as if yesterday or tomorrow were unimportant. I want to
thank you for this," she said as she touched his crystal glass with hers.

"I feel the same," he admitted, taking her hand in his, turning over
her palm. He traced the lines softly, bringing her hand to his lips. "I
want more than a casual affair with you," he admitted. "I want to let
whatever is building between us to evolve naturally. It's far easier to
expose one's body than one's soul to another person. I don't want lust
to get in the way of our really knowing each other. This takes time. Am
I making any sense to you?"

"We have all the time in the world to get to know each other, don't
we?"

"Not in this country we don't," he said with uncharacteristic bitterness.

After paying the bill and leaving a tip, he escorted her back to the
car. This time, when he unlocked the apartment door, he walked inside
and closed the door. As their lips met, with an urgency leaving him
breathless, he felt a burning desire to surrender completely. It was with
the greatest effort that he pulled away from her.

"I'm due back at my base shortly. Get some sleep. I'll call you so we
can talk some more. Okay?"

"When will you return to Jerusalem?"

"I don't know. It's going to be hard for both of us. Be patient. I'll
see you soon, I promise."

The following evening, Neyri called from his base. It was a brief
conversation. He had finally received notification from Harvard of his
acceptance into the graduate program in international relations. It was
his first choice out of the two other universities he had applied to for
entrance.

He managed to call her back later in the evening. They spoke for a
long time, long enough for Jacky to know that he was worth the wait,
more than anyone she had ever known before.

Twenty-nine

IT WAS MAY 1. The hot desert sun burned down on Shulha's unprotected head as she bent to wash the bedding from her father's tent. Afterwards she balanced the basket with fresh laundry on the top of her head. Despite the strain in the lower back, Shulha managed to hang the clean wash on a line strung between two tents.

"I've been looking for you," declared her father, interrupting her work. The Sheikh noticed her advanced pregnancy with concern. Escorting her back to the tent to escape the harsh rays of the sun, he motioned his daughter to be seated on the cushions usually reserved for important guests.

He observed Shulha's face as he passed sweetmeats to her. By his calculations, she would be entering her seventh month by May 10. It was no longer prudent for her to remain in the desert. He had been warned by his son-in-law that the baby was in the wrong position to be born. She would require surgery to assist in the breech birth or it would become dangerous for the mother and the child. Until now all entreaties to return back to her husband in East Jerusalem went unheeded.

"Shulha, how long have you been away from Jerusalem?"

"Five weeks."

"Then it is time to return for the birth of your child."

"I have plenty of time, *Abu*. The baby is not due until July 10."

"What if the baby is born premature?"

"There are plenty of midwives here who can assist me in labor."

"Your husband says it is dangerous for you to remain in the desert, assisted only by a midwife."

"My husband knows nothing! For centuries women have given birth in the desert. Why should I be treated any differently?"

"The baby is in the wrong position, I have been told. The baby will require a competent physician to assist at his birth."

"I do not want to return to East Jerusalem. I have told you this before."

"Yes, Shulha, you have told me, but you have failed to give me the reason why you are avoiding returning to your husband in East Jerusalem."

"Father, you are prying into my heart. This has never been your way before. Why now?"

"Not only are you endangering your unborn child, you are also endangering your own life by stubbornly insisting on remaining with our tribe rather than being where you belong."

"Just where is that, Abu?"

"Beside your husband, wherever he may be."

"He is my husband in name only."

"What has he done to you to turn you against him like this? Surely you know Asa Ibrahimi treasures you."

"You are gravely mistaken, Abu. He loves another."

The Sheikh felt the depth of Shulha's emotions deeply; he was unable to respond without first collecting himself. Sheikh Muhammad reached out to clasp her tiny hand in his old, gnarled fingers, feeling the ache of love he had always felt for his daughter since her birth nearly seventeen years ago. Peering into her dark eyes filled with sadness, he said softly:

"What makes you think so?"

After she told the Sheikh how Asa had betrayed her with a foreign woman, he recalled the warning he had given his son-in-law when he had shown him the Qu'rum caves. Apparently, his son-in-law not only lost this treasure; Asa had shattered her heart in the process. There was only one thing left to do. It was time he interceded on behalf of his beloved Shulha.

"We are returning to Jerusalem at once. Pack your things," Sheikh Muhammad ordered.

"But, Abu . . ."

"Listen to me, Shulha. Why are you so shocked that your Palestinian husband has found himself a woman besides you? Is it not our custom in the desert to take more than one wife? Yet, you are filled with anguish and anger over something that shouldn't shock you at all. Why do you think Asa Ibrahimi would act any differently than a Bedouin?"

"Because I wanted to believe his love for me would ripen and deepen as my love has for him. Because I wanted to believe he would not be in need of anyone but me."

"Such love is so rare, my child!" the Sheikh consoled his daughter as she wept bitterly in his arms.

Hours later, as night fell in the city of Jerusalem, Asa Ibrahimi heard a knock at his front door. His father-in-law and his wife stood on the doorstep, hot, thirsty, and perspiring from their arduous journey. Asa stepped back in the room to admit them, with a solemn expression of remorse on his face.

Muni Ibrahimi greeted the Sheikh and her daughter-in-law with the traditional kisses on both sides of the face, wisely removing Shulha into the kitchen to prepare food for Sheikh Muhammad.

"You look well, my daughter. How do you feel?"

"My seventeenth birthday was yesterday, Umm. I feel as if I am older than my years," she confessed, weeping in her mother-in-law's arms.

In the living room, Sheikh Muhammad did not mince words with his son-in-law.

"Asa, do you remember my warning to you before you married my daughter that all that glitters is not gold? You have made a grave error, my son, in your search for happiness in this society that knows only bloodshed and violence. Yet you persist in believing that only if you become more Westernized in your ways, will you be treated first-class. What continues to frustrate you is your belief you have to prove your worth to others in this society. There is only one person you have to answer beside Allah. Yourself. Stop taking your anger and frustration out on my daughter. Stop blaming my daughter for your problems and your flaws. The hate you feel for yourself has closed your soul like a lid on your own coffin. Take full responsibility for your life and your problems, and stop blaming her for a ruined life. Only then will your life have meaning for you; only then will you be able to rekindle the fire of passion you once felt for Shulha. If you are incapable of doing this, you will not only destroy your life, but my daughter's as well. Do you understand what I am telling you, my son?"

"I understand far more than you think. You warned me that only after you lose something do you realize the treasure you once possessed. I have lost Shulha. Is it too late, Sheikh Muhammad?"

"No, my son, it is never too late, if you are still alive. Do not wait for death to claim your love. Reach out for it now while you have the chance to rectify what you have destroyed."

⁓✲

AFTER THE SHEIKH DEPARTED, refusing to remain in Jerusalem overnight, Asa entered his bedroom. His wife was standing on the small balcony overlooking the walled city of Jerusalem. He walked softly to her, at a loss for words. Since a child, he loved to string words together, absorbing cadence, structure, and the selection process with keen interest. "Precocious" was the word used to describe him as a mere child in love with life, seeing it as a great adventure in an unknown journey. "Gifted" was the way he was described by his high school teachers. Now he stood rooted in anxiety, lest he say the wrong thing to enrage her against him. He stood dumb with fear.

Slowly she turned, as if sensing his presence behind her. Beneath a full moon, he saw a face ravaged by tears. The swollen lids of her eyes brought a lump of anguish to his throat. Remorse enveloped him for betraying his beautiful wife who had once loved him so completely, effortlessly, and innocently.

Since her absence, he had kept asking himself over and over again, why had he betrayed her? When the truth dawned on him—that he had projected everything he hated about himself onto her, and then scorned her in the process—he felt as if he had descended into hell.

Since he couldn't spurn himself, he could spurn her, he realized in the desolation of his loneliness. How easily he had discarded her for things he refused to place on himself! It was so much simpler to blame her for all his ills, as he had previously blamed society. Could words wipe out the sorrow he saw in her eyes? I'm sorry. I betrayed you. Forgive me! How could it?

She broke the silence.

"You are not the man I thought you were. No, let me have my say, please! You have not only betrayed me, you have betrayed yourself. For all your education and the beauty of your mind, you lack the wisdom I possess.

"Your education comes from books. My education comes from an intimate connection with the earth and the desert. It has taught me that the important things in life are simple—shelter, food, family, and love. The years since my childhood living out my life in my father's and mother's tent has taught me to walk humbly yet without loss of my proud place on this earth; to look deeply into my soul in order to see inside the souls of others in truth, respect, and compassion. Most of all, I have learned to love who I am, in order that I may love those around me.

"The desert has taught me there are powers beyond man's imagination, powers we cannot see, only feel. I have felt Allah's presence guiding me toward love. One day you appeared in my father's tent. A light filled my being. Your soul seemed to communicate with my soul, and I longed to be one with you, to be your wife, to bear your children. All I wanted was to love you until the end of my days. I thought you wanted the same. Instead, you began to view me with the tainted eyes of a city dweller, looking down upon my humble origin, despising my nomadic way of life, reducing me to a thing to be scorned and rejected. You thought I would never measure up to your high standards of intelligence, didn't you? Since I could barely read or write, you concluded my vocabulary could not match yours. Yet, how is it I now speak language as you do? Is it not possible that I sought to have you value me by learning to speak like you, to read and write like you? My father hired a wise tutor in Ein Fashkha who taught me daily, as did your mother, unknown to you. When I came to live with you in Jerusalem, your mother continued to teach me on a higher level. It was my way of repaying you for loving me. I kept it secret from you in order to present it to you as a special gift from me to you at the birth of our baby. When I discovered you did not love me, probably never loved me, but wanted me the way one wants to own and possess a thing, my whole world collapsed, along with my marriage and my love.

"As a male Muslim, you can possess as many wives as you desire. So be it. Go possess your blond woman who thrills you with her beauty, sophistication, and knowledge—all of the things I lack, according to you. But you cannot have me as well. It is either her or me. If you choose her, then I beg of you to divorce me so I can return to my father's tent where I belong. If you insist I remain your wife, I will do your bidding, but I will never offer you love or devotion again. Do you understand me?"

"Shulha!" he cried out in anguish, yearning to be heard, to be understood, to be forgiven. "I have wronged you, but I do not want to lose you! I will do whatever it takes to regain your trust, your love, and your devotion. She means nothing to me, do you hear me? Nothing. You mean everything. Forgive me. Stay with me. Let me show you how I can love you. I was too blind, too stupid to see you clearly. I am no longer blind to your essence. I dread that you will not return to me with all your innocence and purity. I beg you to forgive me, to take me back and to love me as you once loved."

She reached out her hand, and with her fingers, she traced the bones of his facial structure. Her fingers touched his lips. He pulled her slowly into his arms, kissing her gently and longingly, unlike any kiss she had ever tasted before.

When he placed her on their bed, his lovemaking was exquisitely tender and slow, as if he needed to stroke every section of her body, opening her to him like petals of a flower responding to sunlight and raindrops. After pouring himself into her warmth, he slipped over to another dimension of reality, where the physical and the spiritual were intertwined in a seamless thread of ecstasy. He clung to her long after their lovemaking was over, acknowledging that what he had been searching for all his life was right in front of his eyes, but he could not see it, not until his eyes opened wide in the precise moment he had lost her.

Thirty

ON AN UNBEARABLY HOT DAY the middle of May, after tutoring in the Old City, Asa discovered his wife in bed, in the middle of a contraction, unable to catch her breath and clutching her huge belly with both hands.

"Shulha, how long have the contractions been going on?" he asked, worriedly starting to assess the situation. He ran to the bathroom, wetting a wash cloth for her sweating forehead, and then he lifted the phone to call the Hadassah obstetrician.

After describing the symptoms, the doctor raised his voice: "GET HERE TO THE HOSPITAL WITHOUT DELAY!"

He dialed his mother's office, relieved to hear her voice: "Umm, Shulha has had contractions for the past twenty minutes. I'm taking her to the Hadassah Hospital on Mount Scopus. Please meet me there."

He hurriedly packed a small suitcase with Shulha's underwear and robe.

"Can you walk down the steps, Shulha?"

When she nodded, he placed a protective arm around her expanded waist, managing to assist his wife down the two flights of steps into his car.

He drove toward the walled Old City only to be met by a new

roadblock, choked by lines of cars and pedestrians attempting to get into the Old City for prayer or into West Jerusalem to run errands.

It was 1:40 PM. Jerusalem was in the midst of a *khamsin,* where the dry desert winds envelope the city in stagnant air, making it difficult to breathe easily on the streets or in the confines of one's apartment. The sun was shining its fiercest rays on his car, which he left running as did the others ahead and behind him.

"Shulha, I'm going to go explain our situation to the soldiers up ahead at the roadblock. If you have another contraction, hold onto my kaffiyeh with all your might. Tear it if you must to help you through the pain, okay?"

"I'll be all right, Asa. Go," she said as she gazed at him with love in her eyes, her voice soft, low, and weak. He bent to kiss her forehead before opening the car door. He walked down the road, his bared head feeling the sun beating down on his scalp, face, arms, and body.

Approaching the nearest soldier who was sifting through the identity papers of the occupant of a beat-up Fiat, Asa implored in flawless Hebrew: "Soldier, I need your help. I have an emergency. My wife is going into labor prematurely. We're several cars deep. I must get her to Hadassah Hospital or we'll have a catastrophe..."

"You'll have a catastrophe, Mister, if you don't walk back to your car and wait your turn like the others to get through."

"But you don't understand! My wife and baby will die if I am held up! The baby is in the wrong position, only a specialist at Hadassah can save her life! Don't you understand what I am saying?"

"Don't you understand there's been another bloody bombing in Jerusalem? Many people, including women and children have been killed. We're not letting any Arabs through until everyone has been checked, and that includes you and your pregnant wife. So step back, let me do my job, and you'll be allowed to pass sooner than if you keep holding everything up by demanding an exception. Understand?"

"Who's in charge here? I demand to speak to your commander!"

"I'm the commander. Now do as I say. Get back to your car and wait!"

A bodily sensation unlike anything he had ever felt before enveloped his being. He had an uncontrollable desire to lunge at the soldier and pound his fists in his face until the face disappeared from his radar. Instead, he turned, walked back to his car with clenched fists, and signaled to the driver behind him that he was turning around.

It took several minutes of careful maneuvering to extricate himself from the tight squeeze he was in, while sweat poured down his face and Shulha's moans were increasing. With his car now turned completely around, he narrowly passed the other cars waiting to get through the roadblock. He drove the back road to Ramallah, praying he could get around that roadblock and take his wife to safety. He drove hastily but carefully to avoid an accident. He felt as if he were choking on fear and an explosive anger. So this is what rage feels like, he thought to himself as he came around a corner, running smack against the Ramallah roadblock at the Kalandia checkpoint, which was even worse than the one he had just encountered near the Old City.

He leaned on his horn, never letting up until two soldiers approached his car, one pointing an M-16 rifle at his window.

"Get out."

"My wife and child will die unless you permit me to pass the roadblock. She is in premature labor. It's a breech birth; the baby is feet first. They can both die. I beg you, let us go through immediately!"

"Your papers, please," the soldier demanded.

While one soldier looked through Asa's identity papers, another asked both of them to get out of the car so they could search it.

"My wife is having contractions. She can't stand up! Have mercy, for God's sake!" Asa cried out with exasperation and frustration.

"Then you get out of the car. Where are her identity papers?"

"She has none."

"No identity papers. How's that?"

"She's a Bedouin, from the Ta'amireh tribe. She comes from Ein Fashkha. She lives in the desert. There are no identity papers . . . please don't delay us . . . let us through . . ."

"Impossible. Call the Red Crescent to take you to the Ramallah hospital. It will take you hours to get through this roadblock."

"Haven't you heard one word I've said to you, soldier? They know nothing about breech births in Ramallah hospital! Our doctor is in Hadassah Hospital on Mount Scopus. He told us not to delay. We must proceed there at once!" he shouted.

"Call Ramallah!" the soldier shouted, turning his back on him.

A piercing scream drowned their voices as another contraction tore through Shulha's abdomen, the unbearable pain crashing through her back, as if rammed by a truck. She bit down on the kaffiyeh to muffle her scream.

Asa flipped open his cell phone, his hands shaking, calling the emergency number in Ramallah. A police dispatch officer responded, telling him an ambulance was on its way, requesting his location and license plate.

Two minutes later, sirens could be heard approaching the roadblock. Due to the multitude of cars at the crossing, it was next to impossible for the ambulance to get through. From Asa's rearview mirror he watched the ambulance attendants running with a gurney up the road toward his car. He got out, waving them down so they would know which car to approach.

Moments later, they extricated his wife from the passenger seat and transported her on the gurney down the road back toward the ambulance with red lights whirling. Asa abandoned his car, jumping in the back of the ambulance as it turned around with sirens blasting to get the woman in labor to the Ramallah hospital.

They arrived minutes later amid sirens and her piercing screams. Shulha was wheeled into the emergency area where two obstetricians and a midwife rolled her into the surgery room where they scrubbed up for the emergency caesarian about to be performed.

They were too late—she was already fully dilated. The baby was born feet first with the cord wrapped around his neck. The surgeons and midwife cleaned up the baby, removing the cord from its neck, placing the baby in a fondling cloth and laying it in the crook of the mother's limp arms. Then they walked out of the operating room to face the father waiting outside the doors.

"The child didn't have a chance. The umbilical cord took its life. A boy . . . "

"What about my wife? How is she?"

"She died . . . together with your son . . . We're so sorry . . . "

PART III

May 2001

Thirty-one

MUNI IBRAHIMI MADE ALL THE ARRANGEMENTS for the funerals of her daughter-in-law and grandson with the Ta'amireh tribe. They were never alone after the burials. The Ta'amireh and Sheikh Muhammad encased Asa and his mother in a protective seal where sunrise followed night, and night followed day. The wisdom of the desert was imparted. God's presence was felt over the land, leading Asa back from the edge of insanity. He finally recognized that the laws of nature and fate intercepted, carving out a rhythm of life where sorrow followed joy, loss followed gain, and sickness followed health, until, ultimately, death followed life.

During the days of mourning, Asa realized how his deep edges had been softened immeasurably by his wife's love. He recalled with burning shame the acquisition of his wife the way one purchases a desired object in the marketplace. Yet, she had loved him with wholeness and sacredness rare in the world, despite the simple level of her existence within nomadic society. It was she who had been the greatest teacher of his life—a woman schooled by life, nature, and all that the desert had to offer: purity of vision and spiritual existence.

In the depth of his bereavement, he asked himself repeatedly: What could he cling to now that Shulha was beyond his reach? Would his memories be sufficient to sustain him when he returned to the city of Jerusalem, a divided city questing for peace but delivering only fire and bloodshed for Arabs and Jews alike? Did it make any difference what he thought any longer, with death looking over his shoulder, mocking him?

Did he actually believe that the two weeks of reconciliation with Shulha—along with the blissful moments of the all-encompassing love he felt for her, and she for him—would last beyond a blip on the screen of his torturous life? He knew in the depth of his soul that he was as good as dead. There was nothing to hope for, or to gain any longer. He felt hardened to the core of his being—hard with grief, loss, hatred, and revenge.

The moment the official period of mourning was over, Asa went in search of his father-in-law. He was nowhere to be found. When he questioned the Sheikh's youngest son he was told:

"My father went to Bethlehem. He will return before nightfall. He asked me to give you a message: Do not to return to Jerusalem until you say goodbye to him in person."

Restless and edgy, Asa mounted his grey mare, a gift of the Sheikh, and rode her hard until he reached the Qu'rum caves. He dismounted and sat on a flat-shaped rock, completely alone with the silence and the beauty of the desert all around him. Within his tortured soul, he felt the pangs of grief beyond anything he had ever endured, even during the months after his brothers and father had been buried. The cumulative losses in such a short span of time were shockingly real, along with the inability to absorb why.

It was not supposed to turn out this way, he argued with himself, and at other times with Allah. Everything in his world had been brought to a dead end. For years, the lack of fulfillment in his life had reminded him of the bitter tasting coffee, a staple in their lives, without the cardamom. Why, why did this happen to my family, to me? he wondered. Did being a second-class citizen rightfully strip him and his family, and his people, of the ability to live ordinary lives in a land belonging to them, not to an occupier who dictated how they should live, how they should behave under the rules of occupation? Did being a second-class citizen mean that it was clearly impossible to seek an identity of meaning in this land? Did being a second-class citizen mean the ability to retain some semblance of normalcy was inoperative because the rules of engagement and the rules of bureaucratic entanglement were constantly changing, confounding their lives with intolerable disappointments, confusion, exhaustion, and bitterness?

Had he not been forewarned by Sheikh Muhammad that straddling two worlds would prove impossible due to the contradictions inherent in such a dual existence? Had it not proved disastrous to him, despite all his attempts to the contrary? For all intents and purposes, his life was over and he felt like a walking corpse. Yet he was still alive and would eventually have to answer the persistent questions that assailed him: Who am I? What am I to do with the life meted out to me? How do I resolve the dilemma of my life? It was approaching evening when he returned to the encampment. The Sheikh was at the entrance to his tent, motioning him to enter.

They sat in silence for a long time. The silence was broken by the arrival of the women serving the light evening meal of goat cheese, olives, and an abundance of dates, eggs, and bread cakes. The two men dipped the bread into the bowl of olive oil. The silence continued until the completion of the meal, when mint tea was served. The Sheikh sank back on his thick cushion, appearing as if he were about to nap. Instead, with his index finger he made a circle on the dirt floor, saying to Asa:

"Our lives are like this circle as we return to our beginnings. Do you remember your first visit here, Asa? I do. You entered this tent searching for your roots, searching for your soul. With my daughter you found the missing parts of yourself, except that you did not realize it fully at the time. It was only after you betrayed her that you came to the realization that what you had been seeking in the outer world you actually possessed. Do you recall my warning to you not to lose your treasure? You did not heed my warning. You were given a second chance with my daughter, and you finally learned the meaning of loving another person with all your being.

"Love, my son, is a treasure so few have the ability to find. How grateful you should be at this moment to have loved. Instead, I observe not gratitude in you, rather, a deep, unrelenting sense of anger and hatred that such a wondrous gift was bestowed on you for only a short while. Against whom will this anger and hatred be directed, I wonder? Against yourself, Asa, or others? Either way, it will be a terrible mistake. Do you hear me, my son?"

"I have nothing further to live for, Sheikh Muhammad."

"You must not think in terms of what life has to offer *you;* rather, what you are obligated to offer back to the world."

"Obligated? To whom?"

"Life is a gift. It must not be squandered. It must not be wasted. You must search within you for a purpose to go on living without Shulha and your son. For it is the way of the earth to be born, and when it is our time, to return to dust. It is not for us to decide it is too soon to die. It is for us to decide how we are going to live until it is time to die. So it is with me, so it is with you. I do not believe we will meet again, my son, so please heed my words with care."

"You are the wisest man I have ever known. I honor and love you deeply, Sheikh Muhammad. I will reflect long on your words. May you and your tribe be protected from further harm. I will leave for Jerusalem at the break of dawn."

The two men stood, embraced, and separated. Asa left the desert, and his father-in-law's house, for the last time, never to return again.

WHEN HE ENTERED HIS APARTMENT IN JERUSALEM, Asa found his mother seated in his father's study. He sat down in a chair opposite the wooden desk. He told her how difficult it was to leave the desert permanently. Then he stood up to go to bed, exhausted from his journey. His final words to his mother were:

"My life has no possible meaning in a country that believes only Jewish women and children should be allowed to live . . . not Arab women and children. They have forgotten that we also bleed when our lives are destroyed . . . we also grieve when our children are snuffed out by their bullets . . . they have forgotten we are human beings . . . so why should we have any mercy on their lives?"

OVER THE NEXT FEW WEEKS, Muni Ibrahimi rarely saw her son. Whenever their paths occasionally crossed, Asa was remote and reluctant to talk. His behavior deeply wounded her.

Mourning over her daughter-in-law and grandson, she believed she was losing her son as well. Recurrent bouts of loneliness and depression assailed her. In all her life, she had never felt more alone. Fear and anxiety over Asa increased in proportion to the distance he was creating between them.

Finally, unable to endure the painful breach in their dying relationship, she determined to stay up all night, if necessary, to talk to him. Jerusalem was in the grip of another *khamsin*. A pall of grey haze had descended over the hills and skyline of Jerusalem during the last four days of June. The stifling heat had been unbearable, unrelieved by the cooling breezes, and descending over the hills and valleys in the late afternoons, leaving the inhabitants of the city sleepless and drained.

By the time Asa returned home, Muni Ibrahimi was limp with fatigue from the weather and her mental state. He stood in the middle of the room looking at his mother as if they were strangers who required an introduction.

"Why are you up at this hour, Umm? Is something wrong?"

"Yes."

"What is it?" he approached the sofa, reluctantly sitting down beside her. Unkempt and with three-days' growth of facial hair, he stared at her with bloodshot eyes. To his mother, he seemed weary to the core of his being.

"Why have you cut yourself off from me, Asa, as if I'm an enemy you are determined to avoid at all costs?"

"I'm trying to keep myself occupied so I won't go nuts!" he exploded. "It has nothing to do with you at all. I'm sorry if I have given you cause for worry. Besides, don't you know worrying is a fruitless endeavor?"

"With what are you occupying yourself, may I ask?"

"I really don't wish to discuss it. It's 2:30 in the morning and I'm exhausted. I'm going to bed, Umm."

"Before you leave this room, there is something you need to see. Please give me a moment. It's in my study."

Muni Ibrahimi opened the middle drawer of the desk, withdrawing a slender piece of paper, handing it to her son.

"What is this?"

"It's a poem by Gibran."

"What makes you think I would be interested in seeing poetry by anyone, especially at this time of night?" Asa snapped at her, his eyes flashing in anger.

"It's not just any poem. It's one copied in your wife's beautiful handwriting. It was to be her gift to you. I know Shulha would have wanted you to have this."

"Why, now, of all times since her death are you showing this to me?"

"In order to help you overcome your grief."

"Is that what you think, that I am still grieving over my dead wife and son?"

"Aren't you?"

"No, Umm, I am not. Good night."

IN THE SILENCE OF HIS BEDROOM, Asa unfolded the slip of paper, noticing the beautiful cursive Arabic script.

With a rapidly beating heart, he read the poem composed by Kahlil Gibran entitled, "On Marriage."[51]

Love one another, but make not a bond of love:
Let it rather be a moving sea
Between the shores of your souls.
Fill each other's cup but drink not from one cup.
Give one another of your bread but eat not from the same loaf.
Sing and dance together and be joyous, but let each one of you
*   be alone,*
Even as the strings of a lute are alone though they quiver with the
*   same music.*
Give your hearts, but not into each other's keeping.
For only the hands of Life can contain your hearts.
And stand together yet not too near together:

For the pillars of the temple stand apart,
And the oak tree and the cypress grow not in each other's shadow.

The sheet of paper fell to the floor like a wounded bird whose wings have been clipped. Asa sat on the edge of his bed sobbing until he felt all of his emotions draining out of him, leaving him empty and hollow, with no knowledge of how to fill the raw, gaping holes that now constituted his life.

Thirty-Two

ON MAY 20, A SKIRMISH IN NABLUS resulted in the death of four men in Neyri's unit. In the rush to evacuate the dead and the wounded, Neyri's jeep overturned on the road, killing his driver. Magen David Adom ambulance attendants delivered Neyri to the Tel Hashomer Hospital in Tel Aviv, unconscious with a severe concussion. During the critical period preceding the CT scan, Jacky remained at his bedside, along with his family.

The neurosurgeon finally appeared, direct from his surgical rounds, to meet with the Ben-Ner family to discuss Neyri's condition. Dr. Paul Medlow, a newly arrived immigrant from America, well-respected and personable, removed a green cap from his full head of salt-and-pepper hair, turning gentle and compassionate eyes on the distraught family huddled around him.

"The results of the CT scan show a subdural hematoma, a midline shift to the brain, as well as intracerebral hematoma, or a blood clot in the brain. The good news is that the Glasgow Coma Scale is high, indicating his coma is not deep and he should be coming around within forty-eight hours. Recovery after such a head injury is in his favor since he is under fifty. The bad news is if we cannot control the blood clot in his brain, it may require surgical removal through a craniotomy. If this should occur, I suggest stabilizing him with anticonvulsants and making arrangements to have the surgery done at the UCLA Medical Center, where they have performed this type of surgery with great success before."

Jacky spent the night sleeping on a hospital chair beside Neyri, talking to him softly from time to time, alternating words of comfort and prayer for the full restoration of his consciousness.

All night long, nurses checked his pulse rate and eyelids, until the 7:00 AM shift and the rotation of nurses, when Jacky finally drifted off to a troubled sleep. In a dream, she was running down a deserted road, chasing after a car speeding away with two children in the back seat. Then the car vanished, swirling dirt, and the empty, lonely landscape enveloped her. Collapsing to her knees in the dust, she cried out: "Don't steal my children from me!" She awakened feeling an intense sense of relief, startled it was only a dream, which made little sense to her since she had no children.

Placing a gentle hand on Neyri's fingers, she felt herself comforted by the touch, brushing away the tears streaming down her face over the frightening road accident. She was terrified to lose him, finally acknowledging the depth of her own love for this man who could have been killed along with his driver and other members of his unit. All she ever wanted, needed, or desired was this man who offered her love, understanding, and comfort so freely and openly. Now he was in the depth of a frightening coma. In panic, she squeezed his hand, whispering softly:

"Neyri, don't leave me, please don't leave me alone. Come back to me, my love!"

Bending her head low over his hand, her tears dropped on his knuckles. She felt a faint pressure. Did she imagine it, she wondered? Tightening her grip, she loosened it, repeating the motion. She leaned over him, peering under his eyelids, as she had seen the nurse doing throughout the long night. There was no movement of his eyes. She removed her finger from his eyelids and sunk back into the chair. It was so little, just a slight pressure, but hope was all she had left to sustain her.

There were no further signs from Neyri over the next couple of hours. After a visit from his parents and brother in the early afternoon, Jacky drove back to Jerusalem. After showering and changing her clothes, she returned to the hospital late in the evening. Close to midnight, exhaustion overtook her.

Once again she had a disturbing dream. This time she was being pursued. She was running through a dense forest. The deeper she plunged into the forest, the greater the panic that she would never find her way out to sunlight and freedom. Just as a hand slid over her throat, she awakened from the dream, feeling sweaty and clammy all over. In the nearby bathroom, she rinsed her face with ice-cold water, trying to piece together the two dreams in rapid succession.

She pushed a lock of wet hair off her forehead, returning to her chair and the midnight vigil. Neyri's near-fatal accident made her reflect over their loving relationship. He had a way of embracing life with a whole-ness that was so refreshing. He treated her as his equal, and he was emo-tionally supportive. He was a strong man with a gentle, soothing touch and all-encompassing warmth that made her feel loved, safe, secure, and respected.

Contrasting this relationship with a marriage without joy or much love, why did she stay for ten years, she wondered? Perhaps, on some level she must have felt she didn't deserve better. What had brought her to such a state, she wondered, knowing she had two loving, support-ive parents who had given her everything. In the process, they had over-protected her, hadn't they? She knew from her own research and books on psychology that overprotecting a child was as crippling as no pro-tection, no holding, and insufficient nurturing.

Why was she still afraid at times to allow her walls to come down before Neyri? Why was she holding back a part of herself even from him? Was it because she had not known him long enough to give her-self completely, or was something else preventing her from opening completely in this new relationship?

She sank back in the chair beside Neyri's inert body, staring at him, at the face that had captivated her the very first time she ever laid eyes on him. She listened to his soft breathing, peering nearer, looking closely at him. Then suddenly she sprang out of the chair as if there were a loose spring. As she paced back and forth in the closed quarters, all the pieces slipped into place for her. His was an open, unguarded face. What he felt inside, he showed openly to all. In contrast, her former husband's face had been a closed book. His eyes had been opaque—the ability to see out but never once allowing anyone, including her, from seeing inside his soul. One man wore a mask; beneath the mask was a false self that had to be protected at all times, necessitating continuous narcissistic stroking, adulation, admiration, and a perfect mirroring, or else all hell would break loose in barbed criticism, harsh tones, and the underlying rage that erupted in the form of extreme judgment against her. Nothing she ever did was right, including the way she breathed. There was an enormous difference between the two men. Beneath the mask worn by her former husband was a false image camouflaging a façade in place of a bona fide self. Subconsciously she had been afraid all men wore masks of deception. Suddenly she found herself breathing with relief, knowing this would never happen with Neyri. He was real. He did not hide behind a façade. This knowledge now freed her to love without fear. She fell into a deep, short sleep, until awakened by the sound of the nurse exclaiming:

"His eyes are open! He's finally coming around!"

"Does this mean he is out of danger?" Jacky blurted out, attempting to shake the sleep out of her eyes. In the next instant, she held Neyri's glance. Tears of relief streamed down her cheeks as she wrapped her arms around him.

"He's coming out of the coma," confirmed the nurse. "I have orders from his surgeon to inject him with anticonvulsant medication, to reduce the risk of seizures," the nurse explained as she gave Neyri the injection.

For the next couple of hours, Neyri was watched carefully by the staff. Severe headaches and vomiting afflicted him until his condition was finally stabilized. He remained in the hospital for one week, during which time the cerebral edema diminished. As soon as the intracranial hypertension was under control, he was told he could resume normal activity, as well as return to his command. He was warned that if headaches, vomiting, or seizures were to recur, he was to be readmitted without delay.

As soon as he was released, Neyri returned to his unit while Jacky resumed her research. Although Neyri was out of danger, she returned to Jerusalem anything but confident. Shaken by recent events and terrified something would happen to him in the last few days before his discharge from the army, she carried a premonition of disaster with her at all times. For no reason at all, she found herself jumpy and nervous. It was the rare moment that they were together. With his imminent release from the army, there was no way he could take leave from his army duties.

The phone was ringing in her apartment when she returned from the Hebrew University. She was relieved to hear Neyri's voice. For once he sounded like his old self. He was very upbeat and excited when he told her:

"Guess where we're headed the first week of June? I just made a reservation with a travel agent in Tel Aviv. We'll be traveling to Greece, to Santorini for two glorious weeks. Have I given you sufficient notice to wrap up your research work, Jacky?" he inquired, sounding lighthearted and joyful.

"You bet! Just make sure your new driver observes all the stops signs and red lights so I don't have to worry about you."

"I told you, everything is going to work out. So stop worrying. Know how wonderful it will be to be alone with you . . . "

Thirty-three

EARLY ON THE MORNING OF JUNE 1, Neyri Ben-Ner was officially released from the Israeli army with a short ceremony at his base. He returned immediately to Jerusalem to finish packing for the trip to Greece. They were due to leave for Athens in a late afternoon departure on El Al.

The flight was short and uneventful. As soon as Neyri and Jacky landed in Athens, they were airborne again, this time in a prop plane taking them to the island of Santorini. The last leg of the trip was by boat. To reach the city of Santorini, they had to climb five hundred steps.

By the time they reached the top, they were already charmed by the beauty of the sea, the sand, and the houses perched elegantly on cliffs jutting out of the mountain. Jacky exhaled, looking around her with a sense of awe and relief. Until this moment, she hadn't realized she had been breathing shallowly, the way people do when they are extremely tense. For the next two weeks, she told herself as she smiled brightly at Neyri, there was nothing to mar their time together.

⁂

THE SAME EVENING of their arrival, they were so entranced with the beauty of Santorini, they stayed up late, dining in a lovely Greek restaurant. Afterwards they strolled through the streets, looking into shops, hunting for bargains, walking hand in hand while eating ice cream without a care in the world. They sat on a bench beneath the stars, in comfortable silence, until Neyri broke it by asking:

"What are you thinking about, Jacky?"

"I didn't realize how much of my energy had been expended on anxiety over your safety, especially after the accident. To know you've fully recuperated and we're actually here together on this gorgeous island fills me with joy and gratitude," she admitted.

"We're so lucky, aren't we? Let's go back to the hotel, shall we?"

Walking back to their room, Neyri discovered the feelings building between them over the past couple months engulfing him. Until meeting Jacky, he had responded to love affairs rather casually. It was a "live for today, for tomorrow you may die" philosophy held by many soldiers and civilians alike. It was an attitude built up by all the wars they had been forced to fight since 1948, making them respond as if they were always living on the edge of disaster. Catastrophe was always around the next corner, so only a fool would postpone the opportunity for sheer physical pleasure.

It had always been his own philosophy as well until he came face to face with Jacky and knew she was different from any woman he had ever known. He couldn't risk losing her to a casual, hasty affair. Instead, the feelings had been allowed to grow, permitting the awareness of a deep attraction turning into love.

The moment the door to their hotel room closed behind them, he gathered her into his arms. He led her to the double bed, kneeling beside her. Slowly he unbuttoned the white silk blouse, unhooking the sheer bra with a flick of his finger. He sucked in his breath involuntarily. Her sensuous body was ready for a night of lovemaking. Her breasts were round and full, the nipples taut, and her stomach flat and firm. She wore black silk bikini briefs beneath the black cotton summer skirt. He tossed his clothes aside, crushing her to him, feeling the rapid beating of her heart against his chest. He lowered his mouth to her breasts, breathing in the taste, feel, and perfumed smell of her exquisite body. He felt her hands gliding down his biceps, across his hairy chest, caressing his mid-section. He lifted her body. She felt weightless, like a feather. He placed her on top of him as he entered. When he heard her gasp of pleasure and her sob of uncontrollable release, he turned Jacky beneath him, thrusting deeply inside, surrendering to her heat as if something were melting within his being in an act of intimacy unlike anything he had ever experienced before.

Jacky touched his forehead, gently caressing his face, his eyelids, lingering at his jaw. She raised herself on her elbow, holding his gaze. She knew, at long last, she was home in an act of lovemaking that was more than a mere physical merging of a man and woman. It was as if her soul were satiated, since there was nothing further it required.

For the first time in her life, she felt whole. This wholeness and completion exposed her former isolation in all its starkness. It required standing alone in the universe, facing life in all its beauty and cruelty, and entering the cycle of ageing toward death. Without a map to guide her or a net to catch her, she would eventually relinquish her life on earth, with all its earthly cares and slip over to the other side where only spirit mattered.

With absolute certainty, she now knew Neyri was hers for only a brief span of time. She would neither fear the depth of her love for him nor fight fate when it was time to part from him. Moments were all that mattered now. Moments would have to last a lifetime, no matter how much she pleaded, no matter how much she begged the fates to allow her an eternity with him. Moments were all they could ever hope to have. Why hadn't she realized this before, she wondered? With this clarity, a lifetime of tears engulfed her being. She wept in joy and in sorrow. Somewhere in the dim recesses of her mind, she knew, now, what it meant to love with her entire being and be loved as deeply in return.

Neyri held her in the circle of his arms, kissing her eyelids wet with her tears, whispering:

"You're all I have ever wanted, all I have ever needed. Stay with me, my love!" he cried out in the darkness.

They lay nestled in each other's arms, sleeping comfortably until, aroused in the middle of the night, they resumed their lovemaking, taking time to savor every touch. At the break of dawn, they arose, showered together, and then indulged in an early morning swim before breakfast. When they entered the dining room both admitted being ravenously hungry.

As they returned to the lobby, Neyri glanced at the headline in the *New York Times:* "SUICIDE BOMBING TAKES THE LIVES OF 21 TEENAGERS IN TEL AVIV." Startled by its content, he grabbed a copy.

"What is it, Neyri?"

"There's been another suicide bombing, this time in Tel Aviv."

They sat in the lobby, devouring the article. As Neyri's face hardened in despair and anger, Jacky became tense and sorrowful, knowing terrorism had once more claimed lives in Israel.

The story read: "The latest suicide bombing at the Dolphinarium, a popular seaside nightclub in Tel Aviv frequented by the youth of the area, took the lives of 21 teenagers, mostly boys and girls who had recently immigrated from Russia. The suicide bomber was a member of Hamas, which took responsibility for this latest carnage on June 1 at the nightclub at . . . " Jacky was unable to continue reading the article, sickened by its content.

"Let's get some fresh air. I suddenly feel like I can't breathe. Let's get out of here," she begged.

Over the next several hours their carefree mood plunged into the depths of despair. Long after the lights were turned out, neither of them could fall asleep. It was obvious that no matter how far or near they were from the shores of Israel, they could not escape hearing about the fate of the country, nor did they want to. It hurt so much to know, once again, that the youth of the nation were being singled out and murdered in a vicious, sick manner. Neyri did not reveal to Jacky that the explosives were packed with rat poison to ensure there would be no clotting of blood among the teenage victims. Among them was the twenty-five-year-old security guard, Yan Blum, a recent immigrant from the Ukraine, survived by a wife and baby daughter. Sixteen of the victims were between the ages of fourteen and nineteen years of age.[52]

"Come to bed, Neyri, there is nothing we can do from here," she pleaded, having been awakened from a troubled sleep by his pacing.

A feeling of sorrow filled his being as he tossed and turned fitfully all night, knowing they were all victims of a catastrophic series of events that he believed would one day embroil the entire world.

IN THE LATE AFTERNOONS, THEY RELAXED at the beach after touring the nearby villages. Every evening, they dined at a different restaurant. It ended all too soon. Making a promise to each other to return one day, they reluctantly packed for their flight back to Tel Aviv.

On their last night in Greece, they walked under the stars. It was difficult to part with Santorini. They walked slowly back to their hotel. Before they reached the entrance, Neyri pulled her into his arms, telling her: "Jacky, I'm so in love with you!" From his jacket pocket, he removed a small box, slipping a sparkling diamond ring on her finger. "Stay with me always...be my wife...I promise to love you, forever...please be mine, Jacky."

THE NEXT DAY, IN THE ATHENS AIRPORT, prior to boarding their flight to Tel Aviv, Neyri called his parents and his brother, to announce their engagement.

Two nights later a small engagement party was held at his brother's home, with friends from Neyri's base, the men from his former unit, and other military in attendance. No date was set for their wedding. It would be sometime before their departure to the States.

A few days after the party, a lingering headache kept Neyri in bed. At first he thought it was due to all the excitement over his engagement. When it persisted for three days without letting up, he gulped down Optalgin tablets for pain. Finally, he made an emergency appointment to see his surgeon at Tel Hashomer Hospital, where another CT scan confirmed what his doctor suspected: elevated intracranial pressure.

"I have contacted the UCLA Medical Center in Los Angeles," the surgeon told Neyri. "They are willing to admit you for testing and a craniotomy on September 15. I strongly advise you to accept, as it's the only hope we can offer you for full recovery..."

Thirty-four

AT THE END OF JULY, BETH DUMONT arranged to meet Asa Ibrahimi. In front of their favorite meeting place, the glass-enclosed Sbarro pizzeria at the intersection of Jaffa Road and King George Street, Beth waited impatiently for his arrival.

The moment he saw her, Asa realized something was wrong. It showed in her eyes; fatigue was evident in her face. He pulled Beth into his arms, feeling a momentary sense of comfort. But it was so fleeting; the emotion vanished the moment he escorted her to an empty table. The Italian pizzeria was bustling with people as usual on a lovely summer evening. He bought two cups of coffee while waiting for their pizza to be prepared.

"What's wrong, Beth? Why did you insist on my seeing you tonight?"

"I'm pregnant," she blurted out nervously, unsure of herself, or his possible reaction to the news.

He stared at her, disbelief etched on his startled face. "Are you sure?" he demanded to know.

"Of course I am! I took a pregnancy test, had a full obstetric exam. Would I tell you if I weren't positive? What's wrong with you?" she angrily retorted.

"How far along are you?"

"Eight weeks."

"Do you intend to get rid of it?"

Beth couldn't believe what she was hearing. Ever since his wife and baby had died, he had turned to her, on and off, for love and comfort. She hoped Asa would now build a firm, lasting relationship. They had been careless the last time they made love, "forgetting" to use protection. She hadn't been concerned, figuring that if she got pregnant, she would deal with it whether he wanted the baby or not. At a minimum, however, she had counted on his concern for their situation. Instead, he appeared cold and remote, a clear indication that he was far from being in love with her as she had believed. What a bloody fool I've been, she thought in dismay, stunned by the implications of her miscalculations.

"Beth, why don't you answer me?" he demanded, sounding annoyed.

"Because I can't catch my breath, that's why, Asa! Just who the hell are you to treat me as if I'm a stranger you just picked up? What's happening to you? I thought we loved each other. I thought this would make you happy, especially after your first baby died!"

"I'm sorry; I didn't mean to upset you. You look upset enough. I'm merely trying to find a practical solution to your problem and . . ."

"You mean, *our* problem, don't you?"

"I can't support you or this baby, not just financially, but emotionally. I'm in no position to offer you anything, Beth, except money for an abortion."

"Keep your damn money! I have no need for it," she snapped, rushing out of the restaurant, intent on getting as far away from him as possible. He ran after her, reaching out to stop her. She jerked her arm from his grasp.

"Stay away from me, Asa, do you hear me? I don't ever want to see you again!"

He whirled her around to face him, as people on the street stopped to stare at them making a scene in public.

"Listen to me, Beth. I'm not rejecting you; I simply can't have a wife and baby in my life right now. I can't for many reasons. None will satisfy you, but you must hear me out. Can we go back to your apartment to talk about this, so I can make you understand how I feel and help you resolve this problem one way or another?"

The next thing she knew, she was sobbing in his arms, throwing her hands around his neck and burrowing her head against his warm chest, unable to stop her tears.

"You'll be okay, I promise you. I'll help you," he consoled.

They took the bus from the downtown area to the Neve Shaanan apartment. After hours of talking, Beth finally told him:

"I'm leaving this country. I'm going back to Ireland. I'm not going to get an abortion, not because I'm Catholic but because I want to keep this baby, to raise it, to love it even if you don't want any part of it. You'd better go home. It's late. I'm exhausted. Frankly, I don't want to talk about it anymore. Please just go, leave me alone," she cried, turning away from him and his pleading eyes.

Minutes later, she heard the door close softly behind him. Lifting the phone, she called her parents in Dublin, praying they would be at home.

"Mom, it's me, Beth. I'm coming home, in the next week or so, depending when I can get a flight out of here. You're happy? I'm so glad. I need you, Mom, more than I've ever needed you . . . you see I'm going to have a baby and the father is . . ."

✦

THE NIGHT BEFORE BETH'S FLIGHT, Asa insisted on coming over to say goodbye in person. He didn't stay long. Beth allowed him to hold her in his arms. She turned her face away when he attempted to kiss her.

He stood awkwardly in front of her, holding a gift-wrapped package.

"What is it?"

"Something I picked up for you and the baby."

"You needn't have bothered, Asa."

"Please promise me not to open it until you're back home in Ireland. Do you promise me?"

"If that's what you want, then, okay, I promise not to open it."

"Maybe one day, Beth, you will forgive me. I see no other way out," he told her, sounding guilty.

"I should have realized this country owns you. You're not free to be who you really are because you're burdened as a Palestinian. I forgive you, Asa. Maybe one day your son or daughter will forgive you as well. What I don't comprehend is why, Asa, are you choosing death over life?"

"It's not death over life. It's death over a living hell."

"You've joined the terrorist movement, haven't you?"

His glance was cold and mocking, chilling her. "What makes you think I'm with the Resistance Movement?"

"Don't lie to me, don't deny it. I have eyes in my head. You're a completely changed man since your wife and baby died at the Israeli barricade. Since that moment, you have allowed bitterness and hatred to eat its way into your soul. The warm, understanding, rational man I once loved has changed into a cold, remote individual whose spirit is consumed with revenge. This country isn't destroying you. You're destroying yourself. That's another reason why I'm leaving. I don't want to watch what it does to you or how many people beside yourself you will destroy. I feel sorry for you. You have choices, like I do. Take a good, hard look at yourself and see what you've become, Asa, before it's really too late."

"You don't know what you're talking about," he said softly, his eyes locking with hers.

"Goodbye, Beth."

THE BRITISH AIRWAYS FLIGHT to Heathrow Airport was uneventful, until the landing. The pilots were instructed to park the aircraft in an isolated section of the airport. All passengers were removed hurriedly from the plane, taken in busloads to the terminal, where they were informed that all luggage was being removed and searched. Beth had two hours to make her connection to Aer Lingus to Dublin, Ireland. The moment she descended the aircraft, three plain-clothes men pulled her aside for questioning.

"Were you given a package to deliver to anyone, Ms. Dumont?" queried the inspector, a middle-aged man from Scotland Yard. While the inspector continued to question her, the other two men examined her passport, tickets, hand luggage, and handbag.

"No."

"Are you absolutely certain? Did anyone hand you a package, asking you to pack it in your suitcase for him?"

"Why, no, I already told you three times. No one gave me a package to... Wait a minute. I was given a present for myself, but not meant for anyone else," she insisted.

"This present you were given, did you by any chance open it before you packed it in your suitcase?"

"Why, no, inspector. I was asked specifically not to open it... until ... until ..."

"Until?"

"Until I reached Dublin."

"Who gave you this 'present,' Ms. Dumont?"

"My former boyfriend," she answered as she drew a tissue from her pant's pocket to wipe the perspiration beaded on her forehead. The palms of her hands were sweating, and her heart was beating rapidly. She was suddenly aware of having been placed in compromising situation, by Asa, yet her mind refused to fully acknowledge where the questioning was leading. She was quaking inside with undeniable fear and disbelief that this was happening.

"Please tell us his name, address, age, and anything else relevant to him."

"Before I do, will you tell me why? What do you suspect is in this package he gave me? Why are you holding me here for questioning and not the other passengers?"

"We have been informed by reliable Israeli security sources that a bomb may have been placed in your luggage. Now will you tell us what we need to know, Ms. Dumont?"

The shock of this information left her visibly pale, trembling and utterly unable to respond. A glass of water was placed in front of her. Shaking her head in disbelief, she cried out:

"No, it can't be true what you are saying! It can't possibly be my boyfriend! He is a Palestinian Arab. If he were going to harm anyone, it would be Israeli Jews, not me. I believe you're making a terrible mistake, inspector."

"Really? Why is that?"

"I'm carrying his child. Why in the world would he give me a present for myself and his baby, pretend it is a gift when it is really a bomb? He has no hatred toward me, only toward Israeli Jews who ... He has no hatred toward me and my baby. ... You are asking me to believe he would intentionally put me and my baby in harm's way?"[53]

"Ms. Dumont, tell us where he can be reached in Israel, so we can have him picked up for questioning before he harms others beside you."

"No, I will not do this until you and your people here at Heathrow inspect my luggage, proving the package my boyfriend gave me is a bomb, as you claim. Then and only then will I give you any further information. What if you are mistaken? He's been picked up by the Israeli patrols before. They beat him; they tortured him to find out information about his brother. I don't want this to happen to him again. What if he's innocent?"

"What if he's not innocent, packed a bomb in your suitcase, planning to kill you and all the passengers on British Air or Aer Lingus? What then, Ms. Dumont? As we're speaking, he could be planning another suicide bombing in Israel where innocent people will be murdered. We need to give the Israeli authorities all the information at our disposal *now*, Ms. Dumont."

"Do you plan to arrest me if I refuse to tell you anything further until my suitcase is located and checked for a bomb?"

"No, Ms. Dumont, we are not arresting you or charging you. We are only holding you for interrogation."

"Then you will have to wait, as I am waiting for the evidence," she stubbornly refused, still protecting him.

Thirty-five

ASA IBRAHIMI HAD SPENT THE LAST TWO DAYS and nights in the basement apartment of a notorious Hamas bomb expert in the Ramallah section of East Jerusalem. The bomb was larger than usual, packed with steel nails, and placed carefully inside Asa's backpack. He was driven to his apartment on Saladin Street, and in broad daylight the car and its driver sped away. When Ibrahimi unlocked the door to his apartment, he prayed his mother would not be home. He breathed with relief when he noticed the silence within his apartment.

He entered his bedroom and carefully placed the backpack loaded with explosives against the closet wall. With a two-day growth, he desperately needed a shower and a shave. Twenty minutes later, he surveyed his reflection in a full-length mirror. Wearing a pair of faded jeans, a black t-shirt, and a white, knitted skullcap, he could easily pass for a Sephardic Jew with his dark, swarthy complexion, with or without the *yamulkah* on his head, he thought. Despite the losses he had endured over the past few months, he still looked young, attractive, and confident. Externals do not count, he told himself as he looked at his reflection with satisfaction. Internally, he was every inch an Arab bent on dying a martyr and killing as many Jews as possible within the radius of his bomb. Satisfied with his appearance, he carefully placed the strap of the backpack on his left shoulder so he could easily place his hands on the device to detonate it at will.

As he descended the steps to his apartment for the last time, he thought of his mother. He had not seen her since dinner several nights earlier. It had been an unhurried meal; as usual she was in bed before 9:00 PM, not aware that anything was amiss. He thought of leaving a note, then dismissed the idea. From the Hamas video filmed yesterday, she would learn all she needed to know about his last day on earth.

On the street, housewives were shopping, children playing, and other pedestrians running errands. The usual at this time of the day, he thought, as he headed on foot to Western Jerusalem, walking casually and unhurriedly. He had no regrets; he had to assume that neither would his mother when she learned the truth. Momentarily, he felt a twinge of guilt as he visualized his mother all alone. In the next instant, he glossed over it. The very act of his martyrdom would be her sole consolation from now on.

At the approach to the Old City, he turned abruptly toward Jaffa Road, to Jewish Jerusalem.

It was Thursday, August 9, 1:30 in the afternoon.

IT TOOK LONGER THAN EXPECTED to remove from the loaded aircraft the luggage of three hundred passengers, and to isolate the luggage belonging to Elizabeth Dumont. A bomb squad was called in.

In the interrogation room, the inspector received a call from the head of the demolition squad, informing him that a bomb had been found in the bottom of Dumont's suitcase. It was the type of device that "technicians" in Ahmed Jibril's Popular Front for the Liberation of Palestine-General Command had used with some success in the 1970s: a radio-cassette boom box barometric bomb timed to explode as the aircraft reached fourteen thousand feet in altitude. The bomb squad had successfully disarmed the bomb in the outskirts of the Heathrow airfield.

The inspector snapped his cell phone shut. He leaned over Elizabeth Dumont's chair, looking straight into her frightened eyes, saying:

"Ms. Dumont, what time was your plane to Dublin scheduled for take-off this morning?"

"Within two hours of arriving at Heathrow."

"That would make it a noon departure today?"

"Correct, inspector."

"Apparently, the bomb discovered in your suitcase, in the package your boyfriend gave you as a gift to take to Ireland, was timed to explode at precisely 1400 hours, 2:00 PM, while en route to England. This barometric-triggered bomb inside your suitcase had a delayed timing device that required being in a pressurized cabin for more than thirty-five minutes for its timer to be set. Fortunately, the timing device malfunctioned, and this malfunction saved the lives of all the passengers and crew on this flight, not to mention your own life and that of your unborn child. I'd say this was some gift your Palestinian boyfriend gave you, wouldn't you agree, Ms. Dumont?"

She burst into tears, gulping back her sobs, unable to comprehend how she had entrusted her life to a man who had no compunction about causing her death and the deaths of hundreds of other passengers on the same flight.

"I'll tell you everything you want to know about him," she cried out in obvious pain and shock. "His name is Asa Ibrahimi. He lives with his mother in East Jerusalem, on Saladin Street #3 ... He was a former graduate student at the Hebrew University ... He has been traveling a lot in the past few weeks, not telling me where he was going or why ... I kept thinking he was going back to his former father-in-law, a Bedouin Arab of the Ta'amareh tribe along the the Dead Sea ... Maybe all along he was going to Gaza to work with Hamas ... I'm just guessing ... You see, his younger brother, Hassam, was a high-ranking member of Hamas, who was assassinated by Israel months ago ... Maybe Asa had connections with his brother's terrorist group ... His mother is a well-respected academic from Bir Zeit University ... All along I believed Asa when he said he didn't hate the Jews ... didn't want to liquidate the country like the other Palestinians ... I believed him ... You see, Asa was intelligent, educated, and gifted. Who could conceive that he would turn such positive energy to destruction? ... To think he wanted to murder me, too, and my baby, his baby ... I simply don't understand why he turned his hatred against me too. Maybe, just maybe, he didn't want his child to follow in his footsteps, to grow up to hate as he hates?" she groped blindly for answers to the unthinkable.

"Maybe life has a different meaning to a militant Muslim who does not value human life as the rest of humanity does," countered the inspector, looking into her grieved eyes and pitying this woman who had been so blatantly used, discarded, and victimized by a ruthless murderer.

AT THE INTERSECTION OF JAFFA AND BEN YEHUDA, Ibrahimi started walking up Ben Yehuda toward the open pedestrian mall. Given the hour of day, it was relatively quiet, no doubt due to the spate of bombings in Jerusalem in recent months. He did an about-face and resumed his walk along Jaffa Road, still crowded with shoppers.

In the opposite direction, Neyri Ben-Ner and Jacky Cohen were walking hand in hand toward Zion Tours on Hillel Street in downtown Jerusalem to book their flight to the States. They decided to depart early in September, flying to Boston after a wedding ceremony on the fourth of September. They planned to stay with her relatives in Harvard, Massachusetts, and then head on to Los Angeles for admittance into the hospital by September 15.

With tickets in hand, they walked toward King George and Jaffa Road, heading for the Sbarro restaurant to join their two best friends for lunch.

In the restaurant, Arnie Davidovitz and David Ha-Levy were seated adjacent to the glass windows, giving them a panoramic view of the downtown area packed with shoppers.

"Here's the contract, David. Look it over and let me know what you think," Arnie said as he passed the Farrar, Straus and Giroux Publishers' contract for their book proposal across the table. He walked over to the cashier and ordered two more cups of cappuccino coffee. When he returned to the table, David's cell phone was ringing.

"Hello? Where are you and Jacky? Okay, we'll order two large cheese pizzas. See you."

"Neyri and Jacky just finished their errands," he told Arnie. "They'll be here in five minutes or so. The book contract and percentage of

royalties look fine to me. Let's wrap it up, sign, and send the contract
back to the publishers, shall we?"

ASA IBRAHIMI WAITED FOR THE LIGHT to change. He walked unhurriedly, as if he had all the time in the world to enjoy the refreshing air.
Every once in awhile, Asa stopped to stare at the store windows laden
with goods. He was sweating; his eyes were glazed as if he had temperature. He mumbled a prayer over and over again: "Allah, give me
courage, give me strength to become a martyr for my people. I must
avenge the humiliation of my people. I must show the Israelis how my
people and I have been murdered in our souls.[54] Soon I will be reunited
with my Shulha and our baby. Beth and our baby will join me . . . in
Paradise." With the back of his hand, he wiped the sweat off his forehead, then continued walking toward the popular Sbarro restaurant,
his own favorite place to meet with fellow students . . . or with Beth.
Soon they would be together, soon this hell on earth would vanish forever . . .

WALKING IN DOWNTOWN JERUSALEM, Neyri and Jacky unexpectedly
met a former Druze paratrooper from the village of Julis in Akko who
had been under his command.

"Say, Commander, it sure is good to see you again!" blurted out the
Druze, in full uniform and on leave from his base for a few days' vaca-
tion in Jerusalem.

"Micraz! What's new, friend? Where are you headed?"

"Just strolling downtown," he answered, eyeing Jacky with admiration.

"This is my fiancée. Jacky, this is Micraz, one of the best paratroopers
under my command."

"Commander, coming from you, that's a compliment I'll never forget! You're sorely missed, *Kuds-Kuds,*" he used the familiar and endear-
ing term in vernacular Hebrew for Commander. "Congratulations, by
the way, to both of you. When did you get engaged?"

"Couple of weeks ago. Why don't you join us? We're headed for Sbarro to meet some friends."

"Could you wait a minute while I go across the street to Bank Hapoalim? I need to withdraw some cash."

"No problem, we'll go with you," Neyri suggested.

They waited for the light to change, crossed King George Street, and headed straight for the bank.

ASA IBRAHIMI OPENED THE DOOR to the Sbarro restaurant and stepped inside the crowded pizzeria. He placed an order for an eggplant pizza topped with extra cheese.

"How long will it take?"

"About twenty minutes."

"I'll wait." Asa Ibrahimi moved aside, surveying the interior of the pizzeria. Every table was occupied. Outside the restaurant, Jacky, Neyri, and the Druze soldier pushed their way past the line of people standing on the street corner.

"Excuse us, we have a table inside."

It was at this precise moment that Asa Ibrahimi caught sight of his former advisor, David Ha-Levy, seated near the window. Sweat started pouring down his face as he edged his way around customers, trying to fade into the background. Abruptly he turned, pushing his way through the crowd.

The bomb inside his backpack detonated prematurely. In the earth-shattering moments following the powerful explosion that pierced the ears of bystanders, shards of glass, metal, and nails showered in all directions. Bodies, blown out of the restaurant, were strewn all over the bloodied street—including the remains of the terrorist. The restaurant—one minute filled with life and repose—was instantly transformed into a gaping, open hole of destruction. Pedestrians in the vicinity of the explosion were in a state of panic and horror. Within minutes, police and ambulances arrived on the scene. Disaster plans were immediately implemented at all major hospitals in the city. All off-duty hospital personnel were called to report to emergency duty.

The air was filled with anguished screams as pedestrians in the street were caught up in the melee of death and destruction. No sooner had the bomb exploded spewing death in all directions, than ambulance sirens could be heard racing away from the scene of downtown Jerusalem, carrying the wounded to hospitals.

Among the victims were 130 wounded, many punctured by steel nails, making surgery a nightmare. Fifteen victims perished, their body parts collected by the Hevrah Kadishah for the purposes of identification and burial.

As the horror unfolded on Jaffa Road and King George streets, phone systems—in particular cellular phones in Jerusalem—crashed as people desperately attempted to uncover the whereabouts of family and friends known to be in the area at the time of the bombing.

By 4:15 PM the streets were jammed with pedestrians standing near the scene of the massacre. Rumors spread through the crowd of a second bombing at the Central Bus station. Once more, police and ambulance sirens were heard on Jaffa Road as people fled in all directions, fearing being caught in another inferno of hell. It was a false alarm, an indication of the level of panic among witnesses in the city of Jerusalem.

Hundreds of Arabs in Gaza and the West Bank, it was learned subsequently, upon hearing of the slaughter in Jerusalem, spontaneously erupted in dancing and singing, firing guns in the air and praising the perpetrators of the bombing. Candies and assorted sweet cakes were handed out to the jubilant crowds.[55]

Hamas and Islamic Jihad claimed joint responsibility. A video taped by Hamas prior to the suicide bombing revealed the bomber to be Asa Ibrahimi, sent from Ramallah on his mission of death. The mother of the suicide bomber, Muni Ibrahimi, refused to speak to the press. She was taken by ambulance to the Ramallah hospital where she was being treated for shock upon learning her son had become a "martyr" for the cause.

During the evening news, the names of the victims who had been positively identified were released to the public:

"Five members of the Schiwascherder family, from Shomrom: Mordehai, 43; Tzila, 41; three children Raiya, 14, Avraham, 4, and Chemda, 18 months.

"Tehilla Maoz, 20, from Jerusalem.

"Michal Raziel, 15, Ramot neighborhood, Jerusalem.

"Judith Lillian Greenbaum, 31, American tourist.

"David Ha-Levy, 40, Talbeiyah neighborhood, historian, Jerusalem.

"Lili Samishvilli, 39; her daughter, Tamar, 8, from Pisgat Ze'ev neighborhood of Jerusalem.

"Yocheved Shoshan, 10, Har Nof neighborhood of Jerusalem.

"Arnie Davidovitz, 52, American, visiting professor, Jerusalem.

"Malka Chana Roth, 15, Jerusalem.

"Giora..."[56]

"IT HAS BEEN ANNOUNCED THAT PLO LEADER Yasir Arafat has condemned the 'killing of innocents,' calling for an immediate cease-fire on both sides. However, Arafat was quoted in recent weeks instructing terrorists under him to ignore his public statements and to continue to murder Jews."[57]

In retaliation for the suicide bombing, the Israel Defense Forces closed the headquarters of the Palestinian Authority in Jerusalem, Orient House, confiscating computer files and documents detailing terrorist activity. The IDF also took over Palestinian Authority Headquarters in Abu Dis, an Arab suburb of Jerusalem, claiming the building served the military arms of the Palestinian Authority, including Force 17.[58]

In a pre-dawn strike, the Israel Air Force bombed Arab police headquarters in Ramallah, since the suicide bomber had been dispatched from Ramallah. No one was reported hurt or killed in the bombing strike.

At a late-night cabinet meeting of the Israeli government, other retaliatory proposals were considered.

SCOTLAND YARD PLACED A CALL THE SAME DAY to Israeli intelligence services, giving them the name of the suspected Arab militant who planted a bomb in the luggage of Beth Dumont en route from Ben Gurion to Heathrow airport.

When Beth Dumont arrived at her parents' home in Dublin, a message to call the inspector at Scotland Yard was waiting for her.

"Ms. Dumont, I'm afraid I have some bad news to disclose to you. Asa Ibrahimi blew himself up along with fifteen Jerusalemites at 2:00 PM Israeli time, with over one hundred wounded in the attack. . . . "

Beth Dumont dissolved into bitter tears, unable to be consoled by either her mother or her father after turning on the news and seeing the replay of events outside the Sbarro restaurant. Closing her eyes, she was able to visualize the interior of the pizzeria and its precise location in the downtown area of Jerusalem. She now fully comprehended how her life was now inexorably changed by the man who had so callously planned her death, as well the deaths of the other passengers en route to Heathrow, and of innocent Israeli Jews in Jerusalem.

Thirty-six

HADASSAH HOSPITAL IN THE EIN KAREM SECTION absorbed the majority of the wounded from the latest bombing attack in the heart of Jerusalem. The Ben-Ner family waited outside the operating theatre, in a waiting area adjacent to the recovery room. Seated in the waiting room crowded with other families of the wounded, worried relatives were consumed by fear. At 9:00 PM, a teenage boy with a transistor radio turned on the evening news, which informed everyone in the room:

"It has just been announced that several of the more critically wounded victims taken to hospitals have died from their wounds..."

Neyri's mother and father were ashen and ravaged by the unknown. Had Neyri and Jacky survived the terrorist attack? Omri had driven in haste from his base the moment he was alerted by his family. He was seated on a chair with his elbows on his knees, locking bleary, blood shot eyes with his wife, Tali.

From time to time, the doors to the operating room would open. An operating room nurse, in surgical cap and gown, would suddenly appear, announcing a patient's name and condition to the family in the waiting area. Many had been there for hours. Too distraught to eat, or dreading to miss any morsel of information about the wounded, no one bothered to disperse for a hasty dinner in the hospital cafeteria.

The only time that people left the waiting room was for trips to the toilets or to the cafeteria, which freely dispensed water, juice, or soda to those who were waiting.

By 10:30 PM Jacob Ben-Ner suggested that the women in the family be driven home while he and his son remained behind.

"The baby-sitter will stay all night if necessary," Tali flatly refused. "I'm going nowhere. We need to be together to know if Neyri and Jacky are out of danger," Tali added, fighting back tears. Miriam Ben-Ner merely nodded her head in agreement.

It was close to 11:00 PM when one of the surgeons pushed through the doors of the operating room to speak to the people stretched wall-to-wall in the waiting room. They pressed him on all sides for answers. The weary-looking surgeon raised his arm for quiet, telling them:

"Out of the 130 wounded, 100 have been treated at Hadassah, the rest at Sha'arei Tzedek. Some of the more seriously wounded required surgical procedures of one kind or another. Several of the more critically wounded died during the operating procedures to save their lives Sixty of the post-operative patients are now being stabilized in the recovery rooms. The remainder have been treated for their wounds and will be released. It will take anywhere from one to two more hours before any of the surgical patients will be revived and removed from the recovery room to beds on the hospital floors. Shortly a list will be posted outside the waiting room with names of those to be released and/or assigned hospital rooms."

Omri Ben-Ner, dressed in army fatigues, approached the surgeon, inquiring:

"What is the condition of my brother, Colonel Neyri Ben-Ner, and his fiancée, an American woman named Jacky Cohen?"

The surgeon shook his head as if attempting to shake the fatigue from his brain.

"I don't know. I'll find out. Wait here, please."

While Omri waited, he thought about how the toll in losses from terrorism was unbearable. The terrorists were not fighting soldiers; rather, they were attacking defenseless civilians from all walks of life who were attempting to simply go about their lives. The terrorists had other plans. They hit at schools, on buses or bus stops, in apartment buildings, in hotels, at celebrations, in cafes, in dance halls, at super-markets, and on campuses of the Hebrew University. Suicide squads now packed bombs with rat poison to ensure that the blood of victims would not clot, and steel nails to rip through flesh and bone and cause maximum damage to a human being. There was no room for com-promise from the point of view of Arab extremists. They had no inten-tion of ever co-existing with the Jewish state. It was all or nothing. Consequently, since 1948, the Palestinians were reduced to the degra-dation of life in refugee camps, which their leaders adamantly refused to dismantle in order to exploit the profound dislocation of their peo-ple for political purposes. The Palestinian people were being used as pawns in a deadly game where there could be no winners, only losers in the continuous rounds of bloodshed, violence, and retaliation, which had become a way of life between the Jewish people and Arafat's Pales-tinian Authority and the various factions of terrorist cells that had evolved into a subculture in the volatile Middle East, Omri thought with bitterness and sorrow.

Moments later, the surgeon walked through the swinging doors, beckoning to Omri Ben-Ner.

"Your brother was covered with shards of glass when he was brought in to Hadassah. Despite a severed artery, a team of surgeons labored for hours and saved his life. It's a miracle he pulled through. His fiancée, the American woman, underwent a long abdominal operation. Steel nails were impacted in her uterus. Consequently, both the cervix and uterus were removed to save her life. Both patients are now in the recov-ery room. You'll be able to see them shortly."

What the surgeon did not disclose to anyone was the atmosphere under which the surgeries for the severely wounded victims took place: The Israeli national anthem of hope and deliverance was sung by the surgeons and nurses alike in a spontaneous response to the carnage they were witnessing for the last couple of hours of this day, never to be for-gotten. This was all they had left—the hope that one day the violence and the destruction of human life would end, and peace and sanity would prevail.

✣

IN THE RECOVERY ROOM, NEYRI awakened from the anesthesia, grog-gily opening his eyes to see his mother, father, and brother peering down at him.

"Tell me . . . is Jacky . . . alive? Please God . . . let her be alive," were his first words.

"She's alive," his brother told him as he leaned over the gurney. "Jacky has been through hell, like you, and through an operation, but she's going to be okay."

"Can I be wheeled over to her?"

Omri nodded, taking the head of the gurney while his parents pushed at the other end of the bed. Tali was standing beside Jacky, who had not yet regained full consciousness. When Tali saw Neyri with his eyes wide open, she bent down to kiss his cheek, telling him:

"Thank God you've survived! Jacky's still heavily sedated. Do you want to be taken to your room now or wait until she wakes up?"

"I'll wait."

"Then we'll all wait with you," Tali responded without hesitation.

"What about David Ha-Levy, Arnie Davidovitz, and a former Druze paratrooper of mine named Micraz?" Neyri asked looking deeply con-cerned.

"What about them?" Omri wanted to know.

"They were in the restaurant with us. You mean you don't know? You don't know if they are alive or dead?" Neyri gasped in anguish and dread.

Nobody answered.

✣

NEYRI AND JACKY WERE PLACED in adjacent hospital rooms. Neyri recovered from his wounds faster than Jacky. His fiancée was emo-tionally and psychologically wounded, more than anything else.

"I can never bear your children. I don't know how to get beyond this . . . do you understand me?" she pleaded with him, devastated by the reality of their situation.

"We will adopt, Jacky. As soon as we land in the States, we will look into adoption agencies, I promise you. We can turn this whole nightmare around by adopting a child who is alone and who needs our love. Don't you see? We can build a family together, just as we planned and dreamed we would," he coaxed, attempting to give her hope.

THEY WERE BOTH RELEASED FROM HADASSAH HOSPITAL within a day of each other. Neyri made sure Jacky was never out of his sight, day or night.

Despite all efforts on both sides to pick up the pieces of their shattered lives, they were unable to do so. It was next to impossible to plan a wedding with two of their best friends still warm in their graves, and Neyri's former paratrooper severely disabled from the terrorist attack.

Jacky was jumpy, filled with anguish and anxiety. After years of exposure to the violence in the Middle East, Neyri had—like other civilians and soldiers in Israel—adopted a thick skin, which allowed him to suppress emotions and achieve a modicum of normalcy in an environment of constant danger. Yet, despite this, it was all Neyri could do to focus on what needed to be done.

Early on the morning of August 23, Neyri suggested they have coffee on the terrace of the YMCA to discuss their plans. Over the rim of his coffee cup, he examined the face of the woman he loved. It was a face that had aged almost imperceptibly, with fine lines around her eyes and mouth. He placed a warm hand over hers, leaning toward her to say:

"Tell me, Jacky, how do you really feel? I need to know."

"Since the suicide bombing?"

"Yes."

"No matter how hard I try to concentrate on our wedding plans, I can't. I keep having flashbacks to the bombing. I hear the horrible sound of the explosion, the screams of the dying and the wounded, and I'm sucked back into a surreal moment when we were just a group of people waiting outside the restaurant, with our limbs and bodies intact and in the next instant, body parts were flying in the street, fifteen people were murdered, including two of our closest and dearest friends. I can't get my life back to the moment before it happened. That's really what I've been trying to do whether I've realized it or not. I want to stop the hands of the clock. I want Arnie and David and the others not to be dead. But I can't stop it. I feel so helpless, so frightened."

"You and I do not have to apologize for being alive. You're suffering from survivor's guilt."

"You're not?"

"Do you think this is the first time I have lost people I love in acts of violence? I have grown up with violence, as has my family, all my friends, and all the people of Israel. You never get used to it—the deaths, the wounds, and the horror of it all. You know as well as I do how much my former Druze paratrooper, Micraz, has suffered since the bombing, with a leg and an arm blown off. He had everything to live for—a career in Zahal, in one of the best units in the IDF. Now with his severe handicap, he will have to struggle every day of his life. He has to go on. So do we. We've learned we must bury our dead, mourn them, and go on living, or else we would be betraying not only their memory but ourselves as well."

"I am not an Israeli. I am an American. My skin is not as thick as yours. I cannot bury Arnie and David one day, and the next day go on living as if my heart weren't shattered."

"My skin is no thicker than yours, Jacky. I don't permit myself to feel as you are feeling, or else I could not function."

"If you aren't willing to suffer pain, you will be unable to feel other feelings, the good feelings like joy and happiness. Doesn't that mean something to you?"

"Of course it does. Israeli reality can often be stark in its contrasts— we mourn our fallen soldiers on one day, and the next day we celebrate life and Israel's Independence Day. We see life starkly, precisely because all of us have witnessed war or the preparations for battles, and after our wars we have buried our dead, and on the morning after we go on living because we have no other choice. To give in to our emotions would be equivalent to relinquishing our hold on reality or our sanity. We are a nation who fights for survival *every single day* we are alive; if we were to give up this fight, what would happen to the Jewish people? So until our enemies stop wishing us extinct, we will continue to live on the edge of life."

"I am in awe of you, Neyri."

"As I am of you, Jacky. Given the circumstances, I think we should dispense with the weddings plans at Yemin Moshe and the King David Hotel, and just have a simple ceremony with my family. What do you think?"

"It would be an enormous relief to me."

"To me as well. Let's head over to my parents and brother to inform them, shall we?"

ON TUESDAY EVENING, SEPTEMBER 4, in Omri Ben-Ner's living room, Jacky and Neyri were married under a *hupah,* a four-poled canopy held by former members of Neyri's paratroop unit. Jacky wore a floor-length gown, a sleeveless sheath in white silk, with a garland of flowers in her hair. Neyri rented a black tuxedo for the occasion. After the brief ceremony, the married couple drove off for two days to Nahariyah, a favorite choice of honeymoon couples.

Just as the sun was setting, Jacky and Neyri walked barefoot along the beautiful Nahariyah beach.

"What are you thinking, Mrs. Ben-Ner?" he teased her.

"Do you realize in just two days we'll be leaving Jerusalem and the Middle East for quite some time. It's almost hard to believe," she admitted. "I shall miss Israel even though I am feeling a sense of relief that we are going to a saner life. It's only for a short time. We'll return next summer. Maybe by then things will calm down."

"Highly doubtful, but we can hope can't we?"

Thirty-seven

PROMPTLY AT MIDNIGHT ON THURSDAY, SEPTEMBER 6, Jacky and Neyri Ben-Ner boarded El Al flight 002 at the Ben Gurion Tel Aviv Airport en route to Logan International Airport in Boston. The flight felt long to both of them after sitting cramped in narrow seats for twelve hours. The moment they landed and retrieved their luggage at the baggage area, they both felt a second surge of renewed energy.

Several hours later, seated in the gazebo in her aunt's garden and viewing the lovely array of flowers, Jacky realized how infinitely relaxed she felt for the first time in months. It was a perfect fall day in Harvard, Massachusetts; a day filled with sunshine and a gentle breeze, in the low seventies with little to no humidity.

From time to time, she glanced at her husband and Aunt Phyllis talking as if they were old friends. She leaned back in her cane chair and sipped hazelnut coffee, filled with gratefulness that their lives had been spared for reasons beyond her comprehension. Back in the greatest country in the world where anything was possible, she wanted desperately to believe there was nothing to fear any longer. They were now safe and secure on American soil, far away from the violence in the Middle East.

SEVERAL DAYS LATER, ON A HOT, HUMID AFTERNOON in Cambridge, Neyri finished a six-mile jog on a path paralleling the Charles River. He stopped on the bridge overlooking the water and a biking path. Joggers pounded by. People lay on the grass or strolled casually with friends and leashed dogs.

He leaned over the railing thinking how this scene contrasted with Israeli life. Here everyone seemed relaxed, as if in low key. It made him realize what underlined the intensity experienced in Israel on a daily basis. It was the direct result of being in perpetual danger while performing normal, everyday activity. The event would be considered routine by any other standard in the world, except Israel, where around the bend possibly lurked a suicide bomber, intent on killing and wounding as many Israeli Jews as possible within the radius of the deadly explosives.

Upon arriving in the States, he discovered that he was required to register at Harvard University before leaving for the West Coast. He purchased the textbooks for his graduate classes at the Harvard Coop in advance of his departure for Los Angeles. Meanwhile, Jacky sought permission from the history Chair to pack up Arnie Davidovitz's office. She had managed, with his help, to pack up only half of the fifteen hundred books on Arnie's office shelves. Initially, it had been emotionally very difficult for both of them to be in Cambridge without their good friend. It left a huge gap in their lives. The pain of Arnie's death was not receding for either of them.

Neyri continued looking over the bridge, watching the strolling pedestrians and reflecting on how strange it was not to hear or speak Hebrew. Moreover, he was aware how deeply he missed his unit in the Paratroop Corps as well as his family and friends. It was becoming apparent to him that America had great strengths, as well as weaknesses. People seemed consumed with filling up the emptiness inside with things. But the reality, he acknowledged, was that Israel was being Americanized, and that a consumer mentality was now becoming just as ubiquitous a phenomenon in the Middle East.

The night before, when he accompanied Jacky to her flat to discuss with the tenants when they would evacuate the premises, several neighbors passed them as they were entering the gated compound. They merely nodded to each other in passing.

He recalled asking with dismay:

"How long have you lived in this apartment complex, Jacky?"

"Little over seven years, why?"

"You don't know any of your neighbors by name?"

"That's the way it is in America. It lacks the warmth of Israel. You'll get used to it."

"I doubt it," was his response.

It was implausible for him to consider living permanently in the U.S. He was bound to Israel the way a child is inextricably bound to his parents. Such bonds never could be severed, even in death, he thought. He wondered, for a brief moment, why he had made the monumental leap from his life in Israel to life as a student in America. He had to remind himself he needed to rest from the burdens Zahal had placed on his shoulders since he was eighteen years old. His young manhood had vanished like a cloud the moment he was inducted in the Golani Brigade and taught to defend and kill in order to protect his people. It had left an indelible mark on his soul, leaving him forever nostalgic for childhood, when his innocence had been intact except for the Yom Kippur War.

Neyri glanced at his watch. It was time to meet Jacky on campus. Once inside Harvard Yard, he walked over to Sever Hall. She was on the telephone when he entered her office. The moment she hung up the phone, she looked upset.

"We have a problem, Neyri. The tenants insist they cannot hand over the keys to my apartment until September 13 at the earliest. What'll we do now?"

"It seems to me you'll have to remain here until the thirteenth, so you can take care of the apartment. We'll re-book your flight out to the West Coast. My operation is not scheduled until the fifteenth, so there's no problem."

"I wanted to fly together with you to L.A."

"We have no choice, Jacky. Where can we go to exchange your ticket for a later flight?"

"There's an American Express travel office on Brattle Street."

"Let's go before it closes.

⚜

EARLY ON THE MORNING OF TUESDAY, SEPTEMBER 11, Jacky borrowed her aunt's Lexus and drove her husband to Logan Airport. Once inside the American Air Lines terminal, Neyri checked the departure time and the gate number for his 7:59 AM flight to Los Angeles.

"Departure is on time. I have less than an hour before boarding, so let's head for the gate," Neyri said as he led the way.

The departure gateway was already crowded with travelers when they arrived. They managed to find two empty seats together.

"I'm so sorry I'm not accompanying you!" Jacky admitted.

"Me too, but it can't be helped. You have enough to do in Cambridge. We'll be together in a couple of days. Promise me you won't worry about clearing Arnie's office or his apartment. Also, remember you must call his lawyer to find out what provisions Arnie made about his apartment and his possessions."

"It's on my list. You'll call me when you arrive in L.A.?"

"Of course. Don't worry about anything. It will all get done in time."

By 7:10 AM, they heard over the loudspeaker a call for passengers to line up.

"Did you remember to pack some of your books?"

He didn't bother to answer. Swooping Jacky up in his arms, he kissed her goodbye with such tenderness it made her regret the decision to re-schedule the flight.

"I love you, Mrs. Ben-Ner," he whispered as Jacky held him tightly in her arms, reluctant to let him go.

"I love you so much, Neyri. Have a safe flight to L.A.," she told him, trying not to burst into tears by their pending separation.

Neyri lifted his black leather carry-on case, and stepped into line for boarding. It was then that he noticed two Arab-looking men lining up as First Class passengers. He edged forward in line, handing in his boarding card. At the last moment, he turned for one last look at Jacky. In the next instant, he entered the plane.

The flight attendant directed him to his aisle, located over the wings. As he passed the First Class section, Neyri scanned the two men, noticing the beefy build of the one in seat 8D, whose hard eyes seemed to bore right through him with unrelenting intensity.[59]

All of Neyri's senses radiated the signal that danger was near. Making his way down the long aisle, he noticed three other Arab-looking men seated in economy class. When he reached row 31, Neyri placed his carry-on luggage in the overhead bin and settled in his seat, all the while thinking about these five men located in two distinct areas of the plane. They were clearly agitated. Why, he wondered? He dismissed the possibility that all five might be afraid of flying. It was not fear he sensed; rather, he detected in these men an aberrant intensity clearly bordering on the repugnant. His thoughts were momentarily interrupted by the flight attendant's announcement over the loudspeaker:

"Please fasten your seat belts, as we prepare to taxi onto the runway for take-off."

JACKY BEN-NER RETURNED TO THE PARKING LOT, feeling a strange sense of loneliness at the separation from her husband. She turned on the ignition and followed the exit signs, attempting futilely to fight back tears. She never knew it would hurt so much to be apart from him. It was exactly one week since they were married in Jerusalem. Over the past seven days it felt as if their bonds of love had not only tightened but deepened as well. They were now tapping into the sacred as well as the spiritual components of their committed relationship, she thought. As she headed in the direction of Cambridge, she started reflecting over his first name "Avner," meaning "father of light," and his nickname, "Neyri," which meant "my light" in Hebrew. With the quickening of her soul, she suddenly realized the full extent of the light and radiance he had brought into her life in the seven months of loving each other. Jacky wished with all her being for the brain operation to be a fait accompli, with the full restoration of his health.

Noticing an empty parking space near Harvard Square, she parked and then began walking toward her favorite restaurant across the street from Harvard Yard, which served the best breakfast in the square. After ordering a take-out breakfast of toasted English muffins and coffee, she headed in the direction of Harvard Hall to tackle packing up Arnie's office. The moment she entered his office overflowing with books, she switched on Arnie's Bose Wave set and tuned to National Public Radio, grateful for the classical music to assist her in the arduous task of emptying his desk and shelves into boxes that the university staff had provided. It took three-quarters of an hour to go through the personal papers left inside drawers and on the top of the desk.

She straightened her back, tense from her concentration and the knowledge that her husband was in the air, flying further and further away from her with each tick of the clock. Something beyond the mere separation from Neyri was churning within her. Being back in Arnie's office, among his personal possessions, was so wounding that she felt fresh tears spurting from her eyes. She walked over to the window facing the Harvard campus, lost in thought. How difficult it was to acknowledge the trauma of Arnie's death, the terrifying suicide bombing in downtown Jerusalem, and the angst of separation from Israel despite the dread of what she had experienced in such a short period of time.

She recalled the way she had felt when she had faced the Western Wall for the first time. She had felt like a stranger in a strange land, aware of the difficulty she encountered with the language, the culture, and a people gathered from 108 different lands. How changed a land from 1948 to the present moment, she thought with dismay. From a time when Israel was seen as a persecuted victim surrounded by an Arab foe intent on utterly destroying it, to a time where Israel is an occupation force that exerts its mighty fist over an impoverished people in order to weaken its tenacious hold on the land, and a military power intent on creating a situation parallel to 1948, when the Palestinians were driven out of the land by war, by fear, by force, and by dread of circumstances. It made her wonder: has Israel come full circle in its greed to possess a land occupied also by another people?

Whatever Israel was doing to wear down the Palestinian people was not working; couldn't the politicians who ran the Israeli government as well as the powerful IDF see it was not working? It wasn't working because Palestinians from all walks of life were resorting to a philosophical stance known in Arabic as *sumud*—clinging to the land, staying put in their homes by all means possible, even when the Israeli army demolished their homes claiming they were built illegally without the proper permits. Throughout all this the Palestinians stayed, moving in with other family members or rebuilding their homes from scratch, once again.[60] No number of roadblocks, curfews, terrifying arrests in the middle of the night, humiliation, second-class status as Israeli Arabs or Palestinian refugees in occupied land, would force them to flee ever again. Even if Israel resorted to "transferring" them out of the country, they would have to be bodily dragged; they would not go by their own volition. Not this time. The Palestinians would not make the same mistake twice—fleeing and then not being permitted to return to their homes, their possessions, and their land.[61] What else was there left for them to experience that would make them break and flee? she wondered. Caught in the act of throwing stones at Israeli patrols, their children were shot in the eyes and legs, not in the chest, the widest area for a sharpshooter to zone in on his victim. They knew it was done intentionally to cripple and to maim rather than to kill, in order to distort the statistics of the current Intifada. Electricity, water, food supplies, and medical supplies were curtailed during sieges and curfews that could last up to a month or longer, creating not only grave hardship but malnutrition as well among the adult and child population. And these occurrences right in front of the Israeli people! Surely they had to know, to see, to question. There were voices, but too few, too little, Jacky thought, as she felt a sense of shame she did not realize she was carrying all these months she had lived in Jerusalem.

It was more than shame—it was the heartbreaking realization that the face of Israel today contrasted sharply with all the expectations of its people at the birth of the nation. Israel had not only lost its innocence and its dream of being a light unto other nations, it had also lost its sense of largess. Above all, Israel was lacking in compassion for the Palestinian people, whose pride and yearning for statehood and independence matched that of the struggling Jews in 1947, before the establishment of the sovereign state of Israel. Why crush rather than accommodate another people ready, at last, to share the land with them? If Israel persisted down the path of no compassion, not only would it destroy another people, it would inevitably cause self-destruction, self-loathing, isolation, and an immoral stance among the nations of the world. How unworthy of Israel!

Surely as the fourth strongest military force in the world, Israel could risk for the sake of peace. In honor of all those who had died to keep Israel safe, Israel could risk for peace. For the sake of the beleaguered living on both sides of the divide, Israel could risk for peace. By the same token, so could the Palestinian leaders and people. A conciliatory gesture, both genuine and heartfelt, could allow one hundred thousand Palestinian refugees to return while simultaneously withdrawing completely, for all time, from the occupied West Bank of Jordan and the Gaza Strip—land conquered and occupied and annexed, not de jure but de facto, since the 1967 Six-Day War between Israel, Jordan, Egypt, and Syria.[62]

She recalled the last penetrating discussion with Arnie Davidovitz in his apartment when she first arrived in Israel and how it had affected everyone who participated in that gathering. Before the group disbanded around the table that night, Arnie told them something that was so earth-shattering in its importance, she recalled it vividly:

"I want to conclude this discussion by pointing out that the real culprit in this conflict is U.S. foreign policy and the uneven-handedness and racist policy of both the United States and Israel toward Palestinians. It is a policy that will haunt both countries in the foreseeable future and perhaps beyond. It is a policy of greed, power, and domination that will, in my opinion, eventually destroy victims and perpetrators alike. One may ask, how did they achieve their objectives? Through propaganda that was devoured especially by supporters of Israel—a propaganda that turned everything on its head, portraying Israel, an uncontested military power in the world, as the insecure, suffering victim of the evil, diabolical, irrational enemy: the Palestinian terrorists, the PLO, and by extension, the Palestinian people. Is it any wonder that the U.S. and Israel are hated by the Arab world?[63]

She thought of Asa Ibrahimi and remembered how he had participated in this lengthy political discussion with them. Five months later, on August 9, Asa Ibrahimi would become a Hamas martyr, murdering Arnie, David, and a multitude of others. Did Asa Ibrahimi know that both of these people were in the restaurant when he detonated the bomb? Her mind was reeling with pain at the waste of human life on that infamous day in the city of Jerusalem. She knew next to nothing about Asa Ibrahimi other than that he was a brilliant student, a man with much promise. What would drive a man to become a human fuse with the express purpose of destroying human life? It seemed to her, Palestinians felt humiliation and powerlessness—two key components in feeling like victims—as if their souls had been destroyed in the process. A suicide bombing is a way of throwing one's death back at the oppressor.[64]

She shivered involuntarily. At 8:28 AM, she heard a knock on the office door.

"Come in, it's open."

✣

THE MOMENT AMERICAN AIRLINES FLIGHT 11 was airborne and cruising at a good altitude, Neyri slipped off his seatbelt, placed the *New York Times* in the seat jacket and turned to the woman seated beside him:

"Excuse me, I need the lavatory."

Neyri Ben-Ner walked down the aisle toward the front of the plane. All during take-off he could not dispel from his mind the Middle Eastern men in first class, whose extremely tense and stone-faced personas disquieted him. His brother Gidi had warned him time and time again when he was in the commandos to know the enemy backward and forward, as well as become an expert in body language. By the time Gidi was a teenager, he had mastered Arabic, teaching Neyri the Palestinian dialect. It had actually come in handy during the Lebanon War when Neyri performed a daring rescue operation in Damur to save four Golani Flying Tiger commandos caught in the path of deadly Palestinian crossfire.

Neyri Ben-Ner stood outside the toilet marked "OCCUPIED." As he inched his way to the business section of the plane, the three men he'd noticed in economy class jumped out of their seats and whipped out cardboard cutters at the same moment that they yelled *"Yallah!"*[65] From the first class section, he distinctly heard the rushing of the cockpit door, along with loud voices and a scream from the cabin. In the next instant, he saw the raw, brute hatred flashing in the eyes of the three terrorist operatives lunging directly at him with Stanley knives.[66]

Suddenly, the Boeing 767 airplane lurched precipitously, banking south toward New York City. Over the loudspeaker, a voice with a foreign accent announced to the frightened passengers:

"This is your new captain speaking. Everyone is to remain calm and in your seats. In the name of Allah, we are heading for a special destination. No one will be hurt if you obey my orders!"[67]

From the back of the plane, a flight attendant cautioned passengers:

"Stay seated. Don't move. Whatever you do, remain seated with your seat belt fastened!" she implored, as she steadily and courageously made her way down the aisle toward the front of the plane. It was 8:29 AM.

Screaming and pandemonium broke out as the hijacked plane, piloted and co-piloted by two Al-Qaeda terrorists, began a sudden and rapid descent in altitude, flying over rooftops of lower Manhattan.[68]

STANDING IN THE DOORWAY OF ARNIE DAVIDOVITZ'S office was the Chair of Arnie's history department, Professor Thomas O'Malley, a man in his early sixties, with a distinguished face, white hair, and a ruddy complexion.

"I stopped by to see if you needed any help, Jacky. I'm sure one of Arnie's graduate students would be willing to box up the rest of his books. How difficult this must be for you emotionally."

"Tom, please, do you have a minute to sit down?"

"Absolutely. If it will be of any help, are you able to talk about the suicide bombing in Jerusalem, Jacky?"

"Thank you, Tom, for your willingness to listen. I'm having recurrent flashbacks. According to my husband, I have nightmares as well. The horrible thing is what such an attack does to your sense of fragility. Time is altered. If we had not accidentally met a former paratrooper of Neyri's in downtown Jerusalem, which delayed our entering the Sbarro restaurant by five minutes, we would not have survived the massacre.

My husband and I lost two of our closest friends among the fifteen dead—not only Arnie Davidovitz but also David Ha-Levy, a well-known Israeli historian. The Druze officer who was in my husband's former unit had an arm and leg blown off by the bomb. It's not something I'll ever get over no matter how much I try or how long I live."

"The streets of Jerusalem have now been turned into a battlefield where civilians are the targets rather than soldiers. How sad for the Israeli people. Regrettably, it parallels events in Ireland when I was growing up in my own country," Professor O'Malley acknowledged with understanding.

> *"We interrupt this program to bring you a special bulletin from National Public Radio:*
>
> *"A commercial airliner has just crashed into the North Tower of the World Trade Center at 8:46 AM. Please stand by for further details."*

"What in the world? Do you think it's a pilot error or a malfunctioning plane?" Tom O'Malley asked in dismay.

"Doubt it. My gut instinct is a terrorist hijacking of a commercial airliner."

"Since you've been living in the Middle East for several months, you're beginning to think like an Israeli."

"Thank God my husband is en route to California, away from the East Coast."

> *"This is NPR news with the latest bulletin: at 8:46 this morning, a commercial airliner crashed into the North Tower of the World Trade Center. We have just had word that at precisely 9:03 AM a second commercial airliner smashed into the South Tower..."* [69]

Jacky shoved the desk chair back, rushing out of Arnie's office with Thomas O'Malley at her heels.

"Where are you going, Jacky?" he called out, following her.

"To the faculty lounge. Perhaps CNN has more information to disclose. My husband's plane . . . may have been diverted . . . he's flying to L.A. I must know what airlines they are talking about . . . I must know!"

"Come into my office. I have a T.V. hooked up."

O'Malley hurried down the hall to his office, switching the television channel to CNN.

Together they watched the news in abject horror as the nightmare was unfolding in Manhattan, amid the flaming towers, the columns of billowing smoke, and the shocking display of disbelief on the faces of the people in the streets of Manhattan, where they'd witnessed the unfathomable.

On CNN, there was a re-play of the first plane imploding the North Tower, followed shortly by the second plane crashing through the South Tower of the World Trade Center. Jacky slowly lowered herself into Tom O'Malley's leather chair. Her eyes remained fixed on the video image capturing the events of that day for all eternity. He noticed that she'd placed her left hand on her neck, as if to verify if she was still breathing.

Tom O'Malley lifted the telephone receiver and bent down to look directly into her face, a face whitened with shock and dread.

"What airline is your husband flying? Do you know the flight number, Jacky?"

She merely shook her head. Then, in a low, flat tone of voice, she said:

"It's not necessary to call American Airlines. My husband is no longer alive."

"Jacky, listen to me, please. There were dozens of flights departing the East Coast this morning from many airports. How do you know your husband was on either of those planes crashing into the World Trade Center?"

Jacky Ben-Ner lifted her large, glazed eyes to his face.

"I just know. He's gone," she said quietly, unable or willing to enter into a plea bargain with God, praying instead for their deliverance from evil.

"He's gone," she repeated.

Thirty-eight

A BRIEF, SOLEMN MEMORIAL SERVICE was held for Neyri Ben-Ner at the Jerusalem Yeshuran synagogue on King George Street on Sunday, September 16, 2001. Among the congregation were members of the military, comrades-in-arms, close childhood friends, relatives and family members. A section was cordoned off for the American ambassador as well.

Jacky was seated beside Neyri's family, looking austere in a black silk suit and a wide-brimmed, black hat. Without a trace of makeup, her face was porcelain white, resembling a statue devoid of life.

The Israeli Consul-General of Boston, Rafi Haas, walked to the podium with tautly held shoulders, and dressed in a pin-striped, charcoal-grey suit, white shirt, and blue paisley tie. The angular planes of his face made him look distinguished. Despite his salt-and-pepper hair, he seemed far younger than his fifty-four years. For over three decades his relationship with Neyri and his entire family had been tight knit. In his youth, he had immigrated to Israel from America. While serving with distinction in the IDF in the late 1960s and 1970s, he was a boarder in the Ben-Ner home.

Rafi Haas lifted his eyes, searching out the bereaved widow and the Ben-Ner family. In a quiet, somber tone, he gave a touching eulogy:

"Not only is the Ben-Ner family bereft of their middle child, a son, and a brother, but a recent bride has become widowed in a tragically short period of time. Israel has lost one of its finest sons and a brave warrior and outstanding officer, and we are all gathered here to pay tribute to Neyri's life and the manner in which he died..."

Shortly after the service and a gathering of the family and closest friends at the Ben-Ner home, Jacky slipped away, needing desperately to be alone. Borrowing her brother-in-law's car, she drove directly to the Old City.

By the time she reached the Western Wall, a soft, diffused light illuminated the city of Jerusalem. Dark shadows crept along the walls of the Temple Mount as Arab Moslems flocked to the Al-Aqsa Mosque for the late afternoon prayers preceding nightfall. The city's pulse beat slower with the advancing twilight. A discernible hush spread over the land.

A tiredness unlike anything she had ever experienced before made her feel burdened and old. She closed her eyes and reflected on how the words chosen by Rafi Haas were a befitting eulogy for her late husband. She knew there would be no closure for a very long time. She uncurled the tightness of her fists and lay the palms of her hands on the concrete ledge overlooking the Western Wall.

It was unearthly quiet here, she thought, feeling drawn into the timelessness of the holy city of Jerusalem, as if she were being transported back to ancient Jerusalem. Close by, through narrow alleyways, past the Moslem Quarters, was the Church of the Holy Sepulcre, the site of the crucifixion, burial, and resurrection of Jesus, sacred to the Christians since the fourth century.

For centuries, she reflected, Jerusalem held people captive in imagination. In any given twenty-four-hour period, one could hear the ubiquitous muezzin calling Arabs to prayer, the tolling of church bells entreating the Christians to mass, the chanting of Jews at the Western Wall lamenting the destruction of the Jewish Temple. Jerusalem had changed hands many times, often under the burden of occupation forces squashing uprisings and revolts up to and including modern times.

It had been only seven months ago that her flight had landed in Israel, bringing her back to the country where she was destined to meet a man she would love deeply and passionately, but have for only a short time. She recalled awakening at sunrise on her first morning back in the country in twenty years. Off the bedroom balcony, she had watched the rising of the sun. It had been as if she were standing before a magnificent painting etched in earth-tone colors with brush strokes of burnt sienna and yellow ochre—a barren earth awakening to the luminosity of a clear, golden, ethereal light that made all other light dim in contrast.

There was a brooding beauty to Jerusalem, she observed as she looked about her. It was as if the city possessed an unfathomable mystery. It was a city of crenellated walls beckoning people from every corner of the globe, holding out the elusive promise of peace and at the same time threatening the Apocalypse—the End of Days—when the entire world would, according to biblical prophesy, be engulfed in its flames.

Two decades before, as a young student, she had been permitted to enter the *Maghrabi,* the door leading to the Temple Mount. Never would she forget how stunned she had been by the vastness of the esplanade—measuring 475 yards in length, 300 yards in width—the beauty, the tranquility, and the contrast to the world she had just left behind. She recalled feeling as if she had departed from earth through the narrow opening of the green door. The Temple Mount was vast in design and scope, encompassing both the Dome of the Rock and the Al-Aqsa mosques, holy to Islam since the seventh century. The Dome of the Rock, a turquoise, hexagonal mosque capped by a gold dome, virtually dominated the area. The site was reputed to have been the place from which the prophet Muhammad had risen to heaven. It was on this exact spot that the Jewish Temple had been erected by King Solomon, destroyed twice—the last and final time in 70 AD during the Jewish revolt against Roman occupation, tyranny, and brutality. The Temple Mount, and the area known as the Holy of Holies, were sacred to Jews in ancient as well as in modern times. It was here that the Jewish high priests had practiced the ancient animal rituals and sacrifices, and where Abraham had prepared to sacrifice his only son, Isaac.

There had been moments in the past when the yearning for peace was so strong within, she could actually visualize it in her mind, like a reel of film in a projection room. With the brutal death of her husband at the hands of Al-Qaeda terrorists, who despised the Zionist state of Israel and its staunchest supporter, the United States, she felt an urgency to stem the horrific bloodshed endemic in Israel and prevent a repetition of the monstrous destruction of lives at Ground Zero in New York City and at the Pentagon in Washington, D.C. But how, she wondered?

The unresolved conflict between the Arabs and the Jews seemed an endless feud of hatred, distortions, and mindless propaganda ad nauseum. Two decades previously, the antagonism and bloodshed had appeared unsolvable at first glance. On closer observation, Jacky knew in the depth of her soul, both sides yearned for peace to descend over the embattled land. Bloodshed, destruction, and wars, in her opinion, were avoidable. If wars were outlawed by human society unconditionally, peace would have a chance, for the first time in history, to spread to all four corners of the globe. It would have to start here, in Jerusalem, the *Ir-Shalom,* the City of Peace, she thought solemnly, as she walked slowly through Dung Gate and back to the car.

Adjacent to Dung Gate, in the valley of Silwan, an Arab village spread out before her. Here the dying rays of the sun lingered on the figure of a young Arab woman holding an infant. Jacky felt tears spring to her eyes, knowing all her dreams of a husband and family were now scattered to the wind, and longing for the strong hands of Neyri and for the life they had dreamed of together.

Wiping away unwanted tears, she raised her hand, waving to the Muslim woman in Silwan. Without hesitating, the woman waved back, offering a shy smile in greeting. Jacky turned, retraced her steps and slid behind the wheel of Omri's car. As she drove the short distance back to her in-laws' home, she felt a calmness descending over her— the first bit of relief since the unspeakable morning of September 11, when all her illusions of safety were shattered forever.

With sudden clarity, she knew what had to be done. It would start with each individual taking the necessary faltering steps toward a more peaceful world by setting individual examples of peaceful co-existence. Eventually, it would mushroom into a collective example in villages, farms, cities and states, among nations and between nations.

Was it really so simple, she wondered, as she shifted gears? Recalling the vision of the Arab woman and child in the valley of Silwan, Jacky knew with resounding clarity and utter certainty that it would have to start with a handshake, a wave, and a smile. Once trust was established, another step could be taken in the direction of peace. An exchange of bread would be necessary between neighbors before an exchange of territory; the tearing down of walls of hatred, distrust, and inequality before an exchange of ideas and the sharing of mutual progress toward peace, prosperity, and accord. It would require another miracle to descend over the golden city of David where peace would reign for a thousand years, and thereafter no thought of war or violence would be conceivable. She envisioned spiritual leaders throughout the world participating in a week-long ceremony of peace throughout the land, with prayers, meditation, candlelight vigils in memory of the slain; music, dancing, and psalms sung in Hebrew, Arabic, Armenian, and Latin. There would be circles of dancers consisting of Palestinians swirling around circles of Israeli Jews, their hands touching briefly, and then the dancing would resume until exhaustion would overtake the participants. In the streets, Arabs and Jews from all walks of life would be joining in the processional of peace in a dance of life, in a dance of joy to have reached this moment in history where recognition, acceptance, and tolerance would be the key components from this day forward. This momentary vision was so stunning in its brilliance, it was as if a blinding light were radiating over her entire body. Shaken from her reverie, she slowly wiped her eyes glazed with tears.

Was it too much to hope or to believe possible? Not only a genuine, lasting peace but a co-existence of normal interchange between Israeli Jews and Palestinian-Israeli Arabs with open borders, tourism, exchange students, teachers, artists; water agreements, medical and research opportunities; trade and cultural interactions along with high-level conferences and leadership to enhance both peoples in growth, development, progress, and a meaningful existence.

Jacky turned off the ignition. She got out of the car. Glancing up at the sky, she saw the sun setting on another day in her life. The ache of grief would be with her for a very long time. She glanced yearningly along the horizon casting the final shadows of evening over Jerusalem.

She walked up the steps, opened the door, and said a silent prayer, closing the door behind her.

epilogue

WHEN JOAB BEN ZERUIAH PURSUED Avner Ben-Ner, the Commander-in-Chief of Saul's army, as far as Hebron, he slew Avner Ben-Ner by stabbing him in his belly.

> *(King) David then ordered Joab and all the troops with him to rend their clothes, gird on sackcloth, and make lament before Avner; and King David himself walked behind the bier. And so they buried Avner at Hebron; the King wept aloud by Avner's grave, and all the troops wept. And the King intoned this dirge over Avner:*

> > *"Should Avner have died the death of a churl?*
> > *Your hands were not bound,*
> > *Your feet were not put in fetters;*
> > *But you fell as one falls*
> > *Before treacherous men!"*

> *And the King said to his soldiers,*

> > *"You well know that a prince, a great man in Israel, has fallen this day... May the Lord requite the wicked for their wickedness!"*
> >
> > SAMUEL II 3:31–3:38

CHAPTER TWO

1 Samuel M. Katz, *Israel Versus Jibril: The Thirty-Year War Against a Master Terrorist* (New York: Paragon House, 1993).

CHAPTER THREE

2 The actual date of this suicide bombing is January 27, 2002. According to an Arutz Sheva news article posted that day and entitled "Another Jerusalem Attack: One Killed" (Arutz Sheva/Israel National News Archives, http://www.israelnationalnews.com): "Pinchas Tukatli, 81, was killed in a suicide terrorist attack carried out for the first time by a woman suicide terrorist who blew herself up in downtown Jerusalem. The number of wounded numbered 172, the majority suffering from shock."

3 Anton La Guardia, *War Without End: Israelis, Palestinians and the Struggle for a Promised Land* (New York: Thomas Dunne Books/St. Martin's Press, 2001). According to La Guardia, Israel avenged the killing of two of its reserve soldiers "by firing missiles from an Apache helicopter directed at Fatah's infrastructure in Gaza. . . . It was much more than revenge, however. It was a display of impotent rage; a public admission of failure" (260).

CHAPTER FOUR

4 Eliahu Elath, in *Israel and Her Neighbors* (Cleveland: The World Publishing Co., 1957), claims that "this feeling of collective responsibility makes the Bedouin exceedingly cautious about destroying human life, since he knows what physical and material retribution will follow, not only to himself, but to his entire family, and often to his whole tribe" (71).

5 Elath, *Israel and Her Neighbors.*

CHAPTER FIVE

6 Schiffmann and Vander Kam (eds.), *Encyclopedia of the Dead Sea Scrolls* (New York: Oxford University Press, 2000).

7 Hershel Shanks, *Understanding the Dead Sea Scrolls* (New York: Vintage Books, A Division of Random House, Inc., 1993).

CHAPTER SIX

8 Karen Armstrong, *Jerusalem: One City, Three Faiths* (New York: Alfred A. Knopf, Inc., 1996).

9 David Lamb, in *The Arabs* (New York, Random House, 1987), reports that "Israel has maintained over the years that the exodus happened because Arab leaders, both inside and outside Palestine, ordered the masses to leave in order to clear the way for the invading armies. The Arabs contend that the flight resulted from a carefully orchestrated Jewish military campaign of expulsion that depopulated 250 villages and several major towns. A classified report prepared by the Israeli Defense Forces in 1948 and kept unpublished until 1986 supports, at least in part, the Arab positions. It says upward of 70 per cent of the Palestinians fled because of Jewish military action or because of related psychological factors. The report cites surprise attacks, protracted artillery barrages and the use of loudspeakers broadcasting threatening messages as elements that precipitated the Palestinians' departure... Often an attack on one village could hasten the depopulation of other nearby villages, for the threat of violence was as strong a weapon as violence itself. 'The evacuation of a certain village because of an attack by us prompted in its wake neighboring villages [to flee],' the report states. The truth probably lies midway between the two sides' claims and the exodus was the result of Jewish militancy and Arab deceitfulness" (212).

10 According to Benny Morris, in *Righteous Victims: A History of the Zionist-Arab Conflict, 1881–1999* (New York: Alfred A. Knopf, 1999): "The affair [of the Deir Yassin Massacre] had an immediate and brutal aftermath. On April 13 [1948] Arab militiamen from Jerusalem and surrounding villages attacked a ten-vehicle convoy of mostly unarmed lecturers, nurses, and doctors on their way to the Hadassah Hospital-Hebrew University campus on Mount Scopus.... For hours the British refrained from intervening and warned the Hagannah not to do so. Three Palmach armoured cars arrived on the scene but were overwhelmed by the ambushers. The

shooting continued for more than six hours, the Arabs eventually dous-
ing the armoured buses with gasoline and setting them alight. When the
British finally intervened, more than seventy Jews had died. Deir Yassin
and the death of Abd al-Qadir had been avenged" (209).

11   Ze'ev Schiff and Ehud Ya'ari, *Intifada: The Palestinian Uprising—Israel's
Third Front.* Translated by Ina Friedman (New York: Simon & Schuster,
1989), 220–227. After many civilian deaths in Israel as the direct result of
the Hamas terrorist organization, its leader, Sheikh Yassin, was eventually killed in a military attack in 2004 by Israel Defense Forces.

12   Raja Shehadeh, a Palestinian lawyer in Ramallah, describes in *Strangers
in the House* (South Royalton, Vermont: Steerforth Press, 2002) how his
family was traumatized after their expulsion from Jaffa in April 1948: "Our
dumbfoundedness had been so petrifying that we could not manage to
continue the life we had lived before. Because of our loss of the part, we
had abandoned the whole. All that remained was a shadow life, a life of
dreams and anticipation and memory. We didn't allow the new generation to make a new life for themselves because we continued to impress
them with the glory of what was, a magic that could never be replicated.
We allowed others to inherit all that had been established because we
failed to see any of it as ours. We defined our loss as total, forgetting that
we still had something; we had ourselves and a life to live" (64–65).

CHAPTER EIGHT

13   "Word for Word/The Interrogator; Psychology and Sometimes a Slap:
The Man Who Made Prisoners Talk," *New York Times,* December 12,
2004. Michael Koubi, chief interrogator of Shin Bet from 1987 to 1993,
interviewed hundreds of Palestinian militants, among them Sheikh Yassin,
who was killed in an Israeli attack in 2004. Koubi reported these facts in
an interview with Michael Bond, editor of the British weekly, *New Scientist.*

CHAPTER TEN

14   Cela Netanyahu, *Self-Portrait of a Hero: The Letters of Jonathan Netanyahu
[1963–1976]* (New York: Random House, 1980).

CHAPTER ELEVEN

15   Carl R. Raswan, *Black Tents of Arabia (My Life Among the Bedouins)* (New
York: Creative Age Press, 1947).

CHAPTER TWELVE

16 La Guardia, *War Without End,* 372: "The Israelis want peace and the end of violence; the Palestinians do not want peace for its own sake, but that ill-defined quality of 'justice.' Palestinians believe they made the historic compromise in 1993 with the Oslo Accords by recognizing Israel and giving up more than three-quarters of the former British Mandate of Palestine. This helps to explain the infuriating Palestinian negotiating tactic of saying 'No' to everything at Camp David that was not a full Israeli withdrawal from the West Bank, Gaza Strip and East Jerusalem."

17 Fatah is a reverse acronym of the Arabic *Harakat Tahrir Falastin,* meaning Movement for the Liberation of Palestine. Uri Avnery, *My Friend, The Enemy* (Westport, CT: Lawrence Hill & Co., 1986).

18 According to Noam Chomsky in *Fateful Triangle: The United States, Israel and the Palestinians,* updated edition (Cambridge, MA: South End Press, 1999), 475: "The army has destroyed the homes of over 3,000 people (often destroying or severely damaging others nearby) on the pretext that a family member is suspected of throwing stones or some other crime. This particularly ugly form of collective punishment, the Israeli press reports, is conducted 'under a law that also does not permit them to rebuild.'"

CHAPTER THIRTEEN

19 David K. Shipler, *Arab and Jew: Wounded Spirits in a Promised Land* (New York: Penguin Books, 1987).

20 Pitirim A. Sorokin, in *The Reconstruction of Humanity* (Boston: The Beacon Press, 1948), maintains that the twentieth century has experienced more wars and deaths from these wars than in all the preceding centuries of life on earth.

CHAPTER FIFTEEN

21 Israel Ministry of Foreign Affairs, "Victims of Palestinian Violence and Terrorism since September 2000," http://www.mfa.gov.il/mfa/terrorism. "Between September 29, 2000 and April 1, 2005 Magen David Adom treated a total of 7,253 casualties as follows: 953 killed, 596 severely injured, 881 moderately and 4,823 lightly injured, among them 11 MDA staff members *(IDF casualties treated by IDF medical personnel are not included in these figures).* Note: This list also includes 18 Israelis killed abroad in terror attacks directed specifically against Israeli targets, and three American diplomatic personnel killed in Gaza."

CHAPTER SIXTEEN

22 Yehoshafat Harkabi, *Israel's Fateful Hour.* Translated by Lenn Schramm (New York: Harper and Row, Publishers, 1988). Harkabi, an expert on Israeli-Arab relations and former chief of military intelligence, maintains: "The solution of the Arab-Israeli conflict requires that both Israelis and Palestinians resign themselves to the arrangement that their respective states in which they will be citizens will occupy only part of their homeland, to which they will both bear sentimental allegiance" (xviii). He further underscores unequivocally: "Israel must withdraw from the occupied territories with their growing Arab population... Given the provocations of 1967, Israel cannot be blamed for its occupation of the West Bank and Gaza, but it should be criticized for attempting to retain them; occupation was justified, annexation is not" (xvi).

23 Harkabi, *Israel's Fateful Hour,* xviii–xix.

24 Amos Oz, *Israel, Palestine and Peace Essays* (New York: Harcourt Brace Jovanovich Publishers, 1992). In his acceptance speech at the International Peace Prize of the German Publishers' Association in Frankfurt, Germany, in October 1992, Amos Oz stated: "The conflict between Israel and Palestine is, I always insist, a tragic collision between right and right, between two very convincing claims. Such a tragedy can either be resolved by total destruction of one of the parties (or both of them), or else it can be resolved through a sad, painful, inconsistent compromise in which everyone gets only some of what they want, so that nobody is entirely happy but everyone stops dying and starts living" (69).

CHAPTER SEVENTEEN

25 Kimmerling and Migdal maintain in *The Palestinian People: A History* (Cambridge, MA: Harvard University Press, 2003), 136–137: "Palestinians would grasp the belief that they were the victims of an immense conspiracy and of a monumental injustice. They would see their plight as representing a breach of the cosmic order. They would seethe in anger, not only against the hated Zionists, but also against their putative allies— their Arab brothers from neighboring countries—and against a wider world that could allow such an injustice... The experience of exile—of a tragedy perceived as both personal and national—would overshadow all else for this generation of disaster (the *jil al-Naqba)* creating both a sense of ennui and ironically, a new form of cultural ferment, largely literary in nature."

26 According to Norman G. Finkelstein in *Image & Reality of the Israel-Palestine Conflict,* 2nd Edition (London/New York: Verso, 2003), 62: "The

Zionists [were able to] pursue with virtual impunity a policy that, as we shall see presently, was openly and relentlessly bent on expulsion." Finkelstein maintains that Plan Dalet (Plan D) "was an expulsion policy to clear hostile forces out of the interior of the Jewish State—most of the [Arab] villages were regarded by the Haganah as potentially hostile" (64). According to Hebrew University Professor Baruch Kimmerling and Joel S. Migdal in *The Palestinian People: A History* (Cambridge, MA: Harvard University Press, 2003): "Although he never declared this outright, the policy of the Sharon government appeared to be intended to gradually and systematically destroy the agreements and the Palestinian Authority institutional infrastructure and leadership, especially rejecting the leadership of Arafat, while carefully and gradually preparing Israeli and world opinion for these moves" (394).

CHAPTER EIGHTEEN

27 Yonah Alexander and Nicholas N. Kittrie (eds), *Crescent and Star: Arab and Israeli Perspectives on the Middle East Conflict* (New York: AMS Press, Inc., 1973), 448–450.

28 Alexander and Kittrie, *Crescent and Star,* 452–454.

29 Raphael Patai, *The Arab Mind* (New York: Charles Scribner's Sons, 1973).

CHAPTER TWENTY-TWO

30 Lawrence Meyer, *Israel Now: Portrait of a Troubled Land* (New York: Delacorte Press, 1982), 242.

31 Meyer, *Israel Now,* 243.

32 David Grossman, *The Yellow Wind.* Translated by Haim Watzman (Toronto: Collins Publishers, 1988), 11–12.

33 Uri Averny, *My Friend, The Enemy* (Westport, CT: Lawrence Hill & Co., 1986). Averny comments that, "I am convinced that this moral problem has to be faced squarely, and that a morally acceptable solution has to be discovered before a political reconciliation and solution can be found" (86).

34 Chomsky, *Fateful Triangle,* 64–79.

35 Avi Shlaim, *The Iron Wall, Israel and the Arab World* (New York: W.W. Norton & Co., 2001).

36 La Guardia, in *War Without End,* argues: "Nobody seems to question whether [the Arab rejection of the 1947 U.N. partition plan] might have been a cardinal mistake. What the Palestinians were offered in 1947 was

far more generous than the truncated, dissected mini-state on offer today" (209).

37   Alan Dershowitz, *The Case for Israel* (New York: John Wiley & Sons, Inc. 2003).

38   Dershowitz states in *The Case for Israel:* "There has always been a small element within the Jewish community that for largely inexplicable reasons has been hypercritical of everything associated with Judaism, Jews or the Jewish State. Karl Marx, Noam Chomsky and Norman Finkelstein come easily to mind" (220). And further, that "Israel is the underdog in one sense. It cannot afford to lose even a single war without exposing its population to genocide and its nationhood to politicide" (227).

39   La Guardia, in *War Without End,* maintains: "With the Al-Aqsa Intifada, matters have become worse. Israeli groups that monitor the Arabic media regularly find appalling examples of anti-Semitic utterances... In the early 1990's, the store in the lobby of the Inter-Continental Hotel in Amman openly sold anti-Semitic tracts, including the notorious Tsarist forgery, *The Protocols of the Elders of Zion,* which purports to describe a vast conspiracy by Jews to dominate the world" (207).

40   Chomsky, *Fateful Triangle,* 456.

41   Chomsky, *Fateful Triangle,* 460.

42   Chomsky, *Fateful Triangle,* 462.

43   According to Morris, in *Righteous Victims,* "Ben-Yehuda [who played a major role in the revival of Hebrew as a spoken language and] who settled in Jerusalem in September 1881, wrote that the goal is to revive our nation on its land... There are now only 500,000 Arabs who are not very strong, and from whom we shall easily take away the country if only we do it through stratagems [and] without drawing upon us their hostility before we become the strong and populous one" (49). Morris argues that "this 'stratagem' apparently bothered a minority of Zionists" (57).

44   Tom Segev, *1949: The First Israelis* (New York: The Free Press, A Division of Macmillan, Inc., 1986).

CHAPTER TWENTY-FOUR

45   Bessel A. van der Kolk, M.D., in *Psychological Trauma* (Washington: American Psychiatric Press, Inc., 1987), indicates that there is an addiction to trauma where "voluntary re-exposure to trauma is very common" (72–73).

46   Chris Hedges, *War Is a Force that Gives us Meaning* (New York: Public Affairs—Perseus Books Group, 2002), 3.

CHAPTER TWENTY-SEVEN

47 Armstrong, *Jerusalem, One City, Three Faiths,* 421.

48 Alvin Rubinstein (ed.), *The Arab-Israeli Conflict,* Praeger Special Studies (Westport, CT: Greenwood Publishing Group, 1984).

49 Yehoshua Harkabi, *Arab Attitudes to Israel.* Translated by Misha Louvish (New York: Hart Publishing Co., Inc., 1971), 65.

50 Grossman, *Yellow Wind,* 91.

CHAPTER THIRTY-ONE

51 Kahlil Gibran, *The Prophet* (New York: Alfred A. Knopf, Inc. 1923), 15–16.

CHAPTER THIRTY-THREE

52 Arutz Sheva, "Dolphinarium Club Terrorist Attack," Arutz Sheva/Israel National News Archives, http://www.israelnationalnews.com (posted June 1, 2001; no longer accessible).

CHAPTER THIRTY-FOUR

53 According to La Guardia in *War Without End:* "At the check-in for El Al flights at Ben Gurion Airport . . . foreign women traveling on their own receive particularly close scrutiny, ever since Nizar Hindawi, a Jordanian working for Syrian intelligence, sent his pregnant Irish girlfriend on to an El Al flight without telling her he had hidden a Semtex bomb in the false bottom of her bag. An El-Al guard spotted the device, saving the lives of 375 people that day in April 1986" (1).

CHAPTER THIRTY-FIVE

54 According to Neil Altman in his article "On the Psychology of Suicide Bombing" (*Tikkun,* Mar–Apr 2005, 15–17), Palestinian terrorists volunteering for suicide bombing missions view themselves and their people as the living dead, murdered psychically by Israeli occupation. Altman concludes that "the Palestinian suicide bomber acts to throw his own death back at his oppressor in an act that is at once retributive and communicative."

55 Arutz Sheva, "Arabs Slaughter 15 in the Holy City," Arutz Sheva/Israel National News Archives, http://www.israelnationalnews.com (posted August 9, 2001; no longer accessible). This article reports that correspondent Ehud Ya'ari, an expert on Arab terrorism, commented that any-

one "who says that the suicide bombings are the Arab response to our taking down their leaders, is simply not reading the map and what they are saying: They are in the midst of a terrorist offensive, continuing from where the 1948 War of Independence left off."

56 Arutz Sheva, "Arabs Slaughter 15 in the Holy City." The other three fatality victims of the Sbarro restaurant suicide bombing, not mentioned are Freeda Mendelson, 62, Romeima neighborhood of Jerusalem; Tzvi Golombek, 26, of Carmiel; and Giora Balash, 60, a tourist from Brazil.

57 Arutz Sheva, "Arabs Slaughter 15 in the Holy City."

58 The PLO's Fatah Force 17 consists of bodyguards for the PLO leadership. According to Schiff and Ya'ari (*Intifada*, 286), Force 17 has also been used for terrorist operations.

CHAPTER THIRTY-SEVEN

59 Muhammad al Amir Awad al Sayyid Atta, an Egyptian citizen carrying a Saudi passport was seated beside Abdul Aziz al Omari, a Saudi citizen residing in Hollywood, Florida. According to Hiro (*War Without End*, 300): "The reason for splitting the hijackers into business and economy class is to enable them to overwhelm the cabin crew at both ends as knife assaults lured the pilots from their cockpit."

60 Raja Shehadeh, in *The Third Way: A Journal of Life in the West Bank* (London: Quartet Books, 1982), acknowledges: "Between mute submission and blind hate—I choose the third way. I am *samid.*" Samid means persevering and steadfast, adopting the stance of *sumud:* to stay put, to cling to their homes and land no matter what happens.

61 For decades, Uri Avnery, a former Israeli Knesset member and a founding member of the Israeli Council for Israeli-Palestinian Peace, has worked tirelessly for peace between Israeli Jews and Palestinians. In *My Friend, the Enemy,* he notes that immediately after the 1948 war ended: "A reconciliation committee was set up by the U.N. and held hearings in Lausanne, Switzerland. There appeared before it a delegation officially representing the Palestinian refugees but which was actually a kind of unofficial Palestinian negotiating team. This group, which included the Ramallah lawyer Aziz Shihaded, approached the Israeli delegate, Eliahu Sasson, and told him that the Palestinians were ready to make peace with Israel. After consulting his government, Sasson rebuffed them bluntly. The government of Israel was not interested in dealing with people who did not represent any government. He would deal with the Kingdom of Jordan only" (58).

62 Harkabi (*Israel's Fateful Hour,* 160) points out that this de facto annexation of occupied territory is contrary to U.N. Security Council Resolution 242 stipulating the full recognition of Israel's existence, the withdrawal of Israel armed forces from territories occupied in 1967, the inadmissibility of the acquisition of territory by war, the need to work for a just and lasting peace, and the just settlement of the refugee problem.

63 According to Chomsky (*Fateful Triangle,* 468–469): "As long as the U.S. remains committed to an Israeli Sparta as a strategic asset, blocking the international consensus on a political settlement, the prospects are for further tragedy: repression, terrorism, war, and possibly even a conflict that will engage the superpowers, eventuating in a final solution from which few will escape."

64 Altman, in "On the Psychology of Suicide Bombing," describes how the psychological portrait of a suicide bomber includes "extreme humiliation." He states, "Palestinians feel that they have been rendered helpless by having their land forcibly taken away, by being confronted with an overwhelming military force." When we consider the motivation for a suicide bombing, "what we must always keep in the forefront of our understanding is that the suicide bomber is killing himself in order to kill others. . . . The bomber is seeking to actualize or dramatize a *psychological* situation occurring in an interpersonal and inter-group context." And the same time, "Israelis have an insatiable craving for military superiority in their need to be assured that they will never again be rendered helpless [like they were in the Holocaust under the Germans]."

65 An Arabic idiomatic expression adopted into Hebrew slang meaning "Let's go!"

66 In *War Without End,* Hiro reports that Wail al Shahri, a Saudi teacher; his younger brother, Waleed al Shahri; and Satam al Sugami, a Saudi student who arrived in the U.S. in May, were all carrying razor-sharp cardboard cutters known as Stanley knives.

67 Hiro reports in *War Without End,* that the terrorist Muhammad Atta, with a total of three hundred hours of flying time, took over control of the cockpit, together with Abdul Omari. The first thing they did was to turn off the transponders so that the flight could not be tracked.

68 As American Airlines flight 11 approached its target, the two hijackers piloting the airplane knew the Boeing 767, weighing 150 tons and carrying fifteen thousand gallons of jet fuel, would be hitting the 110 floors of the North Tower of the World Trade Center at an altitude of 1,368 feet and at 430 to 500 miles per hour. At precisely 8:46 AM, flight 11 slammed into the North Tower between the eighty-seventh and ninety-second

floors, where the Al-Qaeda terrorists knew 15,000 people worked on a given day (Hiro, *War Without End,* 300–309).

69 This was United Airlines flight 175, departing Boston's Logan Airport at 8:15 AM en route to Los Angeles. This Boeing 767, with a passenger list of fifty-six and a crew of nine, was transporting five Al-Qaeda operatives: two in first class—Marwan Yusuf al Shehhi, a Saudi national and a trained pilot residing in Hollywood, Florida; and Fayez Rashid al Bani Hammad from the United Arab Emirates. In economy class were seated Mohald al Shahri, Saudi-trained pilot; and Ahmad al Ghamdi and Hamza al Ghamdi, both Saudi citizens who hijacked this plane at 8:30 AM. When flight 175 slammed into the South Tower, it lodged between the seventy-ninth and eighty-eighth floors, traveling at 540 to 590 miles per hour at impact. The South Tower collapsed first, at 9:59 AM, even though it was struck fifteen minutes later, due to the higher speed of impact, which melted the tower's steel structures. At 10:26 AM, the North Tower collapsed.

The Twin Towers were a symbol of American economic power. Consisting of eighteen million square feet of space, they were utterly destroyed in one and a half hours, shattering Americans' sense of safety and revealing our vulnerability, in what President George W. Bush considered not only an act of terror but of war. The FBI profile of these terrorists indicated they were all well-educated, intelligent, Saudi Arabians in their mid-twenties. (Hiro, *War Without End,* 300–309).

about the author

BARBARA A. GOLDSCHEIDER is a dual Israeli/ U.S. citizen who resided in Talpiot, Jerusalem, from 1971 to 1980. During this time, she lived through hundreds of acts of terrorism, particularly in the two years after the Yom Kippur War, which erupted in 1973. Goldscheider has since served in SAR-EL, the Volunteer for Israel Program in the Israel Defense Forces, three times; first in 1982, and twice again in 1988, after the outbreak of the first Intifada. During the Al-Aqsa Intifada in 2003, she spent six months in Jerusalem doing research in preparation for work on *Al-Naqba (The Catastrophe)*.

While employed for twelve years at Verizon in Waltham, Massachusetts, Goldscheider received three Excellence Awards, including the 2002 Award for Humanitarian Service, in recognition of her relief work at Ground Zero in New York in the aftermath of 9/11. As an American Red Cross national representative (Disaster Service Human Resource), New Hampshire Chapter, she was the recipient of several other awards for her work at Ground Zero from October 17 to November 7, 2001: the 2001 American Red Cross Award; the Derry, New Hampshire Firefighters Award for service to firefighters in New York; and the New

Hampshire Governor Jeanne Sheehan Award. Goldscheider holds a bachelor of arts in English from the University of Rhode Island, having graduated *summa cum laude,* and has been a member of Phi Beta Kappa since 1978. She now resides in Bangor, Maine, doing full-time research and writing.